Molly Malone & Bram Stoker in

The Curious Case of the Irish Yeti

I am a reader

and I celebrated World Book Day 2024

with this gift from my local bookseller

and The O'Brien Press

WORLD BOOK DAY®

World Book Day's mission is to offer every child and young person the opportunity to read and love books by giving you the chance to have a book of your own.

To find out more, and for fun activities including the monthly World Book Day Book Club, video stories and book recommendations, **visit worldbookday.com**

World Book Day is a charity sponsored by National Book Tokens.

Author photograph by Sam Nolan.

ALAN NOLAN grew up in Windy Arbour, Dublin and now lives in Bray, Co. Wicklow with his wife and three children. Alan is the author and illustrator of *Fintan's Fifteen*, *Conor's Caveman* and the *Sam Hannigan* series, and the illustrator of *Animal Crackers: Fantastic Facts About Your Favourite Animals,* written by Sarah Webb. His Molly Malone & Bram Stoker adventures, *The Sackville Street Caper* and *Double Trouble at the Dead Zoo*, are also published by The O'Brien Press. Alan runs illustration and writing workshops for children, and you may see him lugging his drawing board and pencils around your school or local library.

www.alannolan.ie

Twitter: @AlNolan

Instagram: @alannolan_author

Molly Malone & Bram Stoker in

The Curious Case of the Irish Yeti

Alan Nolan

THE O'BRIEN PRESS
DUBLIN

First published 2024 by The O'Brien Press Ltd,
12 Terenure Road East,
Rathgar, Dublin 6,
D06 HD27, Ireland.
Tel: +353 1 4923333; Fax: +353 1 4922777
E-mail: books@obrien.ie;
Website: obrien.ie
The O'Brien Press is a member of Publishing Ireland.
ISBN: 978-1-78849-490-8

Design and layout by Emma Byrne.
Cover illustration by Shane Cluskey.
Internal artwork by Alan Nolan.

8 7 6 5 4 3 2 1
28 27 26 25 24

Printed and bound by Norhaven Paperback A/S, Denmark.

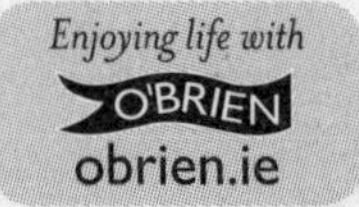

For Rachel

A Short List of Characters Contained Within, provided by the Most Considerate Author for Your Instruction and Delight:

Bram Stoker

The future author of *Dracula*, almost twelve years of age, yearns for adventure and to have stories to tell.

Molly Malone

Eleven years of age, accomplished sneak thief and part time fishmonger.

Billy the Pan, Shep, Hetty, Rose & Calico Tom, AKA The Sackville Street Spooks

Molly's gang, to whom she is part sergeant major, part mother hen.

Lily the Maid

The Stoker family maid, lover of dogs, Irish folklore and scary stories

Madame Florence Florence

A fortune teller, variously known as the Seer of the What-Is-To-Come, the One Who Knows All, the Seventh Daughter of a Seventh Daughter, and the White Witch of Westmoreland Street.

Mr Bertram 'Wild Bert' Florence

A semi-retired Wild West trick-rider, zebra wrangler and pony vaulter, and Madame Flo's husband.

Sir Alfred Mortlock

Captain of the underwhelming England Eleven cricket team.

Mr Grimble and Mr Bleat

Two thuggish Cockney henchmen, both born within the sound of London's Bow Bells.

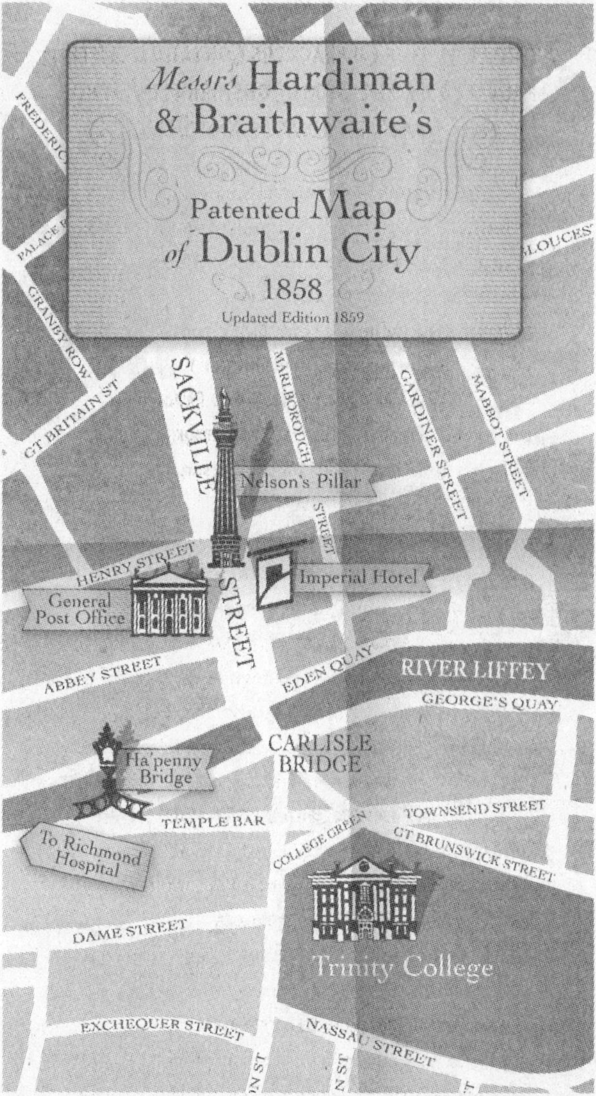

Messrs Hardiman & Braithwaite's

Patented Map *of* Dublin City 1858

Updated Edition 1859

FREDERIC
PALACE
GRANBY ROW
GT BRITAIN ST
SACKVILLE STREET
MARLBOROUGH STREET
GARDINER STREET
MABBOT STREET
LOUCEST
Nelson's Pillar
HENRY STREET
Imperial Hotel
General Post Office
ABBEY STREET
EDEN QUAY
RIVER LIFFEY
GEORGE'S QUAY
CARLISLE BRIDGE
Ha'penny Bridge
TEMPLE BAR
To Richmond Hospital
COLLEGE GREEN
TOWNSEND STREET
GT BRUNSWICK STREET
Trinity College
DAME STREET
EXCHEQUER STREET
NASSAU STREET
N ST
ST

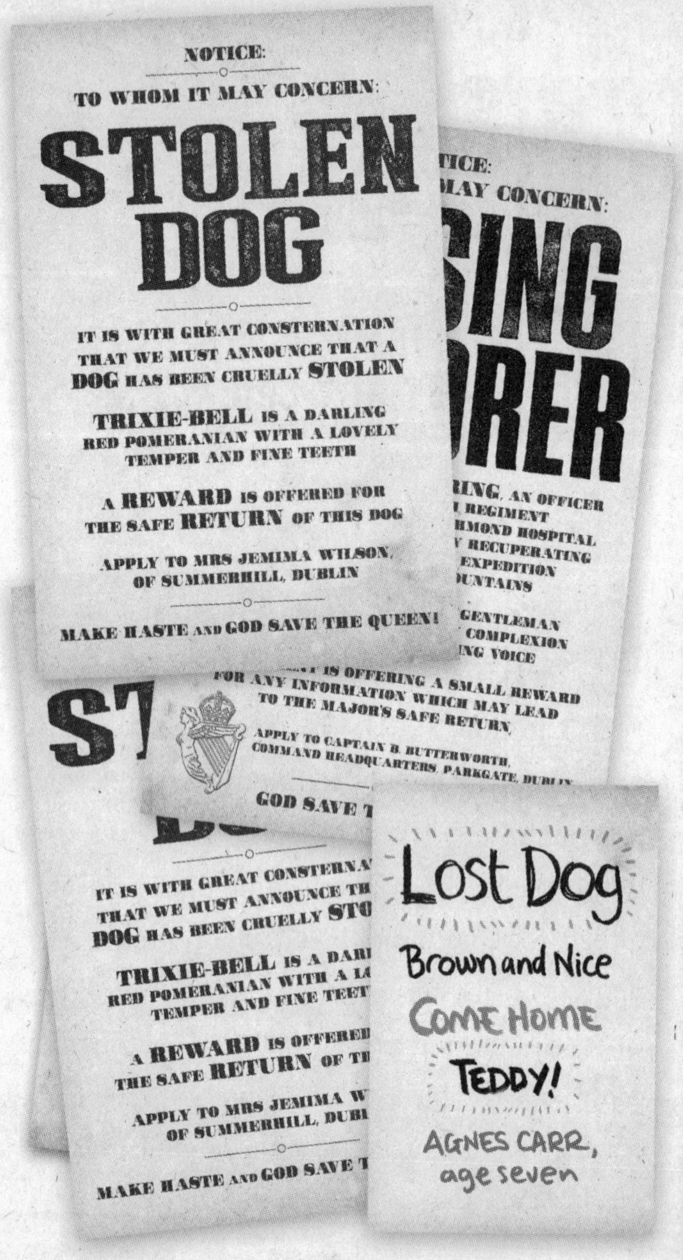

NOTICE:

TO WHOM IT MAY CONCERN:

STOLEN DOG

IT IS WITH GREAT CONSTERNATION THAT WE MUST ANNOUNCE THAT A **DOG** HAS BEEN CRUELLY **STOLEN**

TRIXIE-BELL IS A DARLING RED POMERANIAN WITH A LOVELY TEMPER AND FINE TEETH

A **REWARD** IS OFFERED FOR THE SAFE **RETURN** OF THIS DOG

APPLY TO MRS JEMIMA WILSON, OF SUMMERHILL, DUBLIN

MAKE HASTE AND GOD SAVE THE QUEEN!

TICE:

MAY CONCERN:

SING

ORER

RING, AN OFFICER
REGIMENT
HMOND HOSPITAL
Y RECUPERATING
EXPEDITION
UNTAINS

GENTLEMAN
COMPLEXION
ING VOICE

IS OFFERING A SMALL REWARD FOR ANY INFORMATION WHICH MAY LEAD TO THE MAJOR'S SAFE RETURN.

APPLY TO CAPTAIN B. BUTTERWORTH, COMMAND HEADQUARTERS, PARKGATE, DUBLIN

GOD SAVE T

ST

IT IS WITH GREAT CONSTERNA
THAT WE MUST ANNOUNCE TH
DOG HAS BEEN CRUELLY STO

TRIXIE-BELL IS A DAR
RED POMERANIAN WITH A LO
TEMPER AND FINE TEET

A REWARD IS OFFERED
THE SAFE RETURN OF TH

APPLY TO MRS JEMIMA W
OF SUMMERHILL, DUBL

MAKE HASTE AND GOD SAVE T

Lost Dog

Brown and Nice

COME HOME

TEDDY!

AGNES CARR,
age seven

Prologue:

It's Just Not Cricket ...

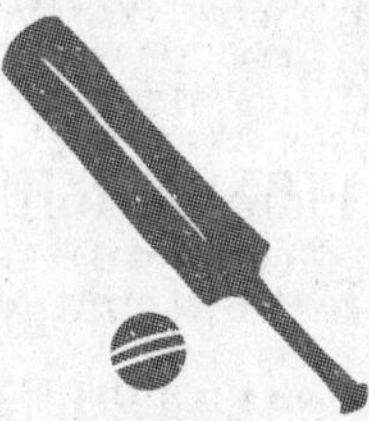

The short, stocky man entered the dark carnival tent and timidly sat down at a small circular table across from the formidable-looking fortune teller. The long, orange ostrich feather at the top of the fortune teller's purple turban waved and bobbed as she fluttered her fingers in mysterious movements over the large, glimmering crystal ball that sat on the centre of the table beside an empty teacup and saucer. The man tugged at his rectangular beard and hesitantly opened his mouth to speak.

'SPEAK YE NOT, SIR ALFRED MORTLOCK!' commanded the fortune teller in an imperious voice. The little man jumped in his seat, whipping the tiny, red-and-yellow-striped hat off his head and wringing it in his diminutive hands. 'I, Madame Florence, KNOW why ye have come,' continued the fortune teller, her eyes wide and her nostrils flaring, 'I know ye are Sir Alfred Harold Mortlock, the Captain of the England Eleven, and ye have travelled to Dublin to battle the Irish cricket team!'

Sir Alfred gasped. Madame Florence closed her eyes and began to make a low, droning HUMMMMMMMMMMMMMMMMMMM-ing noise. The teacup on the table began to rattle in its saucer. The small man whimpered. Flo's eyes snapped open, 'Ye want to know if your team will triumph over the Irish, or will ye be beaten yet again?' Sir Alfred nodded nervously, his face ashen white under his oblong beard and his eyes still fixed on the rattling teacup.

'Mortlock,' said Madame Flo, 'YE SHALL NOT PREVAIL!' Sir Alfred Mortlock leapt out of his chair (in fact, he almost leapt out of his skin) and clasped his cricket cap against his chest.

'Now,' said Madame Flo, 'BEGONE!' The tiny cricket captain slowly backed out of the tent, eyeing the now still teacup and patting his pockets for payment. 'No charge,' said Flo, 'Just remember this: You'll ne-ver beat the Irish! YOU'LL NE-VER BEAT THE IRISH!'

With Madame Flo's chant ringing in his ears, Sir Alfred flung open the tent flap and ran off through Smithfield Market as fast as his little legs could carry him.

DEAR SIRS AND MADAMS

HAVE YOU SEEN MY DOG?

I AM SIMPLY **LOST** WITHOUT HIM

HE IS A COCOA-COLOURED LABRADOR WHO IS FOUR YEARS OF AGE AND ANSWERS TO THE NAME OF TOBY

HE WAS LAST SEEN IN THE GARDINER STREET AREA NOT THREE DAYS SINCE

PLEASE C
HENRY CAVE
GARDINEI

GOD SAVE OUR C

NOTICE:
I IT MAY CONCERN:

SSING LORER

D HERRING, AN OFFICER
YAL IRISH REGIMENT
FROM RICHMOND HOSPITAL
EN LATELY RECUPERATING
ARDUOUS EXPEDITION
ALAYAN MOUNTAINS

IS A TALL GENTLEMAN
R, A RUDDY COMPLEXION
LENT SINGING VOICE

FERING A SMALL REWARD
TION WHICH MAY LEAD
R'S SAFE RETURN,

AIN B. BUTTERWORTH
QUARTERS, PARKGATE, DUBLIN

TO WHOM IT MAY C

MISS EXPLO

MAJOR REDMOND HER
WITH THE ROYAL IRIS
HAS GONE MISSING FROM R
WHERE HE HAD BEEN LATE
FOLLOWING AN ARDUO
TO THE HIMALAYAN

MAJOR HERRING IS A T
WITH BROWN HAIR, A R
AND AN EXCELLENT

THE REGIMENT IS OFFERIN
FOR ANY INFORMATION
TO THE MAJOR'S S

APPLY TO CAPTAIN B
COMMAND HEADQUA

GOD SAVE THE QU

HEAR YE! HEAR YE!

CHAMPION DOG MISSING

His name is Hercules, twice proclaimed the strongest dog in Ireland.

BLACK SPOTS
SHARP TEETH
MEDIUM TAIL
CAN JUGGLE

Needed for mid-week Strongman act – hurry, if you please!

Cornelius the Mighty,
Third tent from the left,
Smithfield Carnival

Chapter One:

A Dog's Life

In which Bram is woken from his beauty sleep when his neighbour confronts a thieving creep.

Bram was awakened by the tinkling sound of breaking glass. He rubbed his eyes, got out of bed and padded barefoot in the darkness to his window. Pulling the curtain to one side he gazed down into Buckingham Street, which at this hour was dark apart from the line of gas lamps that painted the cobblestones in tight, dim circles of yellow light. *It's almost four o'clock in the morning*, thought Bram, *I heard the grandfather clock in the downstairs hallway chime not ten minutes ago!* The tinkling sound came again, followed by an indistinct but angry shout, then by the sound of running footsteps. Suddenly, out of nowhere came a booming explosion that reverberated and echoed off the facades of the fine houses lining the street. Bram instinctively ducked down beneath his windowsill, and when he peeked out again he saw one of his neighbours, Mr Prattle from number seventeen he thought, stalking down the cobblestones wielding a blunderbuss gun. White smoke was snaking from its trumpet-like barrel. 'And don't come back, thief!' cried Mr Prattle in a shrill voice, then he looked around sharply, pulled his dressing gown tight around him and stalked back to his house, 'Beggaring burglars!'

Bram went back to his bed and, striking a match, lit the candle on his bedside table. He fished out a battered, leather-bound book from under his bed, sat down and began to write.

The Diary of Master Abraham Stoker
10th of June, 1859
19 Buckingham Street, Dublin

Dearest Diary,

Another burglary in Buckingham Street!

There have been six break-ins on our street already this week, and this latest one tonight makes seven!

I think it's because so many dogs have gone missing recently – Dublin needs guard dogs, and if houses have no guard dogs to bark and woof and make a fuss, what's to stop the thieves and swindlers from strolling in and taking the family silver or the lady of the house's jewellery?

Well, I can think of one thing that will stop the burglars strolling in ... Mr Prattle's blun-

derbuss! Poor Mr Prattle must have been doing the job of his missing hound – sitting up all night long, keeping a watch out for robbers and ne'er-do-wells. A dog's life, if you will!

But, dear Diary, I *do* wonder where the dogs have been disappearing to. As a point of fact, the whole City is wondering! We Dubliners didn't realise how much we depended on our dogs until they started to vanish.

Lots of old ladies and gentlemen who kept a canine for company are now finding themselves quite alone. Not to mention poor distraught children who dote on their darling doggos. So many cats are no longer being chased and so many bones are going unburied.

Tomorrow is Saturday, my closest friend, so perhaps I will meet up with my other best and closest friend (the much less paper-y one), Molly Malone. Maybe she and I can have a chinwag about the missing mutts and see if we can figure out where exactly they might have

disappeared to.

But for now, dear Diary, I find myself yawning with weariness, so I shall take my leave.

Goodnight (what's left of it!),

Bram

Bram slipped the thin pencil inside the front cover of his diary and placed the book carefully on his bedside table. He got into bed and tucked himself snugly into the covers, then, licking his forefinger and thumb, reached out his hand and extinguished the candle flame.

CHAPTER TWO:

WHERE'S MY DOGGONE DOG GONE?

IN WHICH MOLLY MALONE COMES TO CALL WITH MISMATCHED SHOES AND DISTRESSING NEWS.

Bram was awakened again by another noise – a loud banging on the hall door. This was followed by a softer knocking on his own bedroom door. 'Master Bram,' he heard Lily, the Stoker family maid, say, 'Miss Molly is here to see you. Oh, Master Bram, she's waiting for you in the library; she's in quite a state!'

As soon as he had dressed, Bram flew down the stairs and through the door into the book-lined room where Molly waited, patting down his hair and straightening his tie.

'Bram!' cried Molly Malone, 'What kept you? I've been waitin' aaaages!'

Molly's curly red hair, normally so well brushed, was sticking out at all angles and her green dress was on backwards; Bram also noticed that she was wearing shoes that didn't match – one shoe was brown and one was black. She was clutching a cushion from the sofa and pacing up and down on the patterned Chinese rug with wide eyes that, Bram thought, looked even wilder than usual.

'I say,' he said, cocking an amused eyebrow at his friend, 'somebody got dressed in a hurry.'

'Bram,' said Molly, 'will yeh stop messin' – Her Majesty has gone missing!'

Lily the maid let out a little gasp and dropped

her feather duster. 'Not *Her Majesty*!' she cried and flopped back onto the pink sofa in a dead faint.

'She must have been stolen by dog-nappers,' said Molly, as she held the glass of water to Lily's lips. 'She was sleepin' in the kitchen at Madame Flo's and when Wild Bert went down this mornin' to let her out for a wee, the back door had been forced open, and there was Her Majesty – gone! She's a good-lookin' dog, I'd say loads of people had their eye on her.'

'She wasn't *stolen*,' stammered Lily, pushing the water glass away from her mouth, 'she was EATEN!'

'Eaten?' said Bram, 'Don't be ridiculous, Lily, who on earth would eat a dog?'

'The IRISH YETI!' cried Lily, staggering to her feet, 'A huge, hulking, hairy creature, covered in fur, and as tall as Nelson's Pillar! It shambles around the streets of Dublin after dark – from Summerhill to Sheriff Street, and from Sackville Street to Smithfield – with its eyes glowing purple and its sharp claws glinting in the moonlight, looking for four-legged food! It spends all day hiding from the sun and it only comes out at night. They say his favourite dinner is dog! Oh, Miss Molly, the Irish Yeti has surely opened up his great hungry, drooling jaws and swallowed up your poor little pup!'

Molly opened her own mouth, then closed it again with a CLOPP. She turned to Bram with terror in her eyes. 'Her Majesty!' she cried, 'The Yeti couldn't have eaten my lovely dog! She's far too beautiful to be anyone's breakfast!'

Bram furrowed his eyebrows and walked over to a bookshelf. He ran his fingers down the row of books until his hand rested on the spine of a burgundy-coloured cloth-bound tome. He pulled if off the shelf and held out the cover for Molly to read.

'*Frobisher's Bestiary of Extraordinary Animals,*' read Molly, squinting her eyes at the faded gold foil lettering that decorated the book's cover. 'A bestiary is a book of facts about animals,' Bram began to explain.

'I know what a *bestiary* is, Bram,' snapped Molly, 'What I want to know is what an Irish Yeti is!'

Bram opened the book to almost the first entry. 'Abominable Snowman, The,' he read out loud, 'The Abominable Snowman is an ape-like creature, rumoured to inhabit the snowy Himalayan mountainous regions of Nepal to the north of India, where locals refer to him as "the Yeti".' Molly's eyes sprang open at that word. Lily issued another soft shriek and bit her finger. 'The Yeti,' continued Bram, rolling his eyes a little, 'is described as being colossal in size, measuring a good seven feet tall, with a covering of thick, snow-white fur. Its head is heavy browed, and its eyes are said to be a deep purple colour. Locals in Nepal say that the creature feeds on mountain goats, and some have reported that after a full moon they have woken to find that their goat or sheep herd has been depleted by what they think are hungry Yetis.'

'Oh, Master Bram,' wailed Lily, 'Goats have four legs and so do dogs! The Irish Yeti is hunting our four-legged friends!'

'Is there a picture there in the book?' asked Molly. Wordlessly, Bram turned the open book around so they could see. The picture was of an enormous hairy monster, its eyes wide and angry as it held a terrified goat in its giant claws, and its gigantic jaws wide with rows of razor-sharp teeth as it prepared to devour its decidedly unwilling meal.

Lily screamed and fainted again.

Molly shook her head, 'I can't believe – not for one minute – that there's some Irish Yeti-yoke eatin' all of Dublin's dogs ...'

Bram looked at Lily, lying on the couch. 'Neither can I, Mol, well – not really – but the problem is that if Lily believes that rubbish, most of the people of Dublin probably do as well.' He closed the book and put it back in its place on the bookshelf. 'I think we'd better go on a hunt of our own – and see if we can find out what this Irish Yeti really is.'

'And, more importantly,' said Molly, 'we have to find Her Majesty!'

'Yes,' agreed Bram, 'I think if we track down this Irish Yeti, we're bound to discover what really happened to your dog! But, Mol, before we go, just one thing … don't you think you'd better put your dress on the right way around?'

Chapter Three:

All These Sheep Are Really Getting On My Goat

In which pickpocket Shep and Billy the Pan say 'no' to a mob and say 'yes' to a plan.

KLANGG! KLANGG! Billy the Pan used the bowl of his metal saucepan to hammer in the last nail on his hand-drawn (and extremely badly spelled) MISSING DOG poster and, placing the saucepan back on his head, stood back to admire his handi-

NOTICE:

A SPLENDID SPORTING EVENT

THE IRISH

Ware iz owr dog?

DE FAYMUS DOG

HUR MATCHISTY

Belongin to De Sakvill Strete Spoocks
and Moly Malown

Haz DISSAPEERED

Com home Hur Magisty!

com to Billy the Pan or hiz frend Shep
or hiz udder frend Rose
at Madam Flow's howse in
Smitfeeld tu-day

CRICKET TEAM
VS
THE ENGLAND
ELEVEN

SHALL TAKE

SUNDAY TWE

AT TWO O'CLOC

LEINSTER CRICKET

Gentlemen! Come along and s

GOD SAVE THE QUEEN!

work. The saucepan he wore had a multitude of functions. It made a handy hammer when hammering was called for; it performed as an adequate weapon of the head-KLONK-ing variety when required; and it provided Billy with his main means of income. Billy the Pan, like his father and his grandfather before him, was a beggar, and being a beggar in Dublin was not an easy job – Dublin was overflowing with beggars. Billy's Dad, Georgie the Shovel, had told Billy that he would need a gimmick to help him stand out from the crowd, so Billy had procured a large, slightly rusty metal sauce-pan to wear on his head. When he was out working a begging shift, he encouraged punt-ers to knock their knuckles on his saucepan helmet 'for luck' and to throw a ha'penny to 'Billy the Pan' to seal the deal. Although he was just twelve years old, he made as much as an adult beggar with this caper – especially during late-night shifts when the taverns were closing and their hiccup-ing customers were staggering home.

Shep wiped his dribbly nose with a filthy sleeve and looked up at his taller and older friend, 'Do you think this poster will work?'

Billy put a comforting hand on his pal's shoulder. 'I hope so, Shep. I've made twenty of these yokes and we've spent all day puttin' them up on walls an' signposts all over the city. The picture I drew of Her Majesty is just like her; someone is bound to see it and recognise her and come lookin' for The Spooks.'

Shep wasn't too sure about that; the pictures Billy had drawn of The Sackville Street Spooks' dog weren't *that* accurate – for instance, Shep couldn't remember Her Majesty having green fur.

Suddenly there was a tumultuous noise from behind them, and Billy and Shep jumped out of the way just in time as a flock of sheep thundered by, running wildly down the cobblestones of Liffey Street, following a black sheep at the front of the crowd and making a cacophony of BLEEEEATs and BAAAAs. They were chased by a running, red-faced farmer who was waving his arms and shouting in alarm. 'Slow down, yiz eejits!' he cried at the woolly runaways, 'Watch out for the river! You're heading for the water!' But it was too late: as the first sheep reached the low quay wall of the River Liffey beside the Ha'penny Bridge, it jumped high, sailed over the stone barrier and dropped down and out of sight. There was a distant SPLASHHH as it hit the river water below. The rest of the flock followed their leader and leapt over the wall too, making even more SPLASH-es. Billy the Pan and Shep ran to the side of the river and looked over to see fourteen sheep floating with the current down towards Dublin Bay. The flock seemed surprised, but happy enough to be having a little paddle about, and they BAAAAed gently as they floated. 'ME SHEEP!'

shouted the farmer, hanging over the wall and watching his livelihood float away downstream, 'First me poor sheepdog Fluffy Norah disappears, and now this! This wouldn't have happened at all if that abominable Irish Yeti hadn't eaten me dog!'

'At least sheep can swim,' reasoned Billy, 'If you run you might catch up with them at the Custom House – there's a jetty there and you might be able to snag them!' The farmer nodded quickly and hurried off down the quays in pursuit of his waterlogged livestock, shouting 'Someone has to do something about that flamin' Yeti!'

'He's right, you know,' said Billy the Pan. 'The Smithfield Fair last weekend was chaos – with no sheepdogs to guard them, all the goats, sheep an' pigs broke out of their pens and the poor farmers had to try to round them up themselves. And it was no piece of cake either – it was rainin', and it's not easy to keep hold of a slippery pig!'

'Do you think the Yeti is really eatin' all the dogs, Billy?' asked Shep, then his eyes widened as a new thought occurred to him, 'Holy Moley, did the Irish Yeti eat Her Majesty?!'

'Don't be ridic-less,' replied Billy the Pan, 'there's no such thing as an Irish Yeti.'

Just then another tumultuous racket came from behind the two friends and they turned to see a large crowd of angry-looking, shouty people marching towards them up the quays. At the head of the horde was Billy's father Georgie, his silver-painted shovel held high and glinting in the Dublin sunlight. As they approached the boys could make out what the rabble were shouting; cries of 'SAVE OUR DOGS!' and 'LET'S BIFF THE BIGFOOT!' were reverberating and echoing off the tall Georgian buildings on both sides of the Liffey. People were looking out the windows of the buildings to see what the commotion was on the quays, and some were joining in with the chants of the marching mob, 'DOWN WITH YETIS! DOWN WITH YETIS!'

Georgie the Shovel spread his arms wide to halt the angry marchers, and they came to a stop at the Ha'penny Bridge. Each was carrying a makeshift weapon; some had garden rakes, some swung cricket bats around their heads as if they were in training with Irish Team for the next day's match against the England Eleven, others held the wooden shafts of sweeping brushes. One small gentleman even held an egg-whisk that he brandished in a threatening manner as his eyes darted right and left, looking for any sign of the Yeti.

'Da,' said Billy the Pan, a note of alarm in his voice, 'What's goin' on?'

'The Brotherhood of Beggarmen have been raisin' a crowd,' said Georgie, swinging his shovel onto his shoulder like a soldier's rifle, 'We aren't going to stand for any more of our doggos disappearin'. This Yeti yoke is eatin' them for his tea!'

'Ah, Da,' said Billy, 'why are you gettin' these eejits all riled up like this? You don't *know* that the Yeti is eatin' dogs for his dinner – I don't think there even is such a thing as an Irish Yeti!'

But his father continued, 'I met your friend Wild Bert up at Smithfield, he was ridin' around on his horse Buttercup, tryin' to round up all the goats an' geese an' moo-cows that are runnin' amok up there. He was wavin' his white hat and firin' blanks out of that big silver cowboy gun of his, but the animals weren't takin' one blind bit of notice of him; they were doin' as they pleased! The goats were eatin' the washin' off the washing lines, the pigs were rollin' around in the mucky puddles and the people were trippin' over the geese; and don't talk to me about the cats! With no dogs around the cats are goin' crazy – lyin' lazy in the middle of Sackville Street causin' carriages to come to sudden stops, and keepin' good honest beggars like yours truly up till all hours by wailin' an' singin' on the garden fence all night long.'

Georgie shook his large, hairy head, 'Wild Bert said that Madame Flo opened the door to the outside privy this morning and found a GOAT sittin' on the toilet, lookin' back at her! Toilets smell bad enough, but imagine a goat inside in the jacks, doin' its business!'

This thought of that made Shep giggle, and even Georgie the Shovel, as annoyed as he was, couldn't help smiling at the small, curly-haired boy. 'C'mon, son,' he said to Billy, 'join up with the march. We are headin' for Sackville Street – that's where the Yeti has his lair – and we're goin' to be ready an' waitin' for him!'

'You go on ahead, Da,' said Billy, scratching his chin thoughtfully, 'we'll catch up in a while. I heard he doesn't come out in the daytime anyway; the Yeti only comes out at night, and it won't be dark for hours yet.'

Georgie nodded at his son, hoisted his shovel aloft and, with a shout, the rabble set off towards Sackville Street, chanting loudly as they marched. 'LET'S BIFF THE BIGFOOT! LET'S BIFF THE BIGFOOT!'

Billy the Pan looked down at his friend. 'There's no way that Yeti, even if he *does* exist, could be eatin' *all* the dogs in Dublin,' he said, 'Sure, there are *hundreds* of dogs in the City, maybe thousands!'

Shep nodded in agreement, 'You're right, Billy! Not even a monster as tall as Nelson's Pillar could have an appetite *that* big.'

'I think it's time we found out what's really happenin' to the dogs,' said Billy.

"But how do we do that?' asked Shep.

'To catch a dog-napper, we are going to need some bait,' said Billy, 'and I think I know just the dog for the job!'

Chapter Four:

Are We There, Yeti?

In which Molly and Bram follow a hot lead and squint at a footprint.

Molly and Bram had spent the entire day searching the backstreets of Dublin for any sign of Her Majesty; they had opened every shed door and peered into every window of every closed shop. They had asked every person they passed, but nobody had seen hide nor hair of the dog. The two friends passed the Pro-Cathedral and walked the short distance down Elephant Lane and out onto Sackville Street. The late afternoon sun glinted off the windows of the tall, white stone buildings that lined each side of the wide boulevard – said to be the widest street of all the capital cities of Europe – making the darkening street look like it was lit up by fairy lights.

Nelson's Pillar, the tall stone column topped with the statue of the British Naval hero, stood in the dead centre of the street and cast a long shadow over the façade of the General Post Office. At the top of the Pillar Bram could distantly make out the silhouettes of two sea gulls as they perched high up on Admiral Horatio Nelson's head. They seemed to be fighting. *Probably squabbling over perching rights*, thought Bram with a smile.

The street was quiet, even for a Saturday evening, with a small number of slow-moving horse-drawn carts and carriages slowly moving up and down. Very few street sellers were in evidence, and the ones who were there looked harried and distracted as they called out their wares in quiet, muted voices that were much different to their usual sing-song shouts. 'Tasty Strawberries', 'Fresh Potatoes', 'Pretty Flowers', they mumbled. It was almost as if they were half-afraid to draw too much attention to themselves.

The street was so quiet that a group of small children had started up an impromptu cricket match outside the Imperial Hotel. Usually, the doorman at the hotel would have chased the kids off, in case they frightened the horses tethered to the Hansom cabs that lined the front of the building, but as there were no cabs at all at the kerb that evening, he let them play away.

As Molly and Bram walked by the hotel, the doorman doffed his top hat. 'Ahh, Miss Molly Malone,' he said, a huge grin spreading across his face, 'it's yourself! My Ma says thank you so much for sorting out the problem she was having with *you-know-who* who was up to the *you-know-what* down the *you-know-where* for her – she's very grateful to yeh.'

Bram was baffled by all the *you-know-thats* and *you-know-the-others*, but decided he didn't really *want* to know – Molly was always sorting out problems for other people. He cleared his throat and asked the doorman why the street was so quiet.

'Well, young Master,' said the velvet-coated doorman in a hushed voice, 'the whole town is afeared of the Irish Yeti; people are nervous about coming out during the day – and if you think it's quiet now, you should see Sackville Street when the sun goes down completely – it's as dead as the grave!'

There was a sharp shout of dismay from the street and the small band of cricketing kids hurried quickly out of the way as a herd of escaped pigs rampaged down the road, erasing their chalked-out cricket crease and knocking over their wickets.

The doorman smiled, 'But children will be children – they're excited about the Ireland versus the English Eleven match tomorrow. The whole town should be goin' cricket-crazy, but everyone's afraid to celebrate, what with that blinkin' Yeti eating all the dogs.'

Molly scratched her freckly chin and looked at the youngsters; all were wearing ragged clothes and only one of them was wearing shoes. *If you could call them that*, thought Molly, *there's more holes than leather in them shoes – they are just two scraggy soles tied onto the poor girl's feet with twine instead of laces.* They were very much like the kind of shoes that Molly herself used to wear, and Molly was glad that she and her friends had come up a bit in the world since those days; she could afford her own shoes now, even if the button-boots she now wore were fiddly beyond belief to get on and off.

She beckoned to one of the young cricketers

and he trotted over to her.

'Hey Mol,' said the small boy, a shy smile on his smudgy face, 'Are yous lookin' for the Yeti? Me an' Mickser here have seen him!'

'We have not!' exclaimed another tiny boy in indignation. 'We only seen his footprint!'

'Footprint?' said Bram, excitedly – now they were getting somewhere! 'Where did you see this footprint?' The boy jerked a thumb back over his shoulder, 'Down Tucker's Row! C'mon, we'll show yiz!'

The two boys scurried off down Sackville Street in the direction of the Carlisle Bridge and then hooked a sharp left onto Tucker's Row. They came to an abrupt halt at the entrance to a small laneway that ran behind the Imperial Hotel and pointed nervously.

'Down there, Mister,' said Mickser, 'We saw the Yeti's footprints in the muck at the back of the hotel, just last night.'

The other boy nodded, 'And the bitemarks

of his huge teeth in the rotten vegetables that the cooks threw out the kitchen doors!'

'If this "Yeti" is really an actual, honest-to-Gertrude yeti, I'm pretty sure he wouldn't be eatin' vegetables,' murmured Molly to Bram.

'Certainly not,' agreed Bram, then he looked mischievously at the two small boys, 'he'd be much more likely to eat small boys!'

With that, the two boys yelped in fright and galloped off as quickly as they could back to their cricket match. Molly rolled her eyes but couldn't help smiling at Bram; he really did have a devilish side sometimes! 'Right, Mister Macabre with your gruesome sense of humour,' she said, 'let's go and have a look for these Yeti footprints.'

At the back door to the hotel was a wide patch of gungy mud and vegetable matter that had oozed out of the rusting kitchen bins. The viscous puddle was gloopy and extremely smelly, with bits of brown cabbage, putrid perished leeks and leaves of decomposing lettuce sticking out of the goo. Bram wrinkled his nose and held his hand over his mouth to block the stinky smell, but Molly knelt down and stared intently into the greeny-brown mess. 'Here!' she exclaimed, pointing at the centre of the patch of ghastly gunge, 'Lookit – there's the footprint!' She grabbed the sleeve of Bram's well-tailored jacket and dragged him closer to the gloop. 'C'mon, Quality,' she said to her friend, 'time to get a bit of mud on the knees of your fancy trousers!'

At the centre of the gunky puddle was an enormous footprint, much bigger than a normal man's, with a clearly defined rounded heel at the back and a full set of massive toes at the front.

'Here's another one!' cried Bram, wafting his hand in front of his nose, 'See, that's the left foot and this is the right over here!' He moved towards another patch of malodorous mud a few steps down the laneway. 'And here's another!' he called back to Molly. 'The Yeti seems to be walking in this direction!' They both stared down the dark laneway. Even though it wasn't yet eight o'clock, the thin passage with the high walls on either side was almost as dark as it would be at night. *Hardly any sunlight gets in at all down here*, thought Bram, *it's the perfect place for a Yeti to hide during the day … especially one that hates sunlight!*

He was about to say as much to Molly, but she had already started off down the murky passageway. 'Be careful,' he hissed, 'this alley might be Yeti-central – we might end up face-to-face with Bigfoot!'

Molly turned back to her friend and winked a cheeky wink. 'I know that,' she said with one ginger eyebrow raised, 'In fact, that's exactly what I'm hopin' for; I want to have a word with him about a dog!'

Bram thought about Her Majesty, Mol's

lovely dog with her soft brown fur, big, cute floppy ears and long, lolling, licky tongue – although Her Majesty didn't always smell so sweet, she was the sweetest dog in all of Dublin. And this Yeti (or whatever it was) might have devoured her for dinner! He nodded resolutely, puffed out his chest, drew back his shoulders and followed Molly into the darkness.

Chapter Five:

I Wanna Be Your Dog!

In which Billy the Pan and Shep borrow a hound from Hetty and try to be found by a Yeti.

'No chance!' thundered Hetty Hardwicke, 'There's no way I'm lettin' you use poor Prince Albert as bait to catch the Irish Yeti!' She stamped her foot so hard on the wooden floorboards that she made Prince Albert jump, all four of his paws leaving the ground. He whimpered low and cowered behind Hetty's legs.

'Ahh, c'mon, Hetty,' said Billy the Pan, 'we won't let the Yeti get him. I don't think it's a real Yeti an' anyways.'

'An' you're the only other member of The Sackville Street Spooks that has a dog,' said Shep.

'Prince Albert is just a puppy,' glowered Hetty, 'an' he's only a baby – my little baby – you're not tyin' him to a post and leavin' him out all alone for the Yeti to eat for his dinner!'

'But he won't be all alone,' said Shep in a conciliatory tone, 'me an' Billy will be there with him!'

'Yeah, that's right,' said Billy, 'We wouldn't leave your poor dog all alone – we will be there too.'

'Dressed up as dogs!' said Shep, 'We're goin' undercover; lookit.' He held up two highly unconvincing homemade dog costumes. One seemed to be made out of an old grey carpet or rug, it had two long brown wool stockings stitched onto one end for floppy ears, and a knotted length of ship's rope for a tail at the other. The other costume was made from a ratty brown fur coat to which Shep had attached pointy cardboard ears and a tail made from a branch from a pine tree. The tail moulted pine needles as he held it up to Hetty.

'You two are complete and utter eejits,' she said, and then sighed, 'but if you're willing to put your own lives on the line and risk gettin' eaten by the Yeti, I *suppose* Prince Albert can do the same.' Prince Albert looked up sharply at his mistress and twitched his ears – he didn't look too sure about that!

It was getting dark as Billy the Pan and Shep walked cautiously out onto Smithfield Square. The broad expanse of the Square was deserted – the usual Saturday market had been called off due to everybody being afraid of the Irish Yeti – and the only sound that could be heard was the distant BLEEEEATing and OINKing of stray goats and pigs that, sheepdog-less, had escaped from their owners and were trotting around the side streets, foraging for something edible in the piles of garbage. Both boys were carrying their pathetic canine costumes and Shep held Prince Albert by a rope. The dog was straining against his lead; he *really* didn't want to be there. And, for that matter, neither did Shep.

'Are you sure about this, Billy?' he asked, a nervous stutter in his voice.

'I told ya,' answered Billy, 'no talkin' – from here on out we are dogs. If you want to say somethin', just say *woof*.' Prince Albert did go *woof*, and then, much to the dismay of Billy the Pan and Shep's noses, the dog let out a quiet, but extremely stinky, fart.

'The poor dog's terrified,' said Shep, 'and so am I. What if the Yeti eats us?'

'I keep tellin' you,' whispered Billy, 'there's NO Yeti. Now, tie Prince Albert to that pole, put on your dog disguise, and get down on all fours like a good doggy.'

Grudgingly, Shep did just that, and soon the two boys and their shivering canine companion were standing (or, more accurately in the case of the boys, kneeling) on the cobblestones in the centre of the Square. The moon had begun to rise and, squinting through a small split in the fabric of his hopeless dog outfit, Billy could see shafts of moonlight slide slowly down the redbrick chimney shaft of the whiskey distiller's factory at the side of the Square.

'I'm scared,' came a little voice from beside him.

'Dog language only, Shep,' hissed Billy to his younger pal, 'if we keep in character, we might lure the Yeti out into the open.

'*Woof*,' said Shep.

Suddenly there was the sound of footsteps coming quickly from behind them. *It's him – it must be the Yeti!* Prince Albert whimpered and pulled hard on his rope. Billy wished he had made a larger hole in his dog disguise; he couldn't see anything! Then came the sound of *another* pair of footsteps, joining the first. Billy was puzzled, were there *two* Yetis?

'Free dogs,' said a gruff, deep voice, 'It's our lucky day, Mr Bleat! Not just one, not just two, but *free* dogs!' Billy's ears perked up in astonishment, *this* wasn't a Yeti!

'It most certainly is, Mr Grimble,' said an answering voice, slightly more high-pitched but just as gruff as the first. 'Although it should more propp-ah-ly be referred to as our lucky *night*, seeing as the ol' *fork an' spoon* is high in the sky.'

Fork and spoon? thought Billy; he thought the two voices sounded like they might be from London, but what on earth did they mean by *fork and spoon*?

'An' lucky that it is, Mr Bleat,' said the first voice, 'Uvver-wise we wouldn't be able to carry out our duties, as the ol' *Candy Floss* requires us to.'

'The *Candy Floss*, Mr Grimble?' asked the second voice.

'The *Boss*, Mr Bleat,' replied the first, 'You know, sometimes I fink you ain't a propp-ah Cockney at all!'

'Sorry, Mr Grimble,' said Mr Bleat apologetically, 'I do try, but sometimes I get a bit mixed up wiv me *climbing gang*.'

'*Climbing gang*, Mr Bleat?' asked Mr Grimble.

'*Rhyming slang*, Mr Grimble,' said Mr Bleat.

'Understandable, Mr Bleat,' said Mr Grimble, understandingly, 'most understandable. Now, let's get to work and nab these free canines.'

Billy gasped as two muscular arms grabbed him around the waist, and he felt himself being hoisted high onto someone's broad shoulders. From somewhere beside him he heard a quiet, scared voice saying, '*Woof*,' and he guessed that Shep was also receiving the same treatment from these two mysterious Londoners. He tried to look out from under his grey rug dog disguise, but although he could hear Prince Albert's growling as he was being dragged across the Smithfield cobblestones by an unseen hand, all Billy could see was a sliver of the moon as it shone in the clear night sky. *Yeti?* he thought, *these two jokers aren't Yetis!*

Chapter Six:

Finding This Bigfoot Will Be No Small Feat

In which Molly and Bram come face-to-face with a fur-ocious creature.

'STOP!' hissed Molly and held up her hand. Bram, who had been trudging along with some trepidation behind her, came to a halt.

'What is it?' he hissed back. 'I heard something,' she said softly, 'a grunting noise, coming from behind those bins.' The fairly full moon had risen over Sackville Street and by its watery light Bram could make out the silhouette of tall metal dustbins; the bins were stuffed with smelly vegetable waste and their lids were battered and rusted. A sudden wind whipped up stray pages of newspapers and they flapped over the children's heads like white, papery bats. 'SSHHHH!' said Molly, 'Did you hear that?' Bram shook his head, 'Did I hear what, Mol?' Then he heard it: a low, rumbling GRRUUUMMMMMMBBBBBLE that seemed to reverberate from the inky blackness behind the dustbins. Molly and Bram both took an involuntary step backwards; Bram's foot slid with a squelch on the remains of a wet, rotten turnip that had fallen from one of the bins, and his legs went out from under him. He ended up sitting on his backside on the greasy cobblestones. 'Ow!' he said, more in surprise than in pain.

'Never mind 'Ow!'' said Molly, 'Gerrup quick, there's somethin' alive in there!'

Bram got to his feet, looking annoyed with himself as he wiped his hands on his well-made trousers. Molly grabbed his arm tight. A colossal shape was emerging from the dark shadows behind the rusty bins; a huge man-shaped form that unfolded itself from a crouching position to its full, immense height. It was covered from hideous head to terrifying toe with white, shaggy fur that glinted and glistened in the moonlight. Its massive furry shoulders seemed to grow out of the space where Bram guessed that its ears would have been, if he could have seen them at all underneath the thick fur at either side of the creature's head. The monster's eyes were the most frightening feature of all; placed low under a huge hairy brow, they flashed evilly with purple light. Molly and Bram stood still as statues, rooted to the cobbles under their feet with fear. The Yeti lifted his huge head and seemed to fill its chest with slightly stinky laneway air. Molly gasped, then furrowed her eyebrows and raised her two fists as if ready to fight. Bram expected the Yeti to let out an ear-splitting roar, but instead it made a small whimpering noise. Bram and Molly exchanged puzzled glances.

'THERE IT IS!' A sudden shout surprised the two friends, and they looked around to see a mob marching towards them in the moonlight. The crowd was led by Georgie the Shovel, who, as well as his customary silver-painted spade, was brandishing a wooden torch, the top of which was engulfed in a flickering flame. Behind him the rabble almost filled the narrow laneway from side to side. Some of them were holding torches too; some had lanterns and all of them held a home-made weapon of some description. 'LET'S BIFF THE BIGFOOT! LET'S BIFF THE BIGFOOT!' they chanted as they bore down on the children. Molly and Bram turned back to the Yeti, but he had already lumbered off down the lane and away from the mob in a lop-sided, lurching gait. In the distance they could see his silhouette skidding as he rounded the corner at the other end of the passageway.

'AFTER HIM!' bellowed Georgie the Shovel, and the crowd thundered by Molly and Bram in pursuit of the creature, waving their rakes, sweeping brushes handles and cricket bats as they ran. A small gentleman brought up the rear of the gang, rotating the handle of an egg-whisk and wailing, 'That Yeti ate me dog for his dinner!'

'Did that Yeti sound dangerous to you?' asked Molly.

'No,' said Bram, 'he was huge, but he actually sounded scared.'

Molly nodded. 'I agree,' she said, 'the poor thing looked harmless. I'm pretty sure he isn't goin' around eatin' dogs – he doesn't look the type – and I'm *very* sure he had nothin' to do with Her Majesty disappearing.' Something shiny on the ground caught Molly's eye and bent down beside the bins and fished out from under a cabbage leaf, a small, circular metal object. One side of it was covered by a glass face and two hands beneath the glass spun around as she held it up for inspection in the moonlight.

'Since when does a Yeti need a compass?' said Bram.

'Since never,' said Molly, 'You know, I have a feelin' that this Yeti may not be a Yeti at all.'

'A bogus bigfoot …' said Bram slowly, 'But Mol, Georgie and the gang are going to capture it, and when they do …'

'We will just have to get to it first!' said Molly, 'C'mon Bram, the game's afoot!'

'The game's a Bigfoot, you mean,' replied Bram with a laugh, 'Let's snag this abominable snowman before Georgie the Shovel does!'

* * *

The crowd chased the Irish Yeti across Sackville Street and had nearly caught up with the creature by the tall stone columns that held up the portico of the General Post Office, but the Yeti took a mighty bound with its massive legs and leapt onto a windowsill on the ground floor. He raised a huge arm, grasped the stone at the top of the window with strong, furry fingers and pulled himself up. He raised his other arm and continued to climb up the side of the building, his fingers finding purchase in the crevices between the big stone blocks that made up the building's façade. The crowd skidded to a halt and watched in awe as the creature ascended the outside of the GPO, climbing arm-over-arm like an experienced mountain climber.

'FOLLOW HIM!' shouted a voice from the mob.

'How?' replied Georgie the Shovel, 'None of us can climb like that, straight up a solid wall – I don't think any human could!'

'Let's get inside!' shouted another man, 'We can go up the stairs and catch him on the roof!'

The mob ran as one to the tall wooden doors of the General Post Office, but as hard as they pushed them and rattled them and hit them with cricket bats and egg-whisks, they couldn't get them to budge. There was no way they were going to open without a key!

Molly and Bram ran across the street past Nelson's Pillar and watched from the back of the crowd as the Yeti climbed and the mob banged on the GPO doors. 'They can't get in,' said Bram breathlessly, 'That's good – we need to get to that Yeti before the people with the pitchforks do – they look angry. I don't know what they might do to that poor Yeti if they catch him. The front door being locked has bought us a few minutes; but how do we get to him?'

'That crowd of eejits may not be able to get into the GPO without a key,' said Molly with a grin, 'but remember, Bram, you are in the company of the number-one sneak thief in all of Dublin.'

Bram grinned back, 'No, Mol, in all of Ireland!'

'You're too kind,' said Molly with a small curtsey, 'And who needs a key anyway, when you've got a hairpin?' She took a metal clip out of her curly ginger hair and, with a wink to her friend, trotted over to a side entrance, out of sight of the crowd who were still hammering on the main door. Bram was always amazed by the ease that Molly could open a locked door; with the jerk and fiddle of a hairpin she could have the door of any house, any tavern, any safe, (or, in this case, any side door to Dublin's General Post Office) open in mere seconds. She stuck the hairpin into the keyhole, stuck out her tongue in concentration and, with a quiet KLIKK, the door swung open. The two kids slipped inside and noiselessly shut the door behind them.

'But how do we get up on the roof?' asked Bram, looking around in the darkness.

'Stairs, I suppose,' whispered Molly and led him through an inner door (this time, unlocked) towards where she thought a staircase might be hiding. They found themselves in the high-ceilinged, marble-tiled lobby of the GPO. A row of panelled hardwood counters where post office clerks sold stamps and franked envelopes during working hours ran across one wall, and facing the counters was the tall main entrance door. The noise of the mob hammering and bashing at the other side of the tall door was deafening and the children could hear their relentless chanting of 'LET'S BIFF THE BIGFOOT!' as the door bowed inwards with each BANGG. The light coming through the windows from the crowd's torches and lanterns threw shadows up the towering lobby walls and illuminated a small sign on a door behind one of the counters. 'Stairs!' whispered Bram excitedly, 'It says *STAIRS*! This way, Mol!'

They mounted the stairs two at a time, racing upwards past wood-panelled walls covered in gilt-framed portraits of past Post Masters General and old Lord Lieutenants of Ireland as they ran. They skidded around three landings until they reached the third storey staircase. This set of steps was narrower than the others, and instead of opening out onto another wide landing, this slender staircase was topped with a trapdoor. 'That must lead to the roof!' panted Bram, out of breath from climbing the stairs at such a breakneck speed. 'Let me go first, so,' said Molly, who, much to Bram's surprise, didn't seem to be out of breath at all, 'it's most likely locked, and I still have my hairpin handy!' She bounded up the last few steps and made quick work of the heavy lock. Between the two of them they heaved the trapdoor up and it opened outwards onto the GPO roof with a KER-ASHHH!!

Molly and Bram's two heads peeped up cautiously from the trapdoor opening and they each slowly looked left and right. The roof of the GPO was illuminated by the pallid, cold light of the moon. Three tall, white stone statues, Mercury and Fidelity, with Hibernia in the middle, stood at the top of the portico and stared down at Sackville Street where the mob were banging on the main door with their makeshift weapons and continuing their chants of, 'DOWN WITH YETIS!' and 'LET'S BIFF THE BIGFOOT!'

Huddled behind the statues, pressed tight against the waist-high stone railings of the parapet wall was a huge hairy shape that was trying its best to make itself as small and tiny as possible. Its furry legs were drawn up to its woolly chin, and its shaggy arms were wrapped around them.

'The Yeti!' said Bram softly. The huge creature raised its hairy head and two glowing purple eyes gazed at the two friends.

'Ah, Janey,' said Molly, 'look at him, Bram; he looks so sad.' The Yeti snuffled and wiped where Bram thought his fur-covered nose might have been with a massive, shaggy paw-like hand.

Slowly, with the chants of the angry crowd below echoing around the roof of the GPO, the two friends climbed out of the trapdoor and approached the Irish Yeti …

Chapter Seven:

Two Phony Hounds in the Pound

In which Billy the Pan and Shep come to the rescue of some captive canines.

From underneath the grey rug of his dog costume Billy the Pan could hear Prince Albert whimpering. The bouncy journey he and Shep had been on, hoisted high on the shoulder of the two London hooligans, had ended abruptly when all three of The Sackville Street Spooks, Prince Albert included, had been unceremoniously flung into a large cage with wooden bars. Once the two boys and dog were inside the cage, the two Cockney bully-boys had padlocked its door.

'Fancy a cuppa *fig*, Mr Bleat?' said Mr Grimble. '*Fig*?' asked Mr Bleat, his bushy eyebrows raised. 'Fig *tree*, Mr Bleat,' said Mr Grimble, '*tea*! Do you fancy a cuppa tea?' Mr Bleat nodded his head enthusiastically, 'Oh, yes please, Mr Grimble, that would be very *chicken*.' Now it was Mr Grimble's turn to raise his eyebrows. '*Chicken*, Mr Bleat?' he asked. 'Chicken and rice, Mr Grimble,' said Mr Bleat, '*Nice*! I mean a cuppa *fig* would be very *nice*!' Billy and Shep could hear the two thugs' footsteps as they wandered away in search of tea. 'What was that all about?' asked Shep, mystified by the coded conversation the two London bruisers had been having. 'I haven't a *brew*,' said Billy with a small grin, 'I mean, I haven't a *clue*!'

Billy raised the grey rug covering off his head and had a look around to see where they were. The room he could see through the bars had a high ceiling made of rusting corrugated iron strips and tall weather-beaten wooden walls. All along each wall were rows of cages, just like the one they were locked in. They were piled up on top of each other, four or five cages high.

'Oh. My. Dog …' said Billy the Pan softly.

Shep peeped out from under his dog disguise and gasped. Looking through the bars of each cage were at least three or four dogs; in some there were German shepherds, red setters and Jack Russells, in others there were collies, dachshunds and Dalmatians; still others held springer spaniels, beagles and French bulldogs. One tiny cage even held a teeny, pint-sized chihuahua.

All the dogs looked downcast and dejected, and many of them were whining and whimpering unhappily.

'All the dogs!' whispered Shep, 'Billy, this is where all the dogs of Dublin are! Someone has been dog-nappin' them an' keepin' them here in this warehouse! The Yeti wasn't eatin' them at all!'

'I *knew* there was no Irish Yeti!' said Billy, 'These two jokers have been goin' around, robbin' everyone's *chocolate*!'

Shep looked baffled. '*Chocolate*?' he asked.

'Oh, sorry, I've been listenin' to so much Cockney rhyming slang, I've started to speak it myself.' replied Billy 'I meant *chocolate log*, *dog*! These fellas have been stealin' everyone's *dog*!'

Just then a diminutive gentleman walked into the warehouse. He wore a long white jacket and a white woolly jumper with a wide, maroon-red V-neck, over which hung a long, rectangular beard. On his head was a bright red cap with a single yellow stripe going right the way around and a tiny brim at the front. He took a long look around at the rows upon rows of cages full of whimpering doggos and put both his small hands to his bald head. 'GRRRIIIIMMMMMBLLLE!' he roared, 'BBLLEEEAAAATTTTTT!!!' Several of the doggy prisoners started howling and many of them, Prince Albert included, cowered back in their cages in fright.

Mr Grimble and Mr Bleat trotted out through the doorway of a backroom, holding cups of tea and small side plates with thick slices of buttered fruit cake. 'Why, 'ullo, Sir Alf,' said Mr Grimble. 'Would you fancy a cup of *brie* and a *mice and snake*, sir?' asked Mr Bleat.

'No, Mr Bleat, I do *not* want a cup of tea *or* a slice of cake,' said Sir Alfred Mortlock, his face becoming an alarming shade of red. 'What I *do* want is to know why you two out-and-out dim-witted nincompoops seem to have stolen every last dog in Dublin and stashed them here in these cages??!!'

'Ah,' said Mr Grimble. 'Well, sir –'

Mr Bleat cut in, 'You see, sir–'

Sir Alfred turned an even more disturbing shade of scarlet. 'SPIT IT OUT!!'

'Remember you said that the England Eleven had to beat the Irish cricket team by 'ook or by crook, sir?' said Mr Grimble.

'Yeee-eessss. ...' said Sir Alfred slowly.

'Well, we 'eard that the Irish cricket team captain has a laah-vely dog,' said Mr Bleat.

Mr Grimble nodded fervently, 'Oh, a *laaaaaah-vely* dog that he's ever-so devoted to!'

Mr Bleat nodded so hard it looked like his head might shake off his shoulders, 'So we thought, seeing as *we* are so devoted to *you*, Sir Alfred, seeing as *we* are your most trusted *spanner-and-wrench men*–'

'That's *henchmen*, Sir Alfred,' said Mr Grimble helpfully. Sir Alfred began to turn red.

'So, as your most trusted *spanner-and-wrench men*,' continued Mr Bleat with an annoyed glance toward his fellow *spanner-and-wrench man*, sorry, *henchman*, 'we decided to try and put the Irish cricket team captain off his game …'

'… By stealing his dog, sir!,' said Mr Grimble, 'It would put him right off! He'd be all at sixes an' sevens, as it were!'

'But then, sir, we weren't too sure if we had stolen the right dog, sir,' said Mr Bleat, 'what with dogs looking much the same as each uvver, an' all.'

'Four legs, two ears, one tail,' said Mr Grimble. Sir Alfred's face had turned almost purple.

'So, we thought we'd better steal anuvver couple, just to make sure we'd stolen the right one,' said Mr Bleat.

'And then we stole a few more, just to be extra sure,' said Mr Grimble.

'And then we stole a few more, just to be *extra*, extra sure,' said Mr Bleat.

'And then,' said Mr Grimble, 'before you know it …' He swept his arm around the warehouse that was filled almost to the ceiling with cages full of captive canines.

Sir Alfred's face had now turned beetroot crimson and he tugged painfully on his oblong beard as he remembered the chant he had heard coming from the fortune teller's tent when he had fled Smithfield Market two days before, '*You'll ne-ver beat the Irish! YOU'LL NE-VER BEAT THE IRISH!*'

'You DIMWITS!' he bellowed, 'You BLOCKHEADS! If either of you two blithering IDIOTS owned one more brain cell, it would die of loneliness!' His face was now a deep shade of maroon. He took off his tiny cap and wrung it in his fists. 'There is just one small, tiny problem with your dog-napping plan: The Irish cricket team captain doesn't *have* a dog, he HATES dogs! The Irish cricket team captain has a CAT – she's small and ginger and her name is Bouncer!' Sir Alfred's face was now vermillion. 'Let me get this right,' he thundered. 'You two NINCOMPOOPS tried to steal the Irish cricket team captain's dog to put him off his game – but he doesn't have a dog, he has a miniscule ginger CAT – and *then* you ended up stealing EVERY DOG IN DUBLIN??'

'Oh my,' said Mr Grimble, 'what a *waffle dress*.'

'He means, sir,' said Mr Bleat, helpfully, 'What an *awful mess*.'

Sir Alfred Mortlock finally (and completely) blew his top. The little man threw his tiny hat onto the ground, stamped both his little feet on the wooden floor and started to SCREAM, SCREECH and SHRIEK so loudly that padlocks on the doors of the dogs' cages rattled. Mr Grimble and Mr Bleat, the two Cockney bully-boys, both of whom were at least ten fists taller than their *candy floss* (sorry, *boss*) cowered back into the corner of the warehouse like a couple of horrified hounds.

In the cage beside a shivering Prince Albert, Billy and Shep pulled back the dog disguises from their faces and looked at each other. So, *this* was why Dublin's dogs were disappearing – two eejits had stolen them by mistake! They heard a jubilant bark from another dog cage beside them and all three dogs, one real and two fake, turned to see a dog they knew well.

'Her Majesty!' said Shep, 'Billy, it's Her Majesty – we found her!' Her Majesty's brown furry face had lit up with happiness and her tail was wagging in a frenzy of delight.

Billy the Pan slipped out of his costume. 'Right,' he said, 'it's time to get our dog out of here; and all the rest of these poor aul' dogs too. Shep, will you do the honours?'

'I have my lock-pick right here,' said Shep, taking a long, thin piece of metal from his curly hair, 'I never leave home without it.' He quickly picked the padlock on the cage door and the door swung open.

'Now, let's get Her Majesty out, and then open all the other cages,' said Billy, 'but let's do it quickly, while this little cricket eejit is havin' his tantrum.'

As swiftly as they could the two boys unlocked each of the cages. Her Majesty bounded beside them, her long tongue lolling, happily sniffing and licking her friend Prince Albert. Shep looked puzzled; the newly freed dogs inside the cages were all as still as statues, they looked like they didn't want to come out at all. 'They're prob'ly afraid to come out,' whispered Billy, 'while that Sir Alfred fella is still shoutin' and bawlin' and causin' a scene.'

Sir Alfred's shouts were echoing off the corrugated iron ceiling of the warehouse and his two huge henchmen were cringing in the corner with their eyes tightly shut and their fingers in their ears. Shep, Billy and their two dogs circled around behind them, unseen and unheard in the general bellowing din that the English Eleven Cricket Team Captain was making, until they stood in the centre of the warehouse.

'Let's give these jokers a nice welcome to Dublin,' said Shep. 'I know just how to do it,' said Billy the Pan, 'with a little trick that Molly Malone taught me – a dog whistle, you might call it.'

He put his two fingers in his mouth, took a deep breath and whistled three times: two ear-splitting high notes and then one equally deafening low note.

At the sound of the two high notes the dogs in the cages all sat up, their ears perking and their tails wagging. On the third note they all smiled big doggy smiles and burst through the doors of their cages barking happily and loudly.

Sir Alfred and his two huge thuggish sidekicks looked around from where they were shrieking and cowering just in time to see hundreds of furry delighted doggos galloping joyfully at full speed in their direction – towards the doors and towards home! They were quickly overrun by the shaggy stampede of canines, and Billy could hear their OOFS! and DO'YA'MINDS? and OO-YAHS! as hundreds of dog paws, big and small, swept over them. Bringing up the rear were Billy the Pan and Shep, followed by Her Majesty and Prince Albert. Billy and Shep leapt over the groaning, trampled forms of Sir Alfred and his two henchmen, but Prince Albert took a moment to cock a leg and piddle on Sir Alfred's little red cricket hat, which lay beside him on the sawdust-covered warehouse floor.

The two friends and their two canine comrades followed the furry avalanche of dogs out of the warehouse doors singing, 'You'll ne-ver beat the Irish! YOU'LL NE-VER BEAT THE IRISH!'

NOTICE:

A SPLENDID SPORTING EVENT

THE IRISH CRICKET TEAM VS THE ENGLAND ELEVEN

BOO!

SHALL TAKE PLACE ON

SUNDAY TWELFTH JUNE

AT TWO O'CLOCK SHARP AT

LEINSTER CRICKET CLUB, RATHGAR

Gentlemen! Come along and support your team!

GOD SAVE THE QUEEN!

EXPLORER

MAJOR REDMOND HERRING, AN OFFICER WITH THE ROYAL IRISH REGIMENT HAS GONE MISSING FROM RICHMOND HOSPITAL WHERE HE HAD BEEN LATELY RECUPERATING FOLLOWING AN ARDUOUS EXPEDITION TO THE HIMALAYAN MOUNTAINS

MAJOR HERRING IS A TALL GENTLEMAN WITH BROWN HAIR, A RUDDY COMPLEXION AND AN EXCELLENT SINGING VOICE

THE REGIMENT IS OFFERING A SMALL REWARD FOR ANY INFORMATION WHICH MAY LEAD TO THE MAJOR'S SAFE RETURN

APPLY TO CAPTAIN R. BUTTERWORTH, COMMAND HEADQUARTERS, PARKGATE, DUBLIN

GOD SAVE THE QUEEN!

Chapter Eight:

A Big Hand for the Bigfoot!

In which Molly and Bram befriend a bogus bigfoot and defuse a dangerous disturbance.

Molly looked at the compass she held in her hand and then looked back again at the Irish Yeti. The huge creature looked terrified; it clung to the ramparts of the GPO roof, and its eyes, formerly a flashing purple colour, looked duller in the moonlight. 'I don't know if this is a Yeti or not,' she said to Bram, 'but it's a poor aul' creature either way.'

'Oh, Mol, I'm absolutely sure this poor creature isn't a Yeti,' said Bram pointing to the Yeti's chest, 'I never heard of Yeti fur needing buttons!' Molly looked, and sure enough, there was a line of small glass buttons going down the length of the Yeti's furry tummy.

'And Bram,' she said, 'I don't think purple is this Yeti's natural eye colour!' She reached out a hand and pulled at the purple Yeti eyes; they came away easily and dangled against the Yeti's chest on a short strap.

'GOGGLES!' said Bram, his own eyes wide.

'S-s-s-snow goggles, actually,' said the Yeti. Molly and Bram both gasped. The Yeti shifted around and sat on the roof with his furry back to the balustrade. 'I'm a-a-afraid I've caused the m-m-most awful fuss,' said the Yeti. 'P-p-p-please allow me to in-in-introduce myself,' he continued, 'My name is Major Redmond Herring.' He pulled back his Yeti-fur head to reveal a pleasant looking, if weather-beaten face – a most definitely *human* one! 'These fur hat, coat, trousers and gloves are my protective snow apparel. I even have big fur boots with leather grips on the soles.' He held up a foot so they could see the bottoms of his boots; the thick grips looked like massive toes.

'Bigfoot...' whispered Bram.

'Ah, yes,' said Major Herring, 'I can see how one could mistake my p-p-protective snow clothing for the furry figure of the Abominable Snowman, but I assure you I am not he!'

'You see, I have recently returned from an expedition to the snowy Himalayan m-m-mountains,' he continued. 'And when I say '*returned*' I more accurately mean that I was '*sent home*.' Unhappily, I had a small spot of *snow madness* while I was there – all I could see from horizon to horizon was vast fields of white; it would send anyone a little doo-lally. The rest of the chaps had me shipped back home to the Richmond Hospital for treatment, but regrettably my *snow madness* has the effect of making me rather m-m-muddled from time to time, and I seem to have yet again escaped from the hospital. And now I'm afraid I can't seem to find my way back!' He scratched his head, 'But you have my solemn word, I am NO Yeti.'

Just then there was a loud KER-ASHHH!! as another trapdoor slammed open onto the General Post Office roof. This was followed by a KER-ANNNGG!! and a KER-UMMPPP!! as two more trapdoors opened. A crowd of people, each holding a sweeping brush handle, a cricket bat or an egg whisk started to crawl though each open trapdoor. The mob, led by Georgie the Shovel, moved cautiously towards the Yeti, who, without his fur head and his purple eyes, looked more human in the moonlight.

'Hullo, chaps,' called the Yeti, 'Major Redmond Herring at your service! Thanks so m-m-much for coming to my rescue!'

Georgie put down his shovel in disappointment. 'Alright, folks,' he said with a sigh, 'the Yeti hunt is over, this is just some army fella with terrible dress sense.' He started to walk back towards the trapdoor.

'You mean this fella didn't eat all the dogs?' asked a little man holding an egg whisk, 'Then, what happened to them?'

'I think I know!' said Molly, hanging over the parapet and looking down into the gas-light-lit street below. Down the centre of Sackville Street came a huge, furry swarm of hundreds and hundreds of dogs. There were scores of Labradors, border collies and springer spaniels, there were gazillions of golden retrievers, poodles and Bassett hounds, and each dog was barking and yapping with glee.

'My dog!' cried Georgie the Shovel, spotting his tiny chihuahua dog in the throng below, 'My own little Foo-Foo!' He hastily climbed back down into the trapdoor and was followed by the rest of the mob, all on the way to the street to greet their previously imprisoned canines.

Bram waved frantically at the horde of excited hounds. 'There's Billy!' he shouted. 'And Shep and Prince Albert! And, oh my goodness, Mol! They have Her Majesty!'

Molly Malone squealed with joy and ran to the trapdoor. Soon she was out on Sackville Street being reunited with her slightly smelly (but completely loveable) dog.

Bram looked over the parapet to see his best friend gratefully hugging Shep and Billy, while being licked from ankle to knee by Her Majesty, and smiled a satisfied smile.

'I say,' said a voice from behind him. Bram turned to see Major Redmond Herring, the former Irish Yeti, get to his feet and stand to attention. 'I say,' repeated the Major, 'I don't suppose you know the way back to the Royal Irish Regiment ward at the Richmond Hospital, do you, old chap? It's on Brunswick Street, I think. I believe it may be time that I resumed my treatment.'

'Come on, Major,' said Bram, taking the hulking furry figure by his shaggy glove paw and leading him to the trapdoor, 'I have some good friends downstairs who'd be only too delighted to see you back home!'

'Young man,' said the Major as he climbed through the door, 'you have been of so much help to me; please call me Red.'

Major Red Herring? thought Bram, *That's a fine name for a fake Yeti if ever I heard one!*

* * *

After Molly, Bram, Shep and Billy the Pan had handed the befuddled former Irish Yeti over to the grateful doctors at the Richmond Hospital, and bid farewell (and *get-well-soon*) to Major Red Herring, they strolled down through Smithfield Square back towards the River Liffey.

'So, Billy,' said Molly, 'you're tellin' me that the English Cricket Eleven captain's henchmen tried to spoil the game for the Irish Cricket Team by robbin' a dog when they should have been stealin' a cat, and they ended up dog-nappin' nearly every dog in Dublin?'

'Yeah,' said Billy, adjusting the saucepan he wore on his head as a hat, and bending to pat Prince Albert, 'they were a right couple of eejits.'

Shep giggled. 'Too true!' he said with a wink, 'They were a couple of *buttered jewels*!' Molly raised an eyebrow, 'Huh?'

'*Utter fools*!' laughed Shep.

'Ah yes, the famous Cockney rhyming slang, I've heard of that,' said Bram. He was kneeling on the cobblestones, hugging Her Majesty. 'It was a good night's work for the Spooks, alright,' he said, in between getting licked on the face by the happy dog, 'We freed all of Dublin's dogs … AND we solved the mystery of the Irish *Meatballs and Spaghetti*!'

Bram stood and smiled a slightly smug smile, 'That means the Irish –'

'*YETI*!!' shouted the gang together with a laugh, 'We know!!'

'Now all that's left to do,' said Molly, 'is to go to the cricket match tomorrow and see the English Eleven get beaten by the Irish team – fair and square!'

'You'll ne-ver beat the Irish,' sang Billy the Pan. Her Majesty and Prince Albert started yapping and howling, and the rest of the friends joined in with the chant as they walked along arm in arm, 'YOU'LL NE-VER BEAT THE IRISH! YOU'LL NE-VER BEAT THE IRISH!'

Author's Note On Dublin:

Many of the Dublin locations in this book are as real as can be and can be visited today. Bram's home at **19 Buckingham Street** still stands; there is even a plaque to announce that he lived there, as well as a painting of his most famous character, *Dracula*, on the wall. The **Ha'penny Bridge** is a celebrated Dublin landmark, although it doesn't cost a half penny to cross it today! The grand **General Post Office** is still in **O'Connell Street**, or Sackville Street as it was known in 1859. In the centre of Sackville Street across from the GPO, **Nelson's Pillar** once stood where the Spire of Dublin stands today, and, on the other side of Sackville Street, **The Imperial Hotel** is now the Clery's building. The redbrick **Richmond Hospital** is on North Brunswick Street, close to the Phoenix Park.

Why not visit some of these places the next time you're in Dublin city? They might even inspire you, just like Bram, to become a writer!

The Real Bram & Molly

Bram Stoker

The *real* Bram Stoker was born and raised in Marino Crescent in Clontarf. After school he attended Trinity College in Dublin where was a star athlete. He always had a great love of writing and theatre, and after college he first became a newspaper theatre critic, and, after that, a theatre manager in London ... and then he decided to combine these two loves to write books such as *Dracula*, *The Lady in the Shroud*, and *The Lair of the White Worm*. His wife's name was Florence!

Molly Malone

Molly is *definitely* a fictional character, best known from the famous Dublin song where she roams the City streets selling cockles and mussels, '*alive alive-oh!*' She's a fishmonger in my book too, as well as a born leader, an accomplished pickpocket and 'the best sneak thief in Dublin'. But, to Bram, Molly is much more than that – she's a true and faithful friend.

Acknowledgements

Thanks to my amazing editor Helen, and to all the team at The O'Brien Press. Thanks to illustrator-extraordinaire Shane Cluskey, a genius with a paintbrush and a pot of purple paint! *Banks go Dutch* (*Thanks so much!*) to author and illustrator Gary Northfield, whose suggestion it was to give Mr Grimble and Mr Bleat their wonky Cockney rhyming slang. And lastly, thanks to my long-suffering family, who hear *all* my Molly'n'Bram plots and ideas … whether they want to or not!

Other Books in the Series

Molly Malone & Bram Stoker in The Sackville Street Caper
ISBN: 978-178849-318-5

Molly Malone & Bram Stoker in Double Trouble at the Dead Zoo
ISBN: 978-178849-434-2

Happy
World Book Day!

When you've read this book, you can keep ɿhe fun going by swapping it, talking about it with a friend, or reading it again!

What do you want to read next? Whether it's **comics**, **audiobooks**, **recipe books** or **non-fiction** you can visit your school, local library or nearest bookshop for your next read – someone will always be happy to help.

Changing lives through a love of books and reading.

World Book Day® is a charity sponsored by National Book Tokens

World Book Day is about changing lives through reading

When you **choose to read** in your spare time it makes you

Feel happier | **Better at reading** | **More successful**

Find your **reading superpower** by

1. **Listening to books being read aloud (or listening to audiobooks)**
2. **Having books at home**
3. **Choosing the books YOU want to read**
4. **Asking for ideas on what to read next**
5. **Making time to read**
6. **Finding ways to make reading FUN!**

This month we are

selection of six c

(two 2-in-1s and tv

Mills & Boon® Medical™ Romance

This exclusive bestselling author collection includes:

THE CELEBRITY DOCTOR'S PROPOSAL

by Sarah Morgan

with

A MOTHER BY NATURE

by Caroline Anderson

THE SURGEON'S GIFT

by Carol Marinelli

with

BUSHFIRE BRIDE

by Marion Lennox

EARTHQUAKE BABY by Amy Andrews

TWICE AS GOOD by Alison Roberts

Collect all four!

Praise for
Amy Andrews:

'*Sydney Harbour Hospital: Luca's Bad Girl* is a humorous story with steamy sensuality and heart-tugging pathos. Amy Andrews has written a fun, engrossing and fascinating story of heartache amid all the medical drama which will keep a reader involved in the story and their interest riveted right from the very first page!'
—*Contemporary Romance Reviews*

'*How to Mend a Broken Heart* is a wonderfully poignant tale of old passions, second chances and the healing power of love. It is an exceptionally realistic romance that will touch your heart and make you shed tears. Author Amy Andrews keeps her characters and therefore her readers in a constant whirlwind of emotions with this dramatic, at times heartbreaking, but ultimately uplifting story about taking chances on love's devastating choices, redemption, and triumphing against the odds.'
—*Contemporary Romance Reviews*

Amy also won a RB*Y
(Romantic Book of the Year) Award in 2010 for
A DOCTOR, A NURSE, A CHRISTMAS BABY

EARTHQUAKE BABY

BY

AMY ANDREWS

First published in Great Britain 2005. This edition 2013.
by Mills & Boon, an imprint of Harlequin (UK) Limited,
Eton House, 18-24 Paradise Road, Richmond, Surrey TW9 1SR

ISBN: 978 0 263 90659 2
ebook ISBN: 978 1 472 01219 7

03-0613

Harlequin (UK) policy is to use papers that are natural, renewable and recyclable products and made from wood grown in sustainable forests. The logging and manufacturing processes conform to the legal environmental regulations of the country of origin.

Printed and bound in Spain
by Blackprint CPI, Barcelona

Amy Andrews has always loved writing, and still can't quite believe that she gets to do it for a living. Creating wonderful heroines and gorgeous heroes and telling their stories is an amazing way to pass the day. Sometimes they don't always act as she'd like them to—but then neither do her kids, so she's kind of used to it. Amy lives in the very beautiful Samford Valley, with her husband and aforementioned children, along with six brown chooks and two black dogs. She loves to hear from her readers. Drop her a line at www.amyandrews.com.au.

Recent titles by the same author:

ONE NIGHT SHE WOULD NEVER FORGET
SYDNEY HARBOUR HOSPITAL: EVIE'S BOMBSHELL*
HOW TO MEND A BROKEN HEART
SYDNEY HARBOUR HOSPITAL: LUCA'S BAD GIRL*
WAKING UP WITH DR OFF-LIMITS
JUST ONE LAST NIGHT…
RESCUED BY THE DREAMY DOC
VALENTINO'S PREGNANCY BOMBSHELL
ALLESANDRO AND THE CHEERY NANNY

**Sydney Harbour Hospital*

This book is dedicated to all those at the coal face of rescue work. What you do is truly heroic.

CHAPTER ONE

LAURA'S legs struggled to keep pace with the bed as it was wheeled quickly down the corridor that led from Intensive Care to the operating theatres. The monitor alarms shrilled continuously as the patient's heart rate climbed higher.

Laura squeezed the black bag attached to the patient's breathing tube, administering lungfuls of air to the unconscious, critically ill patient. If he didn't get to Theatre soon, he would die.

She handed over the bag in one smooth movement to the anaesthetic nurse and the surgical team whisked him through the swing doors. They shut firmly, blocking Laura's view. She crossed her fingers as she walked back down the corridor with the other members of the team who had helped her prepare Mr Reid for his operation. Their thoughts were with him.

'How's it looking?' asked Marie Prior, the unit's clinical nurse consultant, as she approached.

'Not good,' admitted Laura.

'Mr Reid's deterioration wasn't totally out of left field. He's lucky you picked up the signs early.'

'It was a close call, Marie. Too close,' said Laura, feeling depleted now the adrenaline rush had ebbed.

'Let's go have a coffee. Come and meet the new psychiatrist. He's doing today's debriefing session.'

Great, Laura thought. Just what she needed!

'He's cute,' Marie cajoled. Laura's reluctance to participate in such activities was legendary.

'Bunny rabbits are cute,' Laura said, completely disinterested in checking out the new kid on the block. 'But I do need a coffee, so I'll go. But I'm not talking about my feelings or how I was a deprived child.'

The psychobabble she could do without. Laura's privacy was too important and, while she recognised that debriefing was essential in her working environment, she preferred to do so casually among the other staff. She dreaded these monthly sessions and avoided them where possible.

'What's his name anyway?'

'John Riley. Dr John Riley.'

An errant, traitorous brain cell kicked into life. Her heart quickened for a few beats before she consciously quelled the disturbing activity taking over her body. John. Not Jack. Goodness, it had been ten years and still just the mention of a similar name was enough to stir parts of her anatomy only he had stirred. Anyway, her Jack Riley was a surgeon, not a shrink.

Her thoughts wandered to Isaac. He was the only man in her life now. She felt the warmth of her love for him flow through her. She wouldn't have it any other way.

Ten minutes later Laura was relaxed, enjoying the playful banter in the staffroom. She had almost forgotten about the sudden turn of events that had sent her relatively stable patient to Theatre. Almost forgotten about the highly stressful period they had all just endured. Not a bed to spare. One patient left and there was barely enough time to clean the bed area before another took their place.

Marie entered the room carrying a steaming mug, chatting amicably with a man following close behind. It was difficult to see him properly. His head was blocked from her view but Laura got the impression of height and bulk. She had chosen her seat carefully. Crammed in beside the bookcase, it hid her to a certain extent. From where the guest speaker's chair was positioned it would be difficult to see all of her unless she leant forward.

Marie quickly hushed the group and introduced her guest.

'Everyone, I'd like you to meet Dr John Riley. He's St Jude's new Director of Psychiatry.'

Everyone nodded and smiled and murmured their interest.

'Actually, John's a bit formal.' His cheerful voice resonated around the room. 'Most people call me Jack.'

Laura's heart stopped. For one dreadful moment she thought she was having a cardiac arrest. That voice. It couldn't be him. Could it? Marie sat down and afforded Laura a full view of his face. Oh, no! It was him! She looked again, and her heartbeat thundered in her ears.

Same olive skin. Same dark hair clipped close to his head. Same brown eyes framed by incredibly long lashes. Dark, soft, compassionate. She watched, fascinated despite herself, as he dug his teeth into his bottom lip and smiled at what somebody was saying.

Same sexy, full lips. The same lips she had kissed softly for the last time ten years ago. Kissed as she had got out of his bed and walked out of his life. He was a psychiatrist now? What had happened to surgery?

'Well, I thought to start off, you might like to introduce yourselves and maybe tell me a little something about your lives.'

Laura watched, her thought processes frozen as people relaxed under his friendly, interested gaze. Somebody cracked a joke and Jack laughed. It was a comforting noise, gently blanketing the room.

Laura knew how that felt. It made you feel safe. Like being cocooned in a blanket on a cold and rainy night. He had made her feel like that. Safe. Reassured.

There were only two more people to go before those eyes would be focussing on her. Laura's mind was in a total dither. She wanted to run but felt incapable of breathing, let alone anything involving major muscle groups.

She had changed a little, sure, in ten years. A different hairstyle, a few kilos lighter. But it was futile to think that he would not remember her. She wasn't flattering herself.

They had shared a momentous, life-changing experience. For a brief period, ten years ago, he had been her lifeline. A superficial change in physical appearance could not obliterate that.

All he had to do was glance out the corner of his eye and he would see her, but he was much too professional for that. His gaze and attention was one hundred per cent fixed on the person who was talking. They had his complete and undivided attention. She tried to sink further from view.

'Ah…one in every crowd,' he joked. 'Something to hide?' Jack shifted in his chair to get a better view of the staff member beside the bookcase.

He recognised her immediately. Felt his eyes widen as shock and disbelief engulfed his body.

'Laura?' The question rasped from his throat.

The laughter in the room subsided as speculation and curiosity took hold.

'You two know each other?' Marie asked.

Jack did not answer. He was speechless. It was her…really her. After ten years of wondering…wishing. Here she was. In front of him.

A little different maybe, considering the last time he had seen her she'd been naked and sated beside him. He remembered his dissatisfaction on waking to find that she had left some time in the night. It felt like yesterday.

There were so many things he wanted to ask, to know. His mind crowded with questions, each more urgent than the previous one. How she was and what had she been doing and why the hell had she left him like that? He had wanted to hold her some more, talk some more, make love some more.

When Marie had talked about a Laura, it hadn't occurred to him that it would be her. His Laura. He had given up reacting to the name years before.

He watched as her eyes widened and he read the plea expressed in their blue depths. Please, don't reveal me.

'Yes,' he answered. 'We go back a bit.'

He was rewarded with a look of such gratitude he forgave himself the little white lie. Good grief, he thought. They don't know. These people, her colleagues, don't know who she is or what she's been through. How had she managed that?

'Well…' He cleared his throat. 'We must catch up…later.'

'Mmm.' Laura nodded.

She listened but did not hear any of the group debrief session. Her thoughts whizzed chaotically around her head at a million miles an hour. It was him. Jack. It was really him!

The same Jack who had occupied too many waking and nearly all her sleeping hours for a decade. What was she going to do? She couldn't think. The beginnings of a headache crawled across her temples.

Somebody laughed loudly, jarring across Laura's taut nerves. She had to admire Jack's skill. He had a knack at drawing people out. The stresses of the last few weeks had affected everyone. It was his job to be their pressure valve, allowing the steam to escape. Ease the tension.

Patients and situations were openly discussed, putting them into perspective. Unlike her, the people she worked with were much more open to this form of communication. They felt it helped and Laura knew, in reality, that these sessions were invaluable. But circumstances had given her a few coping strategies of her own.

'What about you, Laura?'

'Huh?' she asked belatedly, becoming aware of people looking expectantly at her.

'Marie was saying that you were looking after Mr Reid when he tried to clock out today.'

'Yes.'

'How do you feel about that?'

Still shrouded in the mental fog of disbelief, she groped around for a generic answer he couldn't analyse too much.

'Concerned.'

'Is that all?'

For God's sake, she wanted to yell, stop talking to me.

Leave me be. I need to get my head around this. 'Worried for his family.' She shrugged.

'You don't seem very concerned or worried.' Jack observed. Brown eyes watched her carefully from below long lashes.

'Oh?' That's because all I can think about now is you!

Silence filled the space between them. Laura just wanted to get away. She didn't want to indulge in a philosophical debate. She wanted to be gone.

Jack finally spoke. 'He was a long-term patient. He looked like he'd turned the corner. Surely his setback was a shock?'

'This is an intensive care unit. People are critically ill. Sometimes they get worse before they get better.' Now his persistence was really irking her.

'Sometimes they don't get better.'

'Sometimes.'

Jack read her body language loud and clear. Arms crossed, legs crossed, back erect. Subject closed. She didn't want to talk about it. He wondered how often she did that. Laura had been through a major trauma ten years ago. The emotional baggage from that, mixed with a high-stress work environment, was not a good combination. She was a prime candidate for burnout.

She was thinner than he remembered. Her blue eyes still troubled. He wished he'd known her when they had sparkled with life and fun. Before the terrible events of Newvalley. Before they had mirrored the part of her spirit that had died in the tragic building collapse.

Laura was saved further scrutiny by Marie who came to the rescue, diverting his attention with a question. She gulped air into suffocating lungs. His shrewd gaze weighing her up had felt as restrictive as bricks against her chest. No doubt he had been analysing her every word, every gesture.

Five minutes later a beeper rang out, interrupting the conversation. Jack pulled it off his belt, checking the message.

'I'm sorry, folks, I have to take this call.'

'Use the phone in my office,' Marie offered. 'Across the hall.'

Seeing her chance to escape, Laura stood, ignoring the speculative looks from her colleagues. Her shift finished in fifteen minutes but she was sure no one would begrudge her knocking off now. Just a quick word to the afternoon staff about Mr Reid and she was out of here. Too much had happened today—confronting a ghost from her past was beyond her.

Laura grabbed her bag from her locker. She just wanted to get away from the hospital. St Jude's had been her sanctuary for the last eight years. Suddenly it didn't feel safe here either. Jack Riley's presence caused too many complications.

She pushed the lift button. It arrived promptly and she got in.

'Hold the lift, please,' a voice commanded, followed closely by a big hand preventing the doors' closure.

'Laura.' His brown eyes smiled gently.

'Hello, Jack.' Her earlier testiness dissolved as the years melted away.

He took her hand and squeezed it. They stood quite close in the small lift, looking at their joined hands. Her slim, pale one in stark contrast to his, large and tanned. There was so much to say. Where to begin?

'It's nice to see you again.' His voice was husky. 'Can we go somewhere and talk?'

'I'm really tired.' She needed time to think.

He lifted her chin. Yes, she looked done in. He yearned to embrace her. 'Please.'

'OK.' She sighed. 'But not the canteen.'

He raised an eyebrow.

'Gossip.'

He raised the other eyebrow.

'Oh, come on, Jack. You know what a hospital's like! The grapevine will already be working overtime with what happened in the staffroom.'

'Let them talk.' He shrugged.

'No. Attention is one thing I *don't* need,' she said, and marched out of the doors as they opened onto the foyer.

Laura steamed ahead, leading Jack to the deserted area around the staff pool. It was a cool, peaceful haven set in the beautifully landscaped grounds of St Jude's. She sat down at one of the shady, poolside tables, removed her sunglasses and watched him sit down opposite her.

It was a strange moment. Despite brimming with questions, neither seemed to know how or where to start. For now, Laura was content to just be near him as decade-old memories were rekindled. The good as well as the bad.

'Laura…how…how have you been?' He reached for her hand and she allowed him to take it.

'OK.'

'Really?'

'Yes.' She laughed. 'Really.'

'Any nightmares? Flashbacks?'

'The first two years were rough but…I've been good since.'

'That's great.'

'I'm over it, Jack. It's behind me. I've got on with my life.'

'Yes, but it doesn't ever really go away. Does it?'

'Sure it does.'

'You must let me in on your coping strategies.'

Laura looked at the doubt etched on his face. He could think what he liked. She *was* over it. She was.

'So, what have you been up to?' asked Jack.

'Nothing much. Working…living…'

'Is that it?'

No, she wanted to say. I've had your baby and raised him for the past nine years. My life has been very full. She wanted to thank him for such a precious gift. But she was silent. She couldn't just dump something like this in his lap.

She needed to know if his attitude towards having children

had changed. She needed to know him better before deciding whether or not to break the news.

Ten years ago her decision to keep their son a secret from him had been clear-cut. It hadn't been easy, and the importance of her decision had weighed heavily on her. But she'd done the right thing. She had been sure of that. Still, his reappearance in her life clouded the issue again. Had it been the right decision?

'Pretty much,' she answered. 'How about you? I thought you were off to Adelaide to become a hotshot surgeon. When did you become a shrink?'

He was silent as he searched for the right words. 'After Newvalley, I found it difficult to get back into everyday life—you know what I mean?'

Laura nodded. She knew exactly what he meant.

'I did go to Adelaide and I even stuck it out for a year, but, well…my heart wasn't really in it. Surgery had been my passion and then suddenly it seemed so insignificant. Being involved in that rescue effort where so many people died…'

They were both silent for a few moments, reflecting on the lives that had been lost when the earthquake had hit and the parts they had played in the dreadful tragedy. It had been a major catastrophe for Australia, making news headlines for weeks.

'It was totally life-changing. It made me reassess my whole direction,' said Jack.

Laura nodded again. She understood. Her life now seemed to be separated into two different parts. Before the earthquake and after the earthquake. She was not the same girl as she had been in those years and moments before the earth had shaken and the building had tumbled down around her.

He closed his eyes. 'I thought I was losing it for a while. I couldn't sleep and when I did I'd have nightmares. I felt on edge and irritable. I couldn't concentrate properly on my work and that's scary when you're wielding a scalpel! And

I wasn't the one who'd been trapped… I don't know how you've stayed sane all these years, Laura.'

'I had help,' she said.

'So did I, actually. And that's when I knew I wanted to become a psychiatrist. So I studied people's minds instead of their anatomies. And here I am today.'

'Here you are,' she whispered, and squeezed his hand.

'So.' He lifted her left hand and inspected it. 'No wedding ring.'

'No.' She smiled. 'Never married.'

'C'mon Laura, they must be lining up! You're even more beautiful than I remembered,' he said gently, as he brushed his fingers through her fringe.

She closed her eyes and shrugged. 'What about you? No wedding band either?'

'Divorced.'

Laura felt her eyes widen as she sat more upright. He had been married! Surely not? Jack was sexy as hell and no doubt attracted women like bees to a honey pot but, if her memory served her correctly, he had never wanted to get seriously involved.

They had spent hours talking while she had lain beneath the rubble of the backpackers' hostel. Marriage, kids, all that 'settling down' stuff had definitely not been on his agenda. His career had been his only focus. She must have been a hell of a girl!

'Any children?' She held her breath.

'No, thank goodness.' His tone was tense, forbidding.

She tried not to flinch. It seemed he was still not enamoured about the idea of being a father. Oh, Isaac. Obviously her decision to keep quiet about their son had been justified.

'What happened?'

'Long story,' he said dismissively. 'So, are you coming to the memorial service next week?'

'No.'

'You've never been to any.' His tone was accusing.

'I went to the first.' Her tone was defensive.

Their eyes met and held as she remembered that day and what had happened later in his apartment. They'd made Isaac together that afternoon. They had made love like it had been their last night on earth and they the only two people in the world, clinging desperately to each other, trying to find solace and stability in a world that had been turned upside down.

Jack remembered it vividly. He remembered holding her as she had broken down.

'I thought I was going to die,' she had said over and over, as huge sobs had racked her slim body. He couldn't even begin to imagine how she must have felt—trapped for twelve hours before they'd located her and then for a further eight as rescue teams had worked frantically to dig her out.

He'd thought she was going to die too on a couple of occasions as the unstable foundations had rocked and shifted, buffeted by aftershocks rumbling deep beneath the earth. He'd been helpless to do anything but be there with her, hold her hand, talk. That she had survived was a miracle.

Slowly her sobs had subsided and Jack remembered her embarrassment and then the sudden rush of passion that had taken over as two traumatised people had tried to find a haven together. It had been unexpected—spontaneous—and Jack doubted that either of them could have stopped it. It had been sweet and intense and as he sat opposite her now, he knew he wanted to experience it again.

'Sometimes I wish I hadn't gone.' She broke into their memories.

'You don't mean that, Laura.'

No, he was right. She didn't. Isaac had come from that day. The one great thing that had come out of the whole disaster. He had filled her life with love and joy. Isaac's name meant laughter and that's what he had brought to her life—laughter and happiness. Two emotions she hadn't thought she would feel so soon after Newvalley.

'No, I don't,' she conceded.

'Come with me to Newvalley, Laura.'

'No, Jack.'

'It might be good closure, Laura. If not for you, for the others.'

'There are no others.'

'I mean the relatives of the victims, Laura. Every year they turn up and sit around wondering where you are and how you're doing. They'd love to meet with you. See you're OK.'

Laura was surprised. She'd never thought of it from that angle before.

'You could be their closure, too.'

'I don't want to be their closure,' she said tersely, and rose from the table. 'It took me a couple of years of therapy to get to a point in my life where I could put it all behind me. I don't want to go back. Rehash it. I can't be someone else's crutch.'

'So don't be. They won't ask for anything that you can't give them, Laura. They're just people who lost loved ones and feel connected to you because you made it out alive. Let them be near you.'

She shoved her hands in her uniform pockets and paced.

'I can't, Jack. I don't want to remember that time in my life. I want to leave it in the past, where it belongs.'

'It's part of who you are. Deny it at your own peril. It'll creep up on you one day when you least expect it. Post-traumatic stress can be quite debilitating.'

Laura ignored him. She'd heard it all before. 'I can't just leave work at the drop of a hat.'

'When was the last time you had a holiday?'

'A year ago.'

'You'll be burnt out if you're not careful.'

'I'm sure I'm no more at risk than any of my colleagues.'

'They don't have your trauma history.'

'Oh, please!' She rolled her eyes.

'Have you thought about working in a less stressful environment?'

'I love ICU!'

'There are plenty of other areas to work.'

'Nothing that gives me the job satisfaction.'

'Doesn't seem too satisfying at the moment.'

'Oh, Jack. Sure, we get crazy busy and we lose some. But you know what it's like! Nothing gives me a bigger thrill than seeing a critically ill patient get better and go home. Knowing you've been part of that is the best feeling.'

'You still need to look after yourself. It's not uncommon for post-traumatic stress to set in years after the initial incident. Maybe a word to Marie—'

'Don't you dare! Don't you dare interfere with my work.' She glowered at him.

'Steady, Laura. No need to get upset.'

'Oh, for God's sake, Jack. You're back in my life for two minutes and you're interfering already. I think I'm allowed to be a little cross. I'm not a lost, scared twenty-year-old any more. Besides—no one at work knows. I'd like to keep it that way.'

'It's amazing you've been able to keep it quiet. No one ever recognised you?'

'Well, I didn't start here until a couple of years after Newvalley and the hype had died down by then. Plus, most people don't know that my real name is Mary. I've been called by my middle name all my life, but thankfully backpacker hostels check you in as the name on your passport. As far as Australia's concerned, the girl under the building was Mary Scott, not Laura.'

'But…you've never confided in anyone?'

'When you have photographers who'll use every trick in the book to get a picture, it's hard to know who to trust any more. I've had to become a very private person, Jack. When I started here I didn't want any special treatment or be an item of curiosity. I've struggled to keep a low profile. If my past came out, it'd be all around the hospital…the press would find out…'

Jack's face told her he thought she was exaggerating.

'It's true Jack. Every year, my lawyer is still inundated with offers from the media for an interview.'

'You're not serious?'

'Unfortunately, yes. My lawyer thinks I should get an agent.'

'You could be a rich woman, Laura.'

'My memories are private and not for sale. Besides, I have to protect…'

'Protect?'

'Myself,' she said rather lamely, thrown by how easily she had almost let the cat out of the bag. 'And my family and the people I work with. The last thing anybody here needs is a three-ring circus following me around.'

'Some people would kill for that kind of attention.'

'Not me.' She shuddered. 'Those first few months after…the media camped out on my doorstep. That's why I moved to Queensland.'

'I had no idea you were on TV that much.'

'I wasn't. I declined all interviews and avoided the vultures like the plague. But it didn't stop them from trying! Anyway, they finally grew tired of my constant refusals and decided to leave me alone.'

'It must have been hard to get your life back together with that kind of scrutiny.'

'You can say that again!'

So deeply engrossed in conversation were they that Laura and Jack had not noticed the arrival of other people. Splashing in the water alerted them. Laura checked her watch.

'Please, think about coming to Newvalley with me.'

'No, Jack,' she said firmly.

'Well, it's not until next week.' He smiled and stood beside her. 'I'll be seeing you around. You never know, maybe I'll manage to convince you.'

'Don't hold your breath.' She smiled back. Her lips slackened as she became caught up in his intense stare. 'What?'

'Why did you leave that morning, Laura?'

'Oh, Jack, it was a long time ago. Let's leave it in the past, where it belongs.'

'I need to know.'

'Impatient as always.'

'What would you know?' His voice had a hard edge to it now. 'How do you know what I'm like? *You* walked out, remember. You never gave it a chance. Me a chance.'

All the old feelings returned in a rush. It was as if he had stepped back ten years into the morning after. The sadness and disappointment at finding her gone felt as real now as it had then.

'Are you angry with me?' His outburst had surprised her.

'I thought we had something going and then you walk out in the middle of the night and I never hear from you ever again. Yes.' The hard edge remained. 'I *was* upset with you.'

'Well, I didn't notice you trying to contact me,' she pointed out, peeved by his tone.

'I tried. Quite a lot, actually. I rang and you never picked up. I called around and you never answered the door. Eventually I figured you just didn't want to be found, so I gave up.'

Laura was shocked at his admission. Her phone had rung hot, night and day, from the media. She'd stopped answering it. She'd stopped spending time at her flat, too. She'd never known when a journalist was going to show up. She'd rarely been at home those first couple of months and then she'd moved to Queensland to be nearer her mum and dad.

'Look, Jack, you picked a really bad day for this. I have a headache, and dredging up the past is only making it worse.'

'I'm sorry.' He sighed, taking her hand, instantly contrite. He took a deep breath, trying to rein in his chaotic feelings. That he still felt so strongly surprised him. But looking at her closed expression, he knew now wasn't the time to push. He had to bide his time on this one. He didn't want to blow it with her. She would tell him one day. He hoped. He pulled her to him and gently kissed her forehead.

Despite what had just happened, Laura felt a strange awareness creep into her bones. Every part of her body in contact with his became alive at a cellular level. It unsettled her. She stepped back.

'No doubt I'll see you about,' she said as she started to walk away.

'Count on it,' he called after her.

'I won't change my mind,' she threw over her shoulder as she let herself out the pool gate.

Jack watched her retreat until the wiggle of her cute behind was no longer visible. Her movements aroused him. It may have been ten years but his body was responding to her as if it had been yesterday. He ached for her physically but there was a deeper ache that had nothing to do with her body.

She'd certainly convinced herself that she'd dealt with the events of that day in Newvalley. But despite her claim that she was over it, he could sense an inner vulnerability. Maybe it took someone like him, who knew her intimately, to see what she couldn't.

He had a feeling she was a time bomb ready to go off. It was better for her to do that in an appropriate situation, like the service, with him by her side, than have something else trigger it at work or at home. That could be catastrophic for her. Somehow he had to get her to that service.

CHAPTER TWO

WHAT a day! Laura drove to her outer suburban home, not really noticing the route. She went through the motions—stopped at the red lights, went on the green. But she was not concentrating on the mechanics of driving. She was preoccupied with him. Jack Riley. Back in her life again after all this time.

To say it was a shock was a gross understatement. In reality, Laura had known that one day they would meet again. It would be a necessity. There'd come a time when Isaac would want to know his father and she would not deny him that. She had been prepared for that eventuality. But not yet. She hadn't been prepared for it today.

So, what now? she wondered as she turned the small hatchback into the leafy street that had been her home for the last nine years. Seeing him again had dredged up some intense feelings. Laura felt sure that avoiding him was probably the wisest move…for a while anyway. At least until she figured out whether to tell him about Isaac or not. And how to go about it and… Oh, it all seemed such an insurmountable problem. Too complicated.

It had been simple ten years ago when she had first learned she was pregnant. They'd seen each other only twice and one of those times a building had collapsed on her! They hardly had a relationship at all. Yes, they had a special bond. He had been her rescuer, saving her from certain death and risking his life in the process. They were connected, in a cosmic sort of way, but…a couple? With a future?

They had talked a lot during her rescue. From this she had learned that Jack's career was his priority. A marvellous opportunity had come his way to study surgery in Adelaide.

She remembered the note of barely suppressed excitement in his voice, which even several layers of concrete couldn't muffle, as he'd confided his dreams to her. She wasn't going to dash them because they had been irresponsible when making love. She wanted no further sacrifice from him.

Laura knew that it probably wouldn't have been that difficult to track him down, had she been so inclined. But she had not. How could she have done it to him? She had refused to dump what she was certain would have been very unwelcome news in his lap. Heavens! She didn't want him to think that the whole experience had unbalanced her, turning her into an obsessed lunatic, stalking him, professing to carry his love child.

No. She had wanted the best for him. She had wanted for him what he'd wanted for himself. She owed him her life. She hadn't wanted to ask him to give up his. She'd been, in reality, just a one-night stand.

Even so, she'd agonised over her decision. Keeping a child from someone, even one who didn't want kids, was a huge call. Truthfully, she'd hadn't been in the best place emotionally at the time to make such a momentous decision. But she'd made it, truly convinced it was in Jack's best interests.

Laura opened the door, disturbing the quiet within the house. Normally she would have swung by her mother's and picked Isaac up after work, but he was holidaying with his grandparents. They took him away every year at this time.

Usually they took him for a week to their holiday home at Mooloolaba on the Sunshine Coast. But this year they had decided to splurge and take him to Disneyland. They had gone for two weeks. Two whole weeks!

Laura picked up a photo frame with Isaac's cheeky, nine-year-old grin smiling back at her. He looked so like his father. Same big, gentle, brown eyes with long lashes. Tall and olive-skinned. His hair closely cropped, courtesy of a number-two blade. Jack would have to be blind not to see the resemblance.

Isaac. He had kept her sane through the rough times. A baby's needs had to be met regardless of how the mother was feeling. He had been a good distraction. Someone to focus on when coping with the aftermath of Newvalley and the guilt of being the sole survivor seemed too much to bear.

She traced his face with her thumb.

'Oh, Isaac. What should I do?' She missed him. She was looking forward to hearing his voice on the phone tonight. But there was a lot of time to kill between now and then. Too much time to dwell on Jack. She had to stay busy, keep her mind off Isaac's father.

Laura passed the time pulling out weeds while music blasted into her head via earpieces attached to Isaac's Walkman. She sang along loudly, determined not to let her mind wander.

The job took a few hours to complete and it was nearly dark by the time Laura stepped into the shower. She wished she could wash her problems away as easily as the garden dirt being washed down the drain.

With a couple more hours up her sleeve, Laura headed out for a spot of late-night shopping. She walked back through her door with just enough time to unpack the groceries before ringing America.

Laura had prearranged dates and times to ring her parents and Isaac during their holiday. The price of phone calls from hotel rooms was notoriously expensive and international calls even more so. With her parents footing the bill for Isaac, she felt it was one small thing she could do to help with costs.

'Hi, Isaac.'

'Hi, Mum.'

'How are you?'

'Great, Mum. Wow! It's really cool over here.'

'How's Disneyland?'

'Excellent. It's huge!'

'Where are Gran and Pop?'

'They're in bed still. Something about jet-lag.'

Laura laughed, and it echoed around the empty house. Yep. That was Isaac. Always on the go. Jet-lag didn't stand a chance with him. But her parents were in their sixties. She tended to forget that when they were both still so active.

He chatted on about their plans for the next few days. Laura soaked it up. He'd been gone for such a short time but she missed him fiercely already.

'I wish you were here, Mum.'

'So do I, Isaac. So do I.'

A tear squeezed out from under her closed lids as she swallowed a rising tide of emotion. If only he knew how much she wished she had gone with them. Then today's unexpected meeting would never have happened. Eventually she and Jack would have run into each other but, with the hospital grapevine the way it was, she'd have known about his existence first and have been more prepared.

'I'll get Gran. Bye, Mum.'

'Goodbye, Isaac,' she said, amused by his typically abrupt farewell.

'Hi, darling. How are you?'

Her mother's soft voice put Laura on shaky ground. 'Fine,' said Laura. Why did mothers have the power to reduce you to a helpless dependent child all over again, no matter what your age?

'What's the matter?' Her mother's voice rose an octave.

She never could fool her mother. Suddenly Laura wished her mum was beside her. She desperately wanted to be hugged and soothed the way only mothers seem to know how.

'I saw Jack today.'

Silence as wide as the Pacific greeted her statement.

'Oh.'

'Yes…oh.'

'Well, how…? I mean, what did you…? Did you tell him…?'

'Oh, Mum. It's a long story but…no, I didn't tell him about Isaac.'

'What are you going to do, Laura?'

'I don't know, Mum. I don't know.'

'Darling, it's difficult to talk now. Why don't you wait until we get home next week before you decide anything? We can have a proper talk about it then.'

'That sounds sensible to me.'

Laura was too tired and mentally exhausted to think about a solution. Her head started to throb again. What she needed was to sleep, but she was too afraid to succumb. She could control her waking thoughts but her sleeping?

She took some tablets for her headache and drank some warm milk in her silent house. Thankfully her exhaustion helped her to a dreamless sleep.

It was different at Jack's place. He tossed and turned most of the night. His mind had been alive with thoughts of Laura since meeting her again. Shock, amazement, excitement—he had felt them all. Even the bitterness that still lingered over her desertion. But above all he could not believe the overwhelming urge he had to protect her. It was as strong today as it had been ten years ago.

No, no, no! He shook his head, trying to banish her image from his mind. He reminded himself he didn't do involvement any more. Once you got too involved, women wanted more. Before you knew it there was talk of wedding bells and kids…that he couldn't do. Since his marriage break-up and subsequent divorce, Jack had been determined to keep any relationship light and friendly and short.

Anna…he groaned as he thought about his ex-wife and the total mess he'd made of their marriage. Not for the first time he found himself wishing they had never married. He thanked God there had been no children. In fact, the whole issue had been the crux of their marital problems. He could not go through that again.

With his mind so preoccupied with Laura, it was inevitable that the dream would come again. There she lay, trapped, unhurt but unable to get out. She was reaching her hand out to him, her tear-streaked face pleading for his help. He tried to reach for her hand but the more he stretched the further away she became. Her sobs, bordering on hysteria, mocked his attempts to reach her. And then the remaining structure crumpled and…

Jack sat bolt upright in bed. Sweat glistened on his brow and his bare chest. His heart palpated like a galloping stallion and echoed loudly in his ears. He clenched the sheets in his hands and flung himself back on the damp material.

Dawn was breaking through his bedroom window. He sighed and closed his eyes, hoping to get some sleep. Maybe he would see her today.

The next morning Laura sat with Marie and Steve, getting handover from the night shift. They sat at the nurses' station where a central screen displayed information relayed from the bedside monitors.

Marie wasn't taking a clinical load today but, as boss, she liked to keep up to date with the patients. Laura was in charge of the shift and Steve would float between the bed spaces, helping wherever he was needed.

Staffing was a major issue for intensive care units as a one-to-one nurse-patient ratio was essential. Critically ill patients could crash in seconds, necessitating the bedside nurse to be there all the time—just in case. This meant meal breaks through to toilet stops had to be covered by another nurse.

'So,' said Marie as they finished and rose to start work, 'what's the story with you and Jack?'

Even though Laura had been expecting it, she still wasn't quite ready with an answer. Marie had been a good friend over the years, and it was only natural she would be curious.

'Not much to tell really. I knew him briefly ten years ago.' Laura shrugged, trying to be nonchalant.

'Looked a bit more than that. Looked like you knew each other well.' Marie emphasised the last word, giving it just the right amount of innuendo.

'If you're asking me if we had an affair, the answer is no. Prior to yesterday I only knew him for a handful of hours. Probably doesn't even add up to a whole day.'

OK, so she was being economical with the truth, but one night really didn't count as an affair. Did it? Let's be real, she thought, it was a one-night stand. Mindblowingly wonderful but nonetheless…

'But—'

'Marie,' Laura interrupted, smiling to soften her words, 'I really don't want to talk about it.'

'OK, OK.' She laughed, putting up her hands in surrender. 'None of my business.'

Laura breathed a sigh of relief to be let off the hook. Maybe now she could get on with her day. She was here to work after all!

Laura went from bed to bed, checking on patients and helping out where required. Mr Reid was her first port of call. She put on a gown and entered the isolation room. Mr Reid had had a bone-marrow transplant two weeks ago and had developed severe complications. In Theatre the previous day they had found a perforated bowel.

Today the tubes and wires running all over the bed seemed to have multiplied. She helped the bedside nurse who was scrubbing up to access the central line to administer another bag of blood.

The two drains that came from his operative site were half-full of blood. Laura looked at his lab results on the bedside computer and noted with concern the upward trend. If they continued to worsen and he went into full-blown kidney failure, dialysis would be the next step. Poor Mr Reid! He really had an uphill battle.

Laura de-gowned and moved on to one of the two post-op cardiac bypass patients.

'How are you feeling, Charlie?' she asked. Now that his breathing tube had been removed, he could talk.

'Awful.' His voice was barely more than a whisper. 'If I had known I was going to feel this bad, I'd have never gone through with it.'

'I know you feel that way now,' Laura said, squeezing his hand, 'but in a week's time, when you can actually walk around without getting chest pain or feeling out of breath, you'll feel differently. I promise.'

Laura wished she had a dollar for every bypass patient that had told her the same thing. It was a huge operation involving the chest being cracked open and the blood being shunted out of the body through an artificial pump. Most patients described it afterwards as feeling like they'd been run over by a truck. But the improvement in their lives was astounding.

Laura saw Dr Jenny Dexter, the intensive care consultant, arrive and head for the tearoom. She checked her watch. It was time for morning rounds.

The only really routine event on the unit was eight a.m. rounds. It was a multi-disciplinary meeting with all specialities represented. Individual patients' surgical and/or medical teams, as well as those in allied health fields, attended—occupational therapy, physiotherapy, pharmacy, social work. With a full unit, ward rounds often took an hour, sometimes longer.

As team leader, Laura attended. It was Steve's job to relieve the bedside nurse as each patient was discussed, so they could also contribute information. The medical staff and the nurses worked as a close team on the unit. The doctors relied on the bedside nurses and valued their opinions and judgements. The good doctors, anyway.

Laura was surprised to see Jack enter the room. She knew from nursing handover that one of his patients had been admitted overnight but he didn't need to be here himself.

She eyed him suspiciously as he smiled and plonked himself in the chair beside her.

'Don't you have a registrar?' she whispered as she leaned in, immediately regretting the impulse. The smell of his aftershave lured her into the past. How could she ever forget how he had smelt the day they had made love? The mix of aftershave and pheromones had created an intoxicating aroma.

He looked at her and winked. Jenny called for quiet. Laura blinked, snapping back to the present. For heaven's sake! It had been ten years. You'd think the man would have changed his brand of aftershave!

'Right, as you're here first, Jack, we might as well discuss Simon Adams. He's your patient, I believe?' said Jenny.

'I've just taken over his treatment. He's been clinically depressed since his wife died last year.'

'Has he expressed a suicidal tendency before?'

'Initially, yes, but not for some time.'

'Well, something happened yesterday because his eleven-year-old son found him unconscious with two empty pill bottles beside him,' said Jenny, indicating for the night registrar to begin her patient review.

Laura watched Jack as he joined in the discussion. He was quite animated when he spoke, using his hands, sitting forward in the chair. Every movement caused his sleeve to brush against her bare arm. It was like a caress and Laura fought the urge to purr.

His voice was just as she remembered it, too. Deep and rumbling. She knew his voice intimately, even more than his body. For hours, as she'd lain trapped, his voice had been her only connection with the outside world. She knew every lilt and nuance. His voice had kept her from the brink of despair.

'How much longer does he need to be here?' asked Jack as Laura got back on track with the round.

'Because of the potential for cardiac toxicity and lethal

arrhythmia, we'll need to keep him for another twenty-four hours. He should be over the worst of the effects by then.'

'Right, well, I'll go and talk to him now and if you can discharge him to the psych unit tomorrow, we can follow him up properly. I may need to section him if he doesn't voluntarily agree to stay. I hope it doesn't come to that.'

There was a general murmur of agreement and they moved on to the next patient.

'See you outside,' Jack whispered in Laura's ear, and then excused himself.

She took a sip of her hot tea as his aroma invaded her personal space again. She grimaced as the delicate mucous membranes of her mouth protested the temperature of the hot beverage. The discomfort gave her something else to concentrate on.

By the end of the round Laura had noted down three discharges. She emerged from the tearoom organising in her head what would be required and trying to factor in teabreaks and not think about Jack and his aftershave. Thankfully, he appeared to have left.

She noticed a young boy standing beside Simon Adams's bed. It must be his son. Poor boy! He didn't look much older than Isaac. How terrible to find your father like that.

Her heart went out to him. If it wasn't enough that he lost his mother last year, his father obviously wasn't coping. How alone and sad he must be at the moment.

She watched as his young face crumpled and tears spilled from his eyes. The boy turned away from his father and ran blindly towards the front doors.

Laura gave chase, not wanting him to be alone at a time like this or end up lost somewhere in the hospital because he wasn't paying any attention to where he was going.

She rounded the corner in time to witness the boy running smack bang into Jack.

'Whoa there, matey,' he said holding the boy gently by the shoulders. 'What's your rush, Andrew?'

'Let me go. Let me go,' Andrew sobbed, pushing ineffectually against Jack's hold.

'Come on, mate,' Jack said quietly as Laura approached. 'Why don't I buy you a soft drink from the machine and we can have a talk?'

The boy's shoulders sagged as his struggle died and he nodded his head miserably. He walked back to the unit with Laura and she showed him into the 'quiet' room.

It was a small but comfortably appointed room generally used as a place for relatives of new admissions to wait, as well as a place for doctors to talk to relatives about their loved ones. More often than not it was the place where bad news was given.

She tried to engage Andrew in conversation but he sat tight-lipped and head bowed. Laura felt a little inadequate. She had a son about his age, surely she could think of something to say to help Andrew to open up?

Jack arrived with a can of lemonade. He cracked the lid and handed it to the boy.

'Thanks,' he said quietly, and took a small sip.

Jack weighed up the situation as Andrew continued to stare at the floor, hoping he was up to the challenge. Children weren't exactly his forte. Would he be able to reach the boy?

'Tough time, huh?' asked Jack tentatively, initiating dialogue.

'I guess.' Andrew shrugged.

'Want to talk about it?'

Jack held his breath as Andrew stared solemnly into his lemonade can. Just when Jack thought he'd have to try a different tack, Andrew raised his head slowly and fixed him with a stare that belied his young years.

'Why did he do it?'

Laura's heart lurched at the directness of this eleven-year-old boy.

'Your dad's very sad at the moment. He's finding it really hard since your mum died.'

'But he's got me. Why does he want to leave me as well?' Andrew's voice broke.

Jack felt helpless in the face of such earnestness. How did you explain the complexities of adult emotions to children when they dealt in simplistics?

'Andrew, mate, he doesn't want to leave you. It's not about that. He loves you. He loves you with all his heart and all his soul and all his mind. He's just so sad at the moment he's not thinking properly. He just wanted to stop feeling so sad. It's not about leaving you, I promise.'

The boy was quiet as he mulled over Jack's words. 'Can you help him?'

There was that directness again!

'I reckon I can. I reckon we both can. What do you say? Partners?' Jack held out his hand palm up and waited.

Andrew sat unmoving for a moment and then a slight smile tugged at his lips as he raised his hands and gave Jack a high five.

Laura left them chatting about the latest video games, incredibly moved by what she had just witnessed. And this was a man who didn't want children? He had been amazing with Andrew. OK, he was a psychiatrist, he knew the right techniques, but it had been more than that.

He had connected with Andrew, had got down to his level. She thought about how he would be with Isaac. Something told her he would be a fantastic father. Unfortunately he seemed so opposed to the idea, even worse than ten years ago, he couldn't see what was blindingly obvious. He was a natural with kids.

Fortunately the business of the day didn't give her any time to dwell over the conundrum. There were three discharges to organise and for the first time in weeks there was no one to take their places. The tide appeared to have ebbed.

After lunch it was Laura's pleasure to say goodbye to one of their long-term patients, Bill, who after fifty-two days was finally well enough to go to a general ward. He had been in a car accident, sustaining major chest trauma that had developed into severe respiratory collapse. But he'd hung in there and today he was being awarded his get-out-of-jail-free card.

Bill had a tear in his eye as he squeezed Laura's hand.

'Sister, thank you so much. Thank you. You saved my life, you all did. I don't know how I'm ever going to be able to thank you enough.'

'It was a pleasure, Bill.' Laura smiled. 'Our pleasure. Seeing you well again is all the thanks we need.'

As Laura waved him off she reflected on the truth of her words. It was as she had told Jack yesterday. This was why she did the job, for moments just like these. This was what made her job so special.

Despite the busy workload, Laura was constantly aware of Jack's presence. He was spending a considerable amount of time at Simon's bedside, talking to his patient and spending time with Andrew. This was significant given that, as head of the department, he would have a killer schedule. She guessed that now he had built a rapport with the boy he would be reluctant to blow the tenuous relationship by passing the case off to another member of his team.

Jack approached her as she was at Jason Smith's bedside. His nurse had called her over to discuss his deteriorating condition. Jason had been involved in a teenage pub brawl, sustaining several blows to the head. He had a moderate closed head injury that hadn't required surgical intervention, but he hadn't regained consciousness yet. His heart rate was slowing and his blood pressure was rising.

'Laura, can I talk to you about Simon?'

'Not right now, Jack,' she said distractedly. 'I just need to—'

Her words were cut short by Jason's monitor suddenly blaring loudly. She looked over and saw the young man's arms and legs jerking rhythmically. He was fitting.

'Give him a bolus of sedation,' she instructed the bedside nurse. 'Jack, help me get him on his side.'

Jack assisted as the nurse held her finger on the purge button of the syringe driver that delivered a standard mix of sedative drugs.

'How much?' she asked.

'Until he stops,' Laura said.

'He needs some mannitol to reduce the swelling in his brain and we should load him with an anti-epileptic, too,' said Jack, reaching for the suction tubing and inserting the plastic head into Jason's mouth to clear the secretions from his oropharynx. 'Phenytoin,' he ordered.

Laura stared at Jack over the top of their patient's head. He had taken the words right out of her mouth. She felt admiration for him mix with her satisfaction that they were working together as a team.

Jason's movements slowly subsided. Laura handed Jack an airway and watched as he deftly inserted the curved hollow device into Jason's mouth to prevent his tongue from falling back and occluding his airway.

'He needs a CAT scan,' he said, and her admiration grew a little more.

A flurry of activity ensued, the bedspace becoming quite crowded, so Jack excused himself to write in Simon's notes. He watched Laura surreptitiously in the middle of the action, discussing the developments concerning Jason with the rest of the medical team. She was so in control, so focussed. He hoped there wouldn't come a time when an emergency triggered a different response. How would she ever cope with feeling out of her depth?

Laura worked with Steve quickly to get Jason prepared for another CAT scan. The team felt he had probably extended his head injury by having a further bleed, causing an increase in his intracranial pressure. The scan would confirm this.

Everything attached to Jason had to be switched to a portable alternative. Portable oxygen, portable monitor, portable pumps. The process took fifteen minutes. Steve accompanied the bedside nurse to the radiology department, along with the registrar and two wardsmen. Scanning an intensely monitored person was involved and required many hands.

Laura finally got a chance to grab a quick break so she took it gratefully. She sank into the tearoom chair, her mind abuzz with the things still to do.

'Taking a breather?' asked Jack, sitting beside her.

'Jack. Thanks so much for earlier, with Jason. It was good having someone who knew what they were doing by my side.'

Jack smiled and felt the pleasure at her compliment warm his insides. 'I like being at your side.'

Laura smiled back, their closeness of a decade ago returning. She took a deep breath and blinked. This was neither the time nor the place.

'Oh,' she said, 'I'm sorry. You wanted to see me earlier?'

'Doesn't matter. I sorted it, thanks.' He quelled the disappointment he felt as she distanced herself. 'You've had a busy day.'

'No worse than most. Better than some.' She smiled.

He smiled back and Laura felt her stomach flip-flop. Damn the man. It had been ten years and she could still remember how good he had felt inside her.

'*This* is a normal work day?'

'Pretty much.'

'Laura.' He shook his head. 'Do you know *anything* about post-traumatic stress disorder?'

The glow from distant memories faded as wariness took over. 'Probably more than most.'

'So you know that with the traumatic events of Newvalley, you are in the highest risk group.'

'I think we've been through this already. I can handle it, Jack. I've been doing this for a long time. I'm OK.'

'Just hear me out, Laura, that's all I'm asking,' he said, holding up his hands to emphasise the import of his words. 'I do know what I'm talking about here. You trusted me with Jason, right? Please, trust me on this one.'

Laura shut her eyes and sighed. He was right. She owed it to him to at least listen to what he had to say. His professionalism with Jason and his invaluable help with the emergency compelled her to give his words some thought.

'OK, I'll listen.'

'Thank you,' he murmured, grateful for the chance to sway her to his way of thinking. But where to start? Now he had his opportunity he didn't want to blow it.

'See, the funny thing about PTSD is its ability to rear its ugly head when people least expect it. Sufferers can cruise along for years and then something will happen—doesn't even have to be very big—and wham! They're losing it. Big time.'

'I know that, Jack. But it won't happen to me.'

'No.' He nodded knowingly, 'Of course, you're OK. You've dealt with it.'

'I *have*,' she sighed, rubbing her eyes.

'Well, if that was true, going to the memorial service wouldn't be a problem for you. But it obviously is. I suspect that's because there are still some demons lurking. The effects of PTSD can be quite debilitating. Some people can't even get out of bed, let alone hold down a job. Who was the Einstein that recommended you take up this kind of nursing?'

'I didn't ask anyone's permission, Jack. I kind of just stumbled into it and loved it and stayed.'

'Didn't your therapist advise you not to?'

'I didn't start working here until after my therapy finished.'

'Well, that's just as well because anyone worth their salt would know there are two important factors to decrease the risk of PTSD. One…' he held up his finger '…deal with your issues. Two…' he held up another finger '…reduce life stressors. Not hold hands with them, Laura. Reduce them. But you…' he jabbed his finger at her '…go and choose the world's most stressful job!'

'Actually, I think air traffic controller holds that honour.'

'Laura,' he groaned, exasperated. He had to make her see that she could be setting herself up for a real fall.

'Jack.' She sprang up, a frustrated laugh escaping. 'I've given you a fair hearing but enough already! I am not going to crack up on the job! I'm fine. I've been fine for a long time now and you dragging it all up again is not going to help me. Obviously this is more your issue than mine!'

'Laura—'

'Butt…out…Jack,' she whispered loudly, emphasising each word, and left the room without a backward glance.

Great, he thought, contemplating the empty room. That went well!

CHAPTER THREE

TWO days later, Laura was on her seventh day of a nine-day stretch. It was Saturday. She loved weekends in hospitals. Even though it wasn't necessarily quieter on the unit, there was still less hierarchy floating around making life miserable for those at the coalface. The entire atmosphere was relaxed.

She yawned as she came back from lunch. It was almost two o'clock. Today she was the runner and Marie was team leader. Marie didn't usually work weekends, but when they were this short-staffed she did what she could.

So much for the spare beds! Two had filled by the next day. Miraculously one bed still remained empty and it was Laura's fervent hope that it would still be so at the end of her shift. Only an hour and a half to go!

Thankfully Jack had backed off. In fact, she hadn't seen him at all after their tearoom conversation. It did surprise her, however. The memorial service was on Monday and he had seemed so determined to get her there. Hopefully he had heeded her words.

Jenny Dexter put down the phone as Laura approached.

'I'm going down to Casualty. They want me to look at a guy who's just come in. Sounds serious. I'll let you know.'

'Sure,' said Laura. So much for the empty bed!

Ten minutes later the consultant was on the phone. She gave Laura a brief rundown on the patient, who she'd be bringing up immediately. Mr Gordon was a forty-year-old with a rapidly deteriorating condition. Suspected meningococcal septicaemia.

Marie and Laura prepared the bedspace for the man's arrival in record time. They'd just finished when the stretcher pushed through the heavy swing doors of the unit. Laura took one look and knew that the situation was grave. Two women accompanied the stretcher.

While the medical team took over, Laura ushered the reluctant women into the quiet room.

'My husband's going to die, isn't he?' his frantic wife demanded as the other woman placed a comforting hand on her arm.

Choosing her words carefully, Laura said gently, 'Your husband is gravely ill.'

'Don't let them give up on him. Please, don't let them. Don't let him die.' She clutched at Laura's arm.

She searched for a shred of hope to give to the woman.

'Those doctors out there are the best there is, Mrs Gordon. I know they'll do everything they can.'

When she returned to the bedspace Mr Gordon was already intubated and had a central line inserted. Fluids and drugs were being poured into him. His blood pressure was dangerously low and his heart rate very fast, with multiple erratic beats. The area was littered with discarded packaging and used equipment. It looked chaotic but was actually very controlled.

Laura pitched in, passing things hastily requested, often even before they were asked for. The heart trace on the monitor changed to a life-threatening rhythm and what blood pressure there was totally collapsed.

'Start cardiac massage,' Jenny commanded. Marie climbed up on the bed and began compressing Mr Gordon's sternum. One of the doctors disconnected the ventilator and commenced hand-bagging.

Laura charged the defibrillator. She quickly assembled an ampoule of lignocaine. The machine pinged its readiness and she handed the paddles to Jenny, sending up a quick prayer. All eyes watched his chest jump as the joules of electricity tried to jolt the erratic rhythm back to normality. The trace remained the same. Lignocaine was administered as the machine was charged again.

Mr Gordon had been in full cardiac arrest for twenty long minutes when the futility of the situation called for a reluctant end to the proceedings. The atmosphere, which had been charged with pure adrenaline only moments before, was suddenly hollow and heavy. Solemn introspection replaced frenetic activity.

Laura, who had taken over the cardiac massage, stilled. Her shoulders ached from the effort of compressing such a big man's sternum. And her heart ached for another life they couldn't save. She stared down at the gloved hands that formed a barrier between her and the bright purple rash covering the patient's body—the hallmark of the presence of meningococcus.

'Laura? You've been dealing with the family?' asked Jenny.

'Yes,' said Laura.

'Shall we?'

They de-gloved solemnly and washed their hands at the sink. Jack approached as they were drying their hands.

'What are you doing here?' asked Laura, not even her surprise at seeing him managing to shake the gloom from her voice.

'I was paged. The social worker is dealing with a crisis on another ward and it was felt that Mr Gordon's family might need some grief counselling. Has he passed away?'

'Yes,' said Laura

'Oh, dear. How awful.' Jack voice was quiet as he watched Laura intently. He saw the sadness and disbelief etched on her face and had an inkling of how she was feeling.

He had felt similar emotions at Newvalley. How quickly someone could die was always startling. And it didn't matter how many times you'd seen it before, it was always shocking.

The fact that Mr Gordon was a complete stranger to Laura would only make it harder. It just wasn't right that people died among strangers. Surely, in the most desperately dire time of his life, Mr Gordon should have been surrounded by people who knew and loved him?

Such was the nature of the work on an intensive care unit. But Jack knew it didn't make it any easier and as he continued to watch Laura he could see she was having trouble reining in her emotions. Perhaps she wasn't the best candidate to be present when the dreadful news was given to the family. Maybe she'd had enough emotion for one day?

Jenny excused herself to answer a page and Laura found herself waiting for Jenny's return with Jack beside her.

'Do you think it's a good idea that you be the one to break the news to Mrs Gordon?'

'Jenny will do that,' she said, staring straight ahead.

'Yes, but do you really need to be there, too?'

'I'm the only one here who the family vaguely know. Her husband is dead. I think that she deserves to have at least one familiar face around when she's told. Don't you?' Laura's voice was terse. Her body tense.

'You're looking a little shaky at the moment. You're going to need to be a lot more detached than this,' Jack pushed.

'Don't tell me how to do my job,' she snarled, turning to look at him. 'I am a professional. I've been sitting in on awful conversations for years. I haven't broken down in front of a client ever. Ever! And I'm not about to start. When I go into that room I will be perfectly in control.'

'OK, OK. Calm down. I didn't mean to upset you.'

'When you question my professionalism it upsets me!' she said in an angry whisper. 'You think I want to be part of what's going to be said in that room? Because I don't. Every part of me rebels against the idea.'

Laura took a breath and tried to calm her racing pulse and seesawing emotions. Yes, the swiftness of Mr Gordon's deterioration was having an effect on her, but she had to make Jack understand why he was wrong.

She softened her voice. 'But I am a nurse, I don't have a choice here. I am compelled to be there because it's the right thing to do. The only thing to do. I've made a connection with them. I can't just break that connection in their neediest hour because it's emotionally challenging.'

Jack nodded. He understood what she was telling him but was worried about her nonetheless. At least he would be present during the talk. He had been paged for Mrs Gordon's emotional journey but as Jenny rejoined them he knew that Laura's needs took first place.

'Mrs Gordon.' Jenny addressed the woman, her face grim, introducing herself and Laura and Jack.

'No.' Mrs Gordon shook her head wildly, looking from one to the other, knowing from their faces what they were about to say.

'I'm sorry, Mrs Gordon. We did all we could but...your husband died a few minutes ago.'

'No,' she whispered fiercely. 'He can't be dead. He was fine four hours ago.'

Jenny nodded solemnly. 'Mrs Gordon, what we think your husband had, meningococcal septicaemia, it probably got into his bloodstream. Its onset is very quick...'

The woman wasn't listening. She came closer to Laura and grabbed her by the forearms, her eyes accusing. 'You said they were the best. You said they'd do everything they could.' Her voice rose hysterically and she began to shake Laura.

Laura looked into the woman's eyes, wild with grief, and was paralysed by her disbelief and anger. Even the bite of the woman's fingers as they dug into her skin didn't register. She opened her mouth to say something but the words just didn't come.

She had witnessed many emotional moments, working in this field, comforted many grieving people, but most were surprisingly quiet, reserved in their mourning. To feel the full force of such raw emotion directed right in her face was shocking.

Laura could feel the neutral mask she had slipped on start

to fall away. She blinked. Anything to shut out those strangely compelling anguished eyes. Mrs Gordon's friend was trying to drag her away and Jenny was talking calmly so Laura could be released.

'OK, now. Come along, Mrs Gordon.' Jack's soothing but authoritative voice broke through the woman's hysteria. He gently prised her fingers from Laura's arms and held her as she sobbed.

'Go to the staffroom, Laura,' he commanded.

'Wh-what?' She looked at him, puzzled. She stared at him like she'd never seen him before, her mind refusing to function.

'Jenny, get her out of here,' he ordered.

Laura followed Jenny blankly, sitting in the indicated chair in the staffroom, her body on autopilot as she accepted the cup of tea Jenny placed in her cold fingers.

Laura's brain tumbled over and over, like a clothes dryer. The staff television prattled as she stared at the images on the screen before her, but all she could see was Mrs Gordon's utter wretchedness and hear her accusing words.

She felt…overwhelmed. Helpless. Just like those immediate months following the building collapse. Laura tried not to panic. She couldn't go there again. It had taken too long to claw her way back to a semblance of normalcy. What was happening to her? She'd told Jack she was over it and, damn it all, she was!

She drew in a ragged breath and tried to calm her galloping thoughts. I am a professional. I am a professional. The chant helped her retreat from the edge. She felt she'd gained back some control when Jack found her half an hour later.

'Laura,' he said gently. 'Are you OK?'

Laura dragged her gaze to his face. She felt her control teeter and stumble at the concern written there and echoed in his words. She shook her head and he pulled her into his arms.

'It's OK. I'm here.'

'Just like always, huh?' His chest muffled her whisper as he slowly rocked her.

Before she could stop it, her mental proximity to the past had her back in his apartment ten years ago, being rocked and comforted. Smelling him, feeling him. Wanting him.

She felt the beginnings of an awareness, similar to the one that had possessed her back then. The one that had led to her kissing him and touching him and tearing his clothes off.

Laura broke away, putting some distance between them.

'That poor woman, that was awful.' She shuddered. 'Really awful.'

'It was what I was worried about before we went in.'

'What? That she would attack me?'

'No. That emotionally you were a little too raw still. I mean, you were speechless in there. That's not normal, I hope?'

'Of course not,' she dismissed gruffly. The thought that he seemed to know her state of mind better than she did was unsettling.

'So why this time?'

'I've never had anyone eyeball me and intimate that it was my fault before. It threw me…that's all.'

'She didn't mean it, you know. She wasn't attacking you personally,' he said.

'I know that,' she said, exasperated that he felt the need to explain something so obvious.

They sat in uncomfortable silence for a few moments.

'Laura. Laura?' He placed a hand against her cheek and turned her face so she was looking at him. 'Please, come to the service with me.'

Laura began to protest but he hushed her with a finger against her mouth. 'Hear me out, OK?' He rubbed his finger against her bottom lip and she would have given him anything in that moment.

'Forget about all the reasons you should.' He pressed his finger against her lips to still her murmured protest. 'OK, all the reasons *I* think you should. How about just doing it for me? For us. Sure, I think you need this but I can't deny that mostly my reasons for wanting you to go are personal. Think of it as completing the journey that we started ten years ago. Coming full circle. If you don't think you need closure from what happened then, OK. But maybe we need closure, Laura. I don't feel like there was ever any ending to us. You know? I think this is the perfect opportunity for us to put our relationship in perspective. Lay some ghosts.'

Laura was stunned by the words. Despite the distraction of his thumb stroking her lips, she managed to absorb most of them. It was true, their relationship had been left up in the air. More so than Jack realised.

'But…there's work. I can't just leave.'

'I'm sure Marie can spare you.'

Laura pulled away from the eroticism of his caress and the seduction of his soft voice, sitting as far from him as her chair would allow. She just couldn't leave them when they were already short-staffed. 'No, she can't. I'm rostered on for the next two days. Marie needs all hands on deck.'

Marie entered the staffroom. 'Did I hear my name?' She looked from one to the other. 'How are you doing, Laura?'

'Fine,' said Laura.

'You don't look so good,' Marie observed.

'I've been trying to convince her to take time off work. I think she should go to the memorial service on Monday, Marie.'

'What service? What do you mean?'

'To the Newvalley Earthquake Memorial Service.'

Laura glared at him. 'Shut up, Jack,' she snarled.

'You've lost me, I'm afraid.' Marie looked confused.

'We were there.'

'What, at the disaster site? Were you part of the rescue effort?'

'I was,' said Jack. 'Laura was the one being rescued.'

'Jack!'

'Hang on, they only rescued one person. A girl called Mary,' Marie said, obviously confused.

'Mary is Laura's first name,' said Jack.

'*You're* Mary Scott?' Marie stared open-mouthed.

'Yes,' Laura admitted quietly, glaring at Jack.

'Why have you never said anything, Laura?'

'I wanted to be anonymous, Marie. Not a curiosity.'

Marie drummed her fingers on the table, watching Laura as she considered the problem. Laura could see her mind working and almost hear the shuffling going on.

'I'm not going, Marie, we're too busy. You can't spare me.'

'No. You must go. I'll just need to do some rearranging of the skill mix and get onto the agency.'

'Agency will go on our cost centre and throw the budget out.'

'Such is life, Laura. Things happen that aren't under anyone's control and we have to deal with them. You should know that better than anyone. This is one of them. You had a harrowing incident today. We're all stressed at the moment. You can probably afford that least. I think some time off would do you the world of good.'

'I'm fine now. I don't need time off.'

'Laura, think about it. It's perfect timing. With Isaac away, you're a free agent. Take whatever time you need. We'll manage.'

Laura froze at the mention of her son's name. Jack raised an eyebrow. She saw the speculation in his eyes.

'But—'

'That's an order, Laura.' Marie turned on her heel, muttering about making the arrangements immediately. It appeared that was that.

Laura flopped her head back against the chair and closed her eyes. She was going to kill Jack.

'Who's Isaac?'

Scratch that. She was going to kill Marie. She was silent and kept her eyes shut, hoping he'd disappear.

'Is he the man in your life?'

'Yes,' she said, opening her eyes and exhaling, relieved that his assumption had given her an out. Well, it was the truth, he was the man in her life. Little man.

Jack felt like someone had punched him in the gut. Of course she would have someone. Just because she had said she wasn't married, it didn't mean she wasn't involved with someone. She was gorgeous, for heaven's sake!

'Do you love him?' He held his breath.

'More than life itself. There isn't anything I wouldn't sacrifice for him.'

She couldn't help it if Jack's assumptions led him to believe that Isaac was her lover instead of her child. After today's upheavals it all seemed slightly frivolous and funny. She wanted to laugh out loud.

'Are you happy?'

'He has brought so much joy to my life,' she said, looking directly into his eyes.

Her voice sounded so intense, he didn't doubt a word. So? Wasn't that what he wanted for her? All these years of thinking and wondering, his paramount concern had been her happiness. He knew somewhere inside him that he was glad for her, but other emotions were currently more prevalent. Sadness and…regret. Maybe if he had tracked her down earlier? Like he had thought about doing a thousand times.

'Have you been together long?'

'Nine years.'

So soon? So soon after…Newvalley. After them? Jack was stunned. It had taken him four years to marry Anna. Four years to feel together enough for a long-term relationship. Had Laura rushed it with this man? But, then, who was he to judge? At least Laura and Isaac were still together. His marriage had only lasted four years.

'That's a while. Yet you've never married?'

Now the questions were getting a bit too much. She stood and went to the window. Miniature people on the street far below went about their business.

Jack took her silence as a hint that the subject was closed. Maybe that was an issue in their relationship. Maybe she wanted to get married and he didn't. It was common enough. He took in her loveliness and wondered what kind of a fool this Isaac was.

'What about Newvalley?' he asked, changing the subject.

'Oh, Jack, I don't know…' She pressed her face against the glass.

'Please, Laura, I've never asked you for anything.'

'You're going to blackmail me now?' She turned to face him, her voice incredulous.

'No…I just meant—'

'I never asked you for anything either, Jack. I never asked for that building to fall on me and I never asked you to rescue me. I'm just as much a victim of circumstances as you.'

'OK,' He threw his hands out in surrender. 'I'm sorry, that came out wrong. Please…for me. Please, come with me. It would mean a lot.'

Laura found his earnest face hard to deny. Was she just being obstructive for the sake of it? Maybe he was right. Maybe it was time to go back and get some closure.

She couldn't deny the incident today had spooked her. Mrs Gordon's grief had been shocking. Laura couldn't remember feeling this out of her depth since the emotional turmoil of Newvalley.

She was so sure she'd put the past behind her but today's events had aroused the same feelings of disconnection and helplessness that had plagued her a decade ago.

Maybe Jack was right. Maybe she wasn't over it. And, besides, how difficult could it be? More importantly, he was asking her to do this for him. And she owed him. It was probably the least she could do.

'OK,' she agreed, pressing her hot forehead against the

cold glass. Her shoulders sagged. 'Please, don't let me regret this,' she whispered to the glass.

Behind her, Jack raised his fists in victory. Yes! He couldn't explain why he felt they needed this so much. He just knew they did. Maybe in Newvalley they'd find the closure they both needed to move on with their separate lives.

'I'm driving down tomorrow. Keep me company on the drive?'

'Whatever.' She shrugged.

'I probably won't be leaving till around lunchtime.'

'Sure.' Laura quickly scribbled her address on a piece of paper and handed it to him.

'See you then,' he said, a huge grin in place as he backed out the door. 'Tomorrow.'

'Tomorrow.'

Laura groaned and leaned her head back against the glass. Was he right? Would it mean closure? Or would it be opening up a whole new can of worms?

CHAPTER FOUR

SUNDAY morning dragged. The air was heavy with humidity as the dark rainclouds outside gathered momentum. Was the rain symbolic? Was it a bad omen? Laura threw a few things into a small bag, her mind preoccupied with thoughts of Jack.

How was it going to be, spending time with him? He'd been part of her life for ten years and yet these next few days would be the longest time they'd been together. It was crazy—they had a child together, yet they'd barely spent twenty-four hours in each other's company.

Laura took the time to examine her real fear—it would be so easy to fall for him. It almost seemed inevitable in a way, with their history. But Laura couldn't just think of herself. There was Isaac to consider.

She hadn't had a relationship of any kind since Jack. Isaac had needed stability, not a series of men in and out of his life. There had been quite a few vying for her attention but none that had interested Laura and certainly none keen enough to take on someone else's child.

In reality, Laura knew that falling for Jack would be futile. She remembered his terse 'thank goodness' that had accompanied his confirmation that his marriage had borne no children. She was not after a relationship that did not involve a long-term commitment to both of them. They were a package deal.

Isaac had done well with no father figure so far. Better none than an unstable influence. Maybe when he was older, she could start thinking of herself. Maybe.

It was midday when the phone broke the silence.

'Laura, sorry, I've been caught up at the hospital. I've had to section Simon Adams.'

'Oh, no,' she gasped softly.

'He refused to commit himself for voluntary treatment. I didn't have a choice. I have to make sure he's back on track before I let him go home to Andrew.' His deep tones resonated down the line.

'Of course you do,' she sympathised, her ear tingling from the nearness of his voice.

'I'll be there in half an hour, an hour at the most.'

'Fine.'

'Haven't changed your mind?' he teased.

'Often.'

His laughter brought a wry smile to her lips as she hung up. Boy, if his voice on a telephone line could affect her like this, how was she going to cope with his physical presence?

It was three o'clock when Jack finally pulled into her drive in a sporty BMW.

'I'm sorry,' he apologised.

'It's OK,' she assured him, handing him her bag as she met him halfway along the garden path.

'This it?' He looked doubtful.

'Yes,' she said.

'I didn't know women could travel light.'

'This one can.' She laughed.

He walked ahead of her, affording her a full view of his denim-clad behind. He was dressed in jeans and a navy polo shirt. It complemented his olive complexion beautifully. Casual but deadly. He looked fabulously fresh and energetic. The sleeves of the knit shirt fitted snugly around his firm arm muscles. The jeans clung to his bottom and thighs. He turned to go into the house. She stood her ground.

'Where are you going?' she asked casually.

'Thought you might give me a tour.' He gestured to the house.

'I think we should get going,' she said. The last thing she wanted was for Jack to see her home. Isaac's paraphernalia was everywhere. Jack thought Isaac was her lover, and she needed that lie at that moment. It was protection for her. Protection against Jack. Protection against herself.

'It's after three now.' She tapped her wristwatch.

'I get it, you're a sloppy housekeeper.'

'It's a long drive to Newvalley.'

He eyed her suspiciously but let the matter rest. He held the door open and she slid into the leather bucket seat. Laura whistled. 'Head-shrinking pays well, then.'

'I do all right,' he stated.

Conversation was scant as he negotiated the traffic through Brisbane. A brief discussion on whether to take the inland or the coastal route had them agreeing to take the Pacific Highway that hugged the New South Wales coastline. Traffic was likely to be worse, but at least it would be more scenic and there would be shorter distances between towns.

'I'm a lousy travelling companion,' she informed him as they left the bustle behind. 'I'm usually asleep before the engine's warm.'

'That's fine.' He smiled at her. 'You look like you could do with a sleep.'

'Thanks a lot. You sure know how to flatter a girl.'

'I thought you weren't having any sleeping problems.'

'I wasn't until I agreed to this trip.' Laura had tossed and turned all night.

'You look like you haven't slept a wink since.'

'Well, you won't mind if I catch up now, then,' she retorted, irritated by his criticism.

Laura shut her eyes and snuggled her head into the comfortable seat. She fell asleep quickly despite her total inability to do so last night. Driving along like this, with Jack, as the efficient car ate up the distance, she felt so snug and safe. Sleep came easily.

Jack smiled indulgently at her, noticing her soft lips slacken as slumber claimed them. He wanted to kiss them. Now she was asleep he could sneak as many looks as he wanted. She was wearing a summery dress with shoestring straps and a floral pattern. It flared loosely around her toned calves and emphasised her waist and the roundness of her hips.

He set the six-stack CD player to random select and settled in for the long drive. Jack could not believe how right this felt. It was like they were an old married couple setting out for a weekend away. He kept glancing at her. His hand itched to touch her slim shoulder, drop a kiss on it. Slip down the thin strap…

He wanted… Dammit! He suddenly realised what he guessed he'd always known on a subconscious level. He wanted an impossible dream. She was spoken for and he didn't do long-term relationships.

Laura stirred a few hours later as the car slowed, going through a town. She stretched and sat more upright.

'Hey, sleepyhead. Better?'

'Much,' she said. 'Where are we?'

'Ballina.'

Jack slowed the car as they approached a pedestrian crossing. A family was waiting to cross. He stopped the car and the mother smiled gratefully at him. Laura identified with the harassed mother as she tried to usher two small children safely to the other side. They were both more interested in licking their dripping ice creams.

The little boy's ice-cream scoop fell off in the middle of the road, splattering and melting quickly on the hot tar. He began to cry and the exasperated mother had to coax him the rest of the way, while he fretted for his ice cream.

Laura remembered how Isaac had been at that age and sympathised. She felt a pang of regret that she had never had more children. She loved being a mother and would have liked Isaac not to be an only child.

Jack watched the play of emotions on Laura's face at the domestic scene before them.

'You like children?' he asked.

'What's not to like?'

'You'd like to have some?'

She chose her words carefully. 'I can see children in my life, definitely.'

He nodded thoughtfully as he accelerated through the town. Of course she would want kids. He was suddenly overwhelmed by the desire to see her holding his child. He gripped the steering-wheel hard to erase the image from his mind. She would not be having his kids.

'What about you, Jack? You like children?'

'Sure. Couldn't eat a whole one, though.'

She gave him a quelling look.

'I'm being serious, Jack. Your wife…what was her name?'

'Anna.'

'She didn't want kids?'

'Oh, she wanted them all right,' he said, changing gears abruptly.

'You didn't,' she stated, afraid of what he would say.

'Let's just say that I'm not father material.' His voice was edged with bitterness.

'How do you know that?' she asked. She wanted to demand it but, sensing his mood, she softened her voice.

'Trust me. I know.'

'But—'

'Look, if you don't mind, I'd rather not get into it.'

'OK.' She gave him a long look. 'Sure.'

He had really piqued her curiosity now. What did he mean—not father material? How could he know that if he'd never tried? Personally she thought he'd be great, if the way he'd been with Andrew was any indication.

From his reaction it had obviously been an issue in his marriage. She wanted to know more. Needed to know more. For Isaac's sake. Did his marriage break up because he hadn't wanted children? Would Jack feel differently if he found out he already had a child? Or would he reject Isaac because he did not want the role? She couldn't risk that. She had to be sure he wanted to be a father before she even considered telling him the truth.

After an initial awkwardness they slipped into easy conversation punctuated by periods of companionable silence. Nothing personal or controversial. Just inane chatter, about their jobs and the hospital. Nothing that made either of them feel uncomfortable.

They drove on, day blending into night. Jack regaled her with anecdotes from his student days and tantalised her with tales from his overseas travels. They studiously avoided talking about Newvalley and what the next couple of days would hold.

Just before the Port Macquarie turnoff, Jack pulled into a service station for petrol. He got out and stretched his long legs and torso, stiff from inactivity.

'Laura,' he said, getting back in and buckling up. 'I'm beat. Why don't we drive into Port Macquarie and grab a motel for the night? I didn't realise it's nearly nine o'clock—no wonder I'm starving. The service isn't until three tomorrow afternoon—we can travel the last couple of hours in the morning.'

'Um…' She dithered. The sleeping arrangements were something she'd avoided thinking about.

'Or I suppose we could stop for a bite to eat and you could take over the driving.'

Her? Drive his BMW? No way! What if she had an accident? What if someone crashed into her? She thought about her eight-year-old hatchback. His car was way out of her league. What if she liked it too much?

'I don't think so, Jack.'

'Shall we find a place, then?'

'Sure,' she said, trying to sound casual.

They drove the short distance from the highway into Port Macquarie. The main road was lined on either side with places to stay. They could only find one with its vacancy sign illuminated. They drove into the reception area and Jack got out to register. A few minutes later he tapped on her car window, startling her. Her heartbeat doubling from the fright, she rolled it down. It trebled as his proximity invaded her space.

'They only have one room left. Do you want to drive further on and see if we can find another place?'

Laura chewed her lip, her mind racing and her heart rate now thrumming ten to the dozen. Spending the night in the same room as Jack. The thought was appalling and exciting all at once.

Jack watched the indecision play across her face.

'Bothered about what might happen if we're alone?' he asked softly. He saw her lips set into a grim line.

'Are there two beds?'

'Of course,' he said, looking offended.

'Well, I'm sure I'll be able to control myself,' she told him tartly.

'What would Isaac think?'

'Isaac wouldn't care.'

'That's very liberated of him.' I'd care, he thought.

Laura stared into his dark eyes, trying to read his mind. He wasn't giving much away. But she did see his tiredness.

'Go get the room, Jack,' she prompted softly, desperate to break the unnerving eye contact. She watched him walk away and started to breathe again. She hadn't even realised she'd been holding her breath.

Laura gave herself a mental shake—if Jack could be cool about this, then so could she. It wasn't as if they were strangers. They knew each other's bodies intimately and they would be sleeping in separate beds. She'd show him. She'd show Jack that being alone with him didn't bother her one iota.

They entered the stuffy unit and Jack turned the air-conditioning on, adjusting the thermostat to keep the room at a cool temperature. The sky had remained cloudy all day, raining on and off. The humidity outside was terrible.

Jack dumped his bag on the single bed. 'I'll sleep here, you have the double.'

Laura didn't argue. The less she had to talk about the sleeping arrangements, the better.

'There's a Chinese take-away over the road. What do you reckon?'

'I love Chinese.' She smiled.

'Why don't you have a shower while I go get it? What do you fancy?'

'Anything.' She shrugged. 'Whatever you're having.'

He shut the door behind him. Laura decided to take his advice and wash away the travel-weariness. She appreciated his attempt to afford her some privacy and took full advantage. She pulled out her nightwear and grimaced. Well, she hadn't expected to be sharing a room with Jack. It would have to do. When he returned twenty minutes later she was showered and dressed in a very practical, oversized T-shirt that came to mid-thigh.

The exotic aroma made her realise how hungry she was. 'Oh, good. I'm starving,' she said, as he laid the containers on the small table in the corner of the spacious room.

Jack busied himself with the food, trying to hide his reaction to seeing her like this. She was fresh from the shower, hair damp and smelling of soap and shampoo. She seemed much more awake after her sleep in the car and looked about sixteen as she attacked the food with the chopsticks. They didn't really talk. The television news was on and they watched it as they ate, making occasional comments.

'Boy! I'm stuffed full,' she said, stretching herself out as flat as possible in the chair. Her shirt rode up, exposing a shapely thigh. Jack eyed her pose, noticing that she wasn't wearing a bra, and didn't like where his thoughts were leading his body. He stood quickly.

'I'm going to have a shower.' A cold one.

Laura cleaned up, throwing the empty containers in the bin. What should she do now? She looked at the clock.

Almost eleven. Bed, definitely bed, she thought, and slipped between the crisp white sheets.

She could hear the spray of Jack's shower as sleep started to muddle her senses. She marvelled at how comfortable she felt in such domestic circumstances. She had been worried about sharing a room with him but instead she found it very safe and comforting. They were both adults, for goodness' sake! What had happened between them had been a long time ago.

Sleep had almost claimed her when Jack came out of the bathroom.

'Laura? Are you awake?'

'Only just.' She opened heavy lids.

'Do you think we should get a wake-up call in the morning?'

'Might be a good idea. I could sleep for a week at the moment.'

Jack picked up the phone and organised it with the switchboard. By the time he had finished she was in a deep, and by the look of her, contented sleep. Jack couldn't believe she could go to sleep so easily. He was beginning to think they should have found another motel. Having her so close, just a bed away, was too tempting. He could almost reach out and touch her. He could hear her slow, steady breathing and wished he could feel it on his face.

The cogs in Jack's mind rolled back like a tape recorder rewinding, replaying scenes from their past. He remembered making love to her as if it were yesterday. He had never had anything like it, before or since. Totally unexpected. Wild. Passionate. No psychoanalysis or thought of consequences. Just an urgent need satisfied by a frenzied response.

Jack wanted her that badly again now. Lying in the dark, with the background hum of the air-conditioning, watching her chest rise and fall, he was overcome with an urgent need to make love to her. It was only extreme self-control that stopped him getting into her bed. He groaned and rolled over, facing the wall. At least he couldn't see her, even if her breathing pattern was being indelibly imprinted into his brain.

She was under the building again. Trapped. Afraid. But this time Isaac was with her. Isaac as he was as a baby. No, you must save him, she kept pleading with the rescuer. With Jack. Finally he was able to grab hold of Isaac but the earth rumbled and the ground shook and the baby slipped from Jack's tenuous hold.

Isaac dropped. His cries rose up to her as he fell further and further into the gaping hole in the earth. No, she screamed. You must save him, Jack. You must save him.

'No! No! You must save him, Jack!'

'Hey. Hey!' Jack took Laura by the shoulders and gently shook her flailing body. 'Laura, wake up. It's only a dream.'

She opened her eyes and sat up. The dream vanished but the fear lingered.

'Are you OK?' He brushed her sweat-soaked fringe off her face. They were very close, only centimetres apart. Too frightened to talk, she leaned against him and he gathered her close.

'It's OK. It was just a bad dream. It can't hurt you now.'

Her heart banged loudly and she felt Jack would have to be anaesthetised not to feel its erratic rhythm thudding against his chest. 'I haven't had a nightmare for years.' What was going on here? Nightmares were a thing from her past. She'd conquered them years ago.

He could hear her confusion. 'It's on your mind, Laura. You've spent years trying not to think about it and now you're being forced to. It's a perfectly normal reaction.'

He might think so but Laura was frightened. If the dream had been as it always had, she could have coped, but Isaac being there too brought a terrifying new twist to her old nightmare.

It was only a dream, she chanted silently in time with the gentle rocking of her body. It was only a dream. Jack rocked her back and forth, holding her for a long time until her body relaxed and her breathing settled.

He went to put some distance between them and realised she had fallen asleep. He laid her down gently on the bed and got up carefully so as not to disturb her.

'No,' she murmured, reaching for his hand. 'Don't leave me, Jack. Please, stay.' She pulled his arm around her waist and tucked his hand under her.

God help him! He tried to sit as far from her as possible with his arm still attached and wound up with a cramp. He gave in and lay down behind her, fitting himself perfectly into the contours of her back as she lay on her side. It felt heavenly. Like this was the place that he belonged.

She was definitely asleep. Jack glanced at the digital clock—five a.m.! Unfortunately his body, being in such intimate contact with hers, was definitely awake. He doubted he would get any sleep at all between now and their wake-up call at seven. She snuggled her bottom in closer to his groin and softly sighed his name.

If his arousal didn't wake her up, nothing would! He longed to make love to her. It was almost a physical ache to deny himself. But Jack wasn't about to make a move on her. She was obviously unsettled by the prospect of what today would bring. She didn't need him making a pass.

Despite his opinion to the contrary, Jack did eventually relax as the deep evenness of her breathing lulled him to sleep.

At about a quarter to seven Laura rolled onto her back and found herself looking into Jack's face. His olive complexion was dark with the overnight growth of stubble. His black lashes, closed, were incredibly long. Being near him was deliciously tempting. His lips were so close. So hard to resist.

His eyes flicked open. They stared at each other for a short while.

'You caught me,' she said, lowering her eyes to hide her sinful thoughts.

'So I did.' A lazy smile brightened his sleepy face.

She took a deep breath. 'Thank you for being there last night, Jack. That bad dream.' She shuddered. 'It really shook me.'

'Want to talk about it?'

'To who?' She smiled. 'Jack Riley, bed companion, or Dr John Riley, psychiatrist?'

'Which do you prefer?' His voice was loaded with humour and innuendo.

'Neither.' She laughed. 'I really don't want to talk about it.'

The whole thing would be too complicated to explain. Besides, it was behind her now. It was daylight. 'What are you thinking?' she asked, as she watched his expression become pensive.

'How much I'd like to kiss you.'

'Oh.'

Laura's stomach clenched. She'd been feeling perfectly comfortable about being in bed with him like this. It was nothing sexual, more…companionable. She felt safe and snug and it all seemed natural somehow. But his admission had moved them into dangerous territory. His full lips were not far away. She didn't even want to think where that would lead.

'What are *you* thinking?'

'I'm wondering what Isaac's doing.' She had to stop this.

'Oh.' Jack fell back, staring solemnly at the ceiling. Well, that put him in his place! They both lay inspecting the ceiling, silent for a few moments. But he couldn't let it lie there. He had come this far.

'Truth is, I've been wanting to kiss you since I met you again.'

'Oh.'

'Laura, I know we've discussed this before but I have to know. Why did you leave that morning?'

This again. Why? Laura sighed and shut her eyes. Ask an easy question, why don't you?

'Jack, leave it be. It's done now. Leave it in the past, where it belongs.'

He rolled on his side and raised himself up on one elbow, looking down into her face.

'I can't. It's something I've always wanted to know.'

She sighed and rubbed her eyes. 'What purpose would there have been in staying?'

'We could have talked about it. Seen where it could have led.'

'Jack, you were off to Adelaide!'

'You could have come, too.'

Laura rolled her eyes and pulled the sheets around her more firmly. 'Look, frankly, I was a little appalled at what had happened.'

'But it was fantastic, Laura.'

'I don't do one-night stands.'

'Was that all it was to you?'

She shut her eyes, blocking out his incredulous expression. 'I don't know, Jack. I was confused, emotionally overwrought.'

'So are you saying that I took advantage of you?'

'No! Of course not. I just mean…I'd not long been pulled out from under a collapsed building… We'd just been to a very emotional church service… It just happened. In the cold light of day it seemed a little…hasty, I suppose. I didn't want you to think that the whole experience had mentally unbalanced me or that I was going to develop an unnatural fixation on you or insist on a relationship. I wanted you to feel free to pursue the career you'd raved about.'

He stroked her face with his index finger and he watched as she closed her eyes. 'So you did it for me,' he said quietly. He kissed her eyelid. He felt her warm breath against his cheek as a soft sigh escaped her lips. He lifted his head and looked into her blue eyes.

'I want to kiss you.'

'No, Jack, we shouldn't.'

'I know, but I can't help myself. I've wanted this for the longest time.'

She said nothing. Neither did she protest as his lips closed in on hers, for she wanted it, too. A slow heat burned in the pit of her stomach and threatened to scorch her bones. It rendered her incapable of movement. His lips were gentle, soft. The light brush of his mouth on hers promised so much.

They didn't touch except for their mouths. His lips roved over hers, slowly deepening the kiss, savouring the taste of her. She tasted wonderful. He marvelled at the way even such light contact affected his body. His heart pounded and his loins fired into life. Slowly the kiss intensified until they were both breathing hard. He groaned and gave in to the desire to entangle his hands in her blonde tresses, trying to press her mouth even closer to his.

The telephone jangled. Their lips slowed and stilled, the ringing phone dragging them back to reality. Jack broke away and flung himself back against the covers. They lay unmoving for a few seconds, their chests rising and falling rapidly.

He reached out and snatched up the receiver. Laura closed her eyes and ran her tongue over her tingling lips, savouring the faint trace of him.

'Yes,' he snapped. 'OK.' He slammed the receiver down.

Laura's body was trembling lightly in reaction to Jack's kiss. She should have resisted, she should have got out of bed when he'd told her he wanted to kiss her. She wasn't exactly acting like a woman in a long-term, loving relationship. She had practically spontaneously combusted at the first touch of his lips.

She should have pushed him away. She should have reminded him about Isaac. Who he thought was her lover. But was really her son. His son. Oh, dear, how complicated!

'That was our wake-up call,' said Jack, rolling back onto his elbow.

'In more ways than one,' she joked lightly, licking her lips, nervous about his next move.

'We could, of course…pick up where we left off,' he said, lightly caressing her ear lobe with his index finger.

A gleam in his brown eyes and one raised eyebrow made her laugh.

'We've still got some travelling to do,' she reminded him.

'It wouldn't take long.'

'They're not words a girl likes to hear.' She laughed and he joined in.

'OK. I'm going to count to three. If you're still here, beside me, in bed, you're fair game.'

Laura scrambled out. Jack hadn't even reached one. He studied her seriously. OK, he got the message. Even if it was different to the one she'd been giving him a few minutes ago.

CHAPTER FIVE

THEY drove into Newvalley a couple of hours later. Jack found their motel, the Miner's Rest, easily. It was the same one he stayed in every year, he told Laura as he parked the car. It was only a block from where the service would be held and most people who attended chose to stay at the Miner's Rest.

It had built up a reputation over the years, offering special rates, and always reserved a floor of rooms for the annual event so everyone could be together. For most, the memorial service was like a pilgrimage and the Miner's Rest was the focal point.

The people who attended year after year knew each other well. Despite the tragedy that had brought them all together, it was a time of celebration, too. They had become a tight-knit group, almost family, and seeing each other again was a time for rejoicing. Most kept in contact during the year but being face to face was particularly bitter-sweet.

They checked in and Laura breathed a sigh of relief on opening her door to see Jack pass her and open his own—four down and on the opposite side of the passage. Distance. Good, she needed to sleep as far away from him as possible.

Laura knew that they couldn't have a repeat performance of this morning. Next time a telephone might not interrupt them and she doubted whether she was strong enough, particularly in this set of circumstances, to resist him.

She dumped her bag on the floor and undertook a cursory inspection of the room. It was quiet and she suddenly felt at a loose end. She found the remote and flicked the television on, plonking herself down on the bed. At least it was a distraction.

A knock roused her a short while later. It was Jack.

'A few of us…' he gestured to about ten people behind him '…are going down for some lunch. Why don't you join us?'

He saw the panic in her eyes as the curious crowd behind him jostled for a better position.

'I'm…I'm not hungry,' she stumbled, avoiding eye contact with the strangers. Her stomach chose that moment to let out a thundering growl, no doubt heard by all. He raised an eyebrow then nodded and smiled, gently squeezing her hand. Laura felt relieved.

'Why don't you have a nap and I'll wake you in time for the service?'

As Jack walked away he shook his head in amazement. He'd just recommended Laura indulge in a classic form of avoidance. Still, in a few hours she would be confronting some carefully buried ghosts. He doubted if sleep would be the easiest commodity to find tonight. She might as well get it while she could.

Laura shut the door and sagged against it. She could still feel their eyes, feel their curiosity and speculation. It hadn't been rude or unkind but it had been intense. She had spent the last ten years of her life dodging people's scrutiny. How was she going to cope with it today?

She threw herself on the bed and resolutely shut her eyes. It felt surreal, being back in Newvalley. She would never have thought a pretty coastal town that was supposed to be nothing more than a four-night stop on her backpacking trip would be such a defining landmark in her life.

Jack's knock woke her at two o'clock.

'You look more rested,' he observed as she opened the door. She looked sexy as hell actually, with her hair all tousled and her sleepy face free of make-up. 'We'll have to leave in three-quarters of an hour. Can you be ready by then? We normally walk, it only takes five minutes.'

'Sure.' She smiled and he turned to go. 'So, did you talk about me?' she asked quietly.

He turned back. 'Laura…it wasn't like that.'

'Oh? How was it then?'

'They were curious and excited. Very excited. They're eager to meet you.'

Laura floundered for a reply.

'I'll be with you, Laura.' He placed a hand on her shoulder. 'Get dressed,' he ordered, gently turning her around and pushing her towards the bathroom.

Laura felt a little more composed when Jack called back for her. She'd chosen to wear a navy dress. It was classic and simple, straight through to mid-calf, emphasising her slimness, sleeveless with a halter neck, adorned with five white daisies with yellow centres. They gave the dress a splash of colour. Navy strappy sandals completed the outfit.

She applied some mascara and lipstick and ran a comb through her short blonde hair. Laura loved how manageable it was at this length—low maintenance. Her hair had been longer when Jack had first known her.

A low whistle greeted her when she opened the door. Her eyes darted quickly behind Jack. She almost sighed aloud in her relief that he was alone.

'You're ready, then?'

'Yep,' she said, squaring her shoulders. 'Let's do it.'

They didn't speak on the ride down in the lift. They were halfway to the revolving doors in the foyer when Jack stopped abruptly. Laura followed his gaze. A group of people milled just beyond the doors. He swore under his breath and dragged her into the nearby boutique.

'They're reporters, aren't they?' she asked, feeling a knot tighten her stomach. She remembered how pushy they could be in their packs and apprehension clawed at her.

'Yes. I think they may be waiting for you.' He waved away the shop assistant about to help them.

'But…how do they know…?'

'They may have overheard some of us at lunch—the press stay here, too.'

'Thanks a lot, Jack. I really don't need this today.'

Jack groaned inwardly. Laura was cranky. And she looked like she was about to bolt. He tried to find the words to apologise but wasn't sure Laura was in the mood to listen. Her stony silence stretched like a long rocky path between them.

Jack's gaze fell on a display of hats behind her. He left her stewing and picked out a stylish straw hat with a very large brim. He bought it from the curious assistant.

'Here, put this on. It should help to conceal your identity a little.'

'I've got a better idea,' she snapped. 'How about I just go back to my room?'

He smothered an exasperated oath and crammed the hat down on her head. 'You're going,' he said firmly, like he was talking to a stubborn child.

She'd have protested if he'd given her a chance, but before she knew it he was dragging her by the hand towards the doors and out through the crowd of milling reporters.

Laura was aware of being jostled and everyone calling her name at once. A strange sense of *déjà vu* settled around her. Mary, how have you been? Mary, how do you feel?

Cameras clicked and whirred, dazing her. She dropped her head and hid beneath the generous straw brim. The noise of a multitude of shouted questions and the crush threatened to engulf her.

'Stand back!' Jack commanded, trying to shield her. 'No comment.'

They finally barged free. 'Bloody animals,' Jack growled, glaring behind him at the mob following at a short distance. Laura gulped in big lungfuls of air.

'Are you OK?' He peered under the hat brim to assess her.

'Yes,' she gulped, clutching her trembling hands to her chest. 'Let's just go and get it over with.'

They walked briskly along the two city blocks, arriving with five minutes to spare. Laura stopped to catch her breath, stilling as she took in the scene.

The site where the backpackers hostel had stood was now a memorial garden. It looked very different to Laura's last memory of it. The sound of drilling and sirens replaced by trickling fountains and birdsong. Mountains of rubble and twisted wreckage replaced by lush grass and flowering borders.

Laura found it hard to believe that a decade had elapsed since tons of concrete had held her entombed. That on this beautiful, tranquil piece of land, chaos and tragedy had reigned.

As Jack led her towards the centre plaque, snippets of her ordeal flashed before her eyes. The noise of drills, the distant calls of people desperately searching for survivors, the smell of dust and the cloying claustrophobia of cold concrete slabs.

A marquee had been erected near the plaque. Jack guided her into this shady area. People turned and stared. A hush fell over the gathering and they parted to let them through. Rows of chairs were set up before the raised podium. Jack ushered her to the front row, where it appeared two seats had been reserved for them. She would have preferred to sit unnoticed at the back but she sat down, grateful to be off wobbly legs.

About to take her hat off, Laura noticed a clutch of television cameras, relegated to a cordoned-off area a short distance away. The cameras appeared to be trained squarely on her. Best to leave it on, she thought as Jack squeezed her hand.

'Lovely to have you here, my dear.' A middle-aged woman tapped her shoulder from behind. Laura turned, uncertain what to do or say. She was humbled by such a genuine sentiment from a stranger.

'Thank you,' she mumbled quietly, and turned back.

The ceremony was plain and simple. Some local dignitaries spoke, as did representatives of different churches. At the end each victim's name was read out and a member of their family lit a candle.

Fifty-six names. Each one felt like a physical blow to Laura as tears blurred the dots of flame into one. She felt sick and hollow and…guilty. Why? Why had she survived when everyone else had perished? What freaky cosmic force had been at work that day to have spared her?

Laura didn't notice people standing, milling around, chatting.

'Laura.' Jack broke into her reverie.

'Hmm?'

'I know a few people who'd like to meet you.'

'Sure.' She shrugged, operating on autopilot. It was now or never.

He helped her up and led her to a small group of people. He introduced her around. The names didn't register. The last woman was the one who had spoken to Laura earlier. Her name was Gwen Johnston.

She was Irish. Laura hadn't noticed that before. She reminded Laura of her mum. Plump with a big bosom and cheerful disposition. Suddenly Laura would have slain a dragon to have her mother by her side.

'It's truly fantastic that you came, Mary. We think about you every year. Me, there isn't a day that goes by that I don't pray for you. Neve would have liked that.'

Laura's felt the hairs on the back of her neck prickle. A broad Irish accent teased at her memory.

'Neve?' she enquired.

'My Neve died in the collapse. She was only nineteen. Backpacking around Australia she was. I fly over from Belfast every year.'

'Neve,' Laura repeated, as if she'd been struck dumb. Memories of Gwen's daughter swept into Laura's mind. It was as if the mention of her name had opened some invisible floodgates and now her mind was awash with a torrent of swirling, gushing images.

Laura's legs began to shake. She clutched Jack's arm for support. She felt the group around her fade away. The peripheries of her vision blackened.

'Laura? Are you OK?' Jack asked but a ringing noise in her ears blocked out the words.

'Neve,' she whispered as she slumped against Jack, then lost consciousness.

'Stand back,' he commanded the group as he laid her gently on the grass. 'Gwen, kneel down and pop her legs up on your lap, please.'

'Is she all right, Jack?'

'Just fainted,' he said, feeling for Laura's pulse. Out of the corner of his eye he saw the media contingent get wind of something happening in the marquee.

'Come closer,' he ordered. 'Shield her from those vultures.' He gestured with his head.

Someone handed him a cool, wet cloth and he placed it on her sweaty brow.

'Laura.' He called her name softly.

'Oh, dear. I should never have mentioned Neve. Why did you let me prattle on so?' Gwen fretted.

'It's OK, Gwen. I think it was just the emotional toll of the whole day. It's not your fault.'

'Oh, dear…' she said again.

'Laura,' Jack said softly.

She slowly came to, murmuring and rolling her head from side to side. Jack was relieved when she opened her eyes and focussed squarely on him. Her eyes looked confused and uncomprehending at first but then he watched them change and her cheeks flame as realisation dawned.

'Oh…I'm sorry,' she said, struggling to sit up.

'Lie still, Laura,' he ordered. 'You fainted. Just take it easy for a moment. Here.' He thrust a cool drink towards her lips and supported her into a semi-upright position. 'Drink this.'

She drank greedily. Dry from the hot, humid day.

'Better now?'

She nodded and sat up further, still using Jack for support. She took her feet off Gwen and apologised for dirtying her dress.

'Don't be silly, my love.'

Laura felt embarrassed and self-conscious sitting on the ground, looking up at the concerned faces forming a protective barrier around her. It was time to get back up to everyone's level.

'Help me up, please,' she said to Jack.

Laura felt woozy and held onto Jack, steadying herself, waiting for the spinning to stop. Slowly the ground stopped moving and she could focus again.

'I'd like to go now,' she said to Jack.

'Sure.'

Jack left her with Gwen while he organised a taxi. He didn't want Laura to walk even though it was only a short distance. Also, he wanted to protect her from the media.

Jack arrived back promptly and Laura was grateful to be heading back. She needed time to think about this new discovery. To analyse it properly. To be suddenly hit by a flashback so real about a person you'd completely forgotten was unnerving.

Forgotten, or suppressed? Laura thought of Neve's last moments and how the end had come, and realised that suppressed was more apt.

Laura was thankful for the protective huddle that surrounded her on the short walk to the waiting cab. These people had met her for the first time only half an hour ago, yet they were already guarding her privacy. As the cab door shut, Laura sagged gratefully against the cool seat and took off her hat. She brushed her hand through her hair, slightly damp where the hat had been.

'What happened back there? Did you have some kind of a flashback?'

She should have known he would know. She looked at him and was struck suddenly by his resemblance to Isaac. Jack's teeth worried his bottom lip, just as Isaac's did when he had something on his mind.

'Something like that,' she admitted, sighing.

'What did you remember? Was it something to do with Neve Johnston?'

'Uh-huh.'

'Want to talk about it?'

'Not really,' said Laura, feeling suddenly weary.

'It'd help.'

'I know,' she said, and squeezed his hand. 'But I need time to think about it first. Sort it out in *my* head first.'

'Fair enough.' He shrugged.

They alighted at the motel a minute later.

'Why don't you come and have a drink at the bar with me?'

'No.' She shook her head. 'I think I'd like to be alone for a while.'

Jack watched her go. He was overcome with an urge to wrap her up in his arms and protect her. She always had aroused his most basic male instincts. He so badly wanted to be there for her these next few hours. Today had been momentous for her and it wasn't over yet.

He thought about the Neve incident. Had she known Gwen's daughter? Maybe they had become friendly while they'd been staying at the hostel? She'd never mentioned a Neve to him. Had she suppressed it? Was this the reason why she'd never fully moved on?

The psyche was an interesting thing, full of self-protection mechanisms. Fifty-six strangers dying was easier to cope with than fifty-five strangers and one friend. Had she suppressed her memories of Neve because the guilt of surviving when her friend hadn't was too intense?

Jack walked to the bar and ordered a beer to stop himself from going to her.

CHAPTER SIX

LYING fully clothed on the bed, Laura could no more have stopped the memories than have held back the tide. Images of Neve Johnston with her lilting accent and red hair floated before her. Laura had definitely known her. She had arrived the day before and they had talked briefly about their plans. No, they hadn't been bosom buddies but Laura had liked her instantly.

The hostel accommodation had varied from family rooms through to open dorms. Laura had the top bunk in a four-bed room. Neve was in an identical room next door. When the earthquake hit and the building collapsed, Laura had been alone, writing postcards. All the women sharing Neve's room had been in. Neve had been the only one to survive the impact.

Laura remembered Neve's hysteria as she'd yelled and cried out to the others. Laura had tried to calm her but hadn't been able to make herself heard over the other girl's hysteria. Eventually the futility of it all had quietened Neve's panic. Then they'd begun to talk.

They had both been in a similar situation. Not hurt but entombed by rubble and debris that couldn't be shifted by hand. When they'd realised they couldn't dig themselves out, or even reach each other, they'd spent a lot of time reassuring themselves that help was on the way.

Once she had calmed down, Neve had made her laugh. She'd had a dry wit and a gregarious nature that was infectious. They'd talked about their lives and hopes. Having somebody there with her had made the experience much less frightening.

Laura reached down and pulled the blankets over her, chilled by the memory of what had happened next.

About two hours into their situation the first aftershock had ravaged the crumpled structure. It had been frightening and Laura had shut her eyes and prepared to die. The noise had been deafening and she had heard Neve's screams melding with hers to form one frightened howl.

Then, just as suddenly, the rumbling had stopped. Except Neve's screams didn't. Laura tried to talk to her. To get her to tell her what had happened. Laura could only assume that the aftershock had shifted some rubble.

Neve's cries had stopped suddenly. Laura had spent the next hour crying and calling out to her. But there had only been silence. Laura had felt fear take grip as the realisation she was alone had dawned. It had grown out of control. She'd cried then, in fear. Fear of being trapped. Fear of never being found. Fear of dying.

Laura supposed that she must have cried herself to sleep because when she awoke some time later, she could hear the distant voices of people and activity above her. Laura began to yell again. Yell for her life. From that moment on she had no memory of Neve Johnston. Until now. She had put Neve aside in order to survive.

Laura shivered and pulled the blankets closer. How was it possible to blank such a thing out? For ten years? Because it was too horrible? Too horrible then and no better now? What else had she suppressed? Once again she was left with why. Why, why, why? Why did Neve die and she live? Why was she spared?

Not that she welcomed death, because she didn't. Her most basic instinct as she'd lain trapped had been to survive. But she'd felt a connection with the others that hadn't made it and had wondered at the seemingly senseless lottery of life that decided who stuck around and who didn't.

From the moment of her rescue, Laura had felt that she had been spared for a greater purpose. And yet she had never fulfilled it. She felt she had bargained with the gods and not made good on her promise. What was her purpose in life she had been spared for? What was she supposed to do to justify her rescue?

She searched her mind for something, anything that would confirm her survival had been warranted. Isaac sprang to mind and she smiled a watery smile.

Yes, he was her greatest achievement. Bringing a wonderful child into the world, nurturing and loving him and seeing him touch other people's lives was a true accomplishment. Maybe this purpose she was suddenly obsessed with didn't have to be grandiose. Could something as simple as giving life be enough?

If that were the case then her career could count as well. Couldn't it? She'd helped save many lives over the years. Given the gift of life many times. That was something special when she thought about it. It was easy to just dismiss it as part of her job, but for a lot of people her contribution had been priceless.

These thoughts cheered her slightly but a feeling of restlessness remained. Laura kicked back the covers. She had to get out. Going over and over this in her mind was driving her crazy. The four walls of the room suddenly seemed suffocating. She changed into shorts and a crop top and left at high speed.

She walked briskly through the streets as the last fingers of daylight curled across the sky. She didn't know where she was going and was surprised to find herself in the memorial gardens.

They were peaceful now, compared to the earlier activity. She walked slowly around them, her mind preoccupied with Neve. She walked up to the central stone monument and absently ran her hands over the cool plate, listing the names of those who perished.

Neve Johnston. Nineteen. Laura turned away as a well of emotion threatened to break through. She wandered aimlessly around, admiring the great job they had done in creating this beautiful monument. Trees had been planted for each of the victims, representative of their country of origin.

Laura found Neve's tree. The little plaque at its foot said NEVE AGNES JOHNSTON. VISITING FROM IRELAND. GONE TOO YOUNG.

Laura slumped to the ground, fingering the raised print of the plaque as tears cascaded down her face and sobs racked her body. They consumed her, falling unabated. She was oblivious to everything.

Through her gut-wrenching misery Laura heard someone call her name and then two arms enfolded her shoulders. Laura assumed it would be Jack, her rock, but as she turned to accept his comfort she looked into Neve's mother's face.

'There, there, dear,' she soothed, and Laura gratefully surrendered to the comfortable broad chest. She wept inconsolably. She wept for Neve and the others. She wept for herself and the burden of guilt she had carried all these years.

Some time later Laura managed to rein in her emotions. All that remained were the last few dying hiccoughs. She took the tissue that Gwen offered.

'You knew my Neve, didn't you, dear?'

'Yes.' Laura nodded. 'But I never realised it until today.'

'It's been a truly awful day for you, hasn't it, Laura? May I call you Laura?'

'I wish you would. I really don't know who you're talking to when you call me Mary.'

Gwen laughed. Neve's laugh.

'Tell me.'

'I…I'm not sure…'

'I need to know, Laura,' she said quietly but firmly. 'Not knowing is terrible. She was my daughter, I loved her. If you know anything about her in her last days…I'm hungry for it. Nothing you could tell me could be worse than wondering about her for the last ten years.'

As a mother, Laura could understand that sentiment. But

thinking again about the last terrifying moments of Neve's life, she wasn't sure every grisly detail was necessary.

Laura took a deep steadying breath and told Gwen everything she knew about her daughter—almost. They sat side by side on the grass under Neve's tree, talking, crying and laughing.

'Neve was so strong. She was constantly trying to cheer me up and keep me positive and focussed on our rescue.'

'She always did have a great sense of humour,' Gwen said, her voice whimsical.

Laura laughed as a sudden snatch of their conversation came back to her.

'Yes. You know what she said, Gwen? It really cracked me up. She said, "That'd be right. Lived nineteen years in one of the world's most dangerous cities and don't have a scar to show for it, and yet I come all the way to Australia and nearly get killed by a bloody great building falling on me head."'

Gwen threw back her head and laughed. Laura joined her, once again cracking up over Neve's joke. Then Gwen asked the question Laura had been dreading.

'Laura, I need to ask you this now. Up until today we assumed that Neve was killed instantly, along with everyone else. Please, I need to know—did she suffer at the end?'

'No,' Laura lied, looking Gwen square in the eye. 'The first aftershock hit a couple of hours after the initial collapse. We were talking one second and she was gone the next. It was very quick, Gwen.'

Tears filled the older woman's eyes and ran down her cheeks.

'I prayed every day that she hadn't suffered.' Gwen hugged Laura. 'Thank you, my dear. God bless you.'

If He didn't strike her down first, Laura thought. She just hadn't known how to tell Gwen the truth. Surely she had suffered enough over the years, coping with the loss of her daughter. Was it so wrong? Looking at the joy and contentment on the other woman's face, Laura couldn't regret the lie.

A short while later, as twilight blanketed the city, the two women walked back to the motel in reflective silence.

They parted at the entrance to the bar. Laura rode the lift up to her floor and let herself into her room. Feeling at a loose end, she flicked the television on and channel-surfed. The news was showing footage of the memorial service.

Laura cringed at how much of the report was devoted to shots of her. Thank goodness for her hat. She was barely recognisable. Then the screen was full of older footage of the carnage wrought by the earthquake and the devastated hostel site.

It had been a decade since Laura had seen this footage, both on the television and with her own eyes. Her skin broke out in goose-bumps and her hands started to shake. She groped behind her for the bed. It was like a bomb had exploded under the hostel.

She felt claustrophobic just looking at the film. She realised that she was scrunching the quilt cover in her hands. She could smell the dust again and feel the fear of dying curl through her gut.

Then the images changed and there she was, being hoisted out of a hole amidst the wreckage. Lying on a stretcher, a drip being held by one rescue worker. Looking at the total devastation, Laura wondered how she had got through the ordeal.

Then the camera focussed on Jack, holding her hand as they lifted the stretcher through the rubble. And there was her answer. Jack had got her through it. From the time he'd located her, he'd been with her every step of the way. Even through the years, through his son, he'd been with her.

Laura was overwhelmed by the sudden urge to see him. She needed to be with the one person who had been there for her all this time. It suddenly seemed so clear. It was as if everything that had happened over the intervening years had been leading her to this moment.

Jack was the only one who really understood. She should be with him. She needed to be with him. He was the only one who could offer her what she intrinsically craved. Comfort.

Ten years ago she had found a safe haven in his arms. With the overwhelming events of today and the disturbing images on her television, nothing else seemed to matter now but rediscovering that comfort.

Jack opened the door promptly to her knock. He was clad only in a pair of shorts.

'H-hello, Jack,' stumbled Laura, not expecting to find him semi-naked.

'Laura. I've been worried about you.' Standing before him, blue eyes slightly red-rimmed, she had a vulnerability that called to his most primitive instincts. His heart lurched. He wanted her. So much. Too much.

'Can I come in?'

Staring intently into her eyes, some part of him somewhere deep in his psyche knew why she had come. Knew that if he stood aside a chain of events would be started that he mightn't be able to control. The first domino would fall. Don't let her in, he told himself as she returned his gaze unwaveringly.

He stood aside. She walked past him, her arm lightly grazing his naked chest. Her perfume caressed his senses. It was intoxicating. She smelt good enough to eat. He gave himself a mental shake at the images that invoked.

'You've been crying,' he said as he shut the door.

'Yes. Gwen and I had a long talk.'

'Want to tell me about it?'

'No. I think I'm all talked out.'

There was silence as he watched her warily. She was looking at him with an openness that hadn't been there since that night ten years ago. Time failed to progress. Clocks didn't exist in the world they now found themselves in.

He couldn't bear it any longer. 'What now, Laura?'

'Make love to me, Jack.'

He expelled the breath he hadn't known he'd been holding. Yes. He had known she would speak those exact words. And he wanted to. So very much. He wanted to cross the short distance that separated them and make them one. But some inexplicable force held him back.

Things had been different when they had made love all those years ago. The trauma had been too close, too all-consuming and his depth of knowledge hadn't been as great. As much as loving Laura tonight, all night, would be infinitely right, Jack knew that it would be the absolutely wrong thing to do.

With the distance that the years had provided, and his psychiatric training, Jack knew that Laura was far too emotionally vulnerable to take such an important step. Having sex to see you through pivotal life situations was not a healthy way of dealing with issues. It didn't make them go away, it only shelved them for a while.

Laura was craving something from him that could lead to an unhealthy dependency. Besides, he wanted more than that. He wanted all of her, all of the time. Not just some of her at times when she wanted to use him to obliterate painful memories.

'I don't think that's a good idea.' His voice was quiet, calm. The complete opposite of the emotional squall lashing his insides.

She took three steps towards him until they were just touching. 'Don't you want to make love to me?'

'Ah-h…' Like he wanted his next breath

'It's been a while since I've played wanton seductress, but…' She wrapped her arms around his neck and rubbed her pelvis suggestively against his. 'I think I remember what an aroused man feels like.'

Jack took a deep breath. It was a mistake, because now his senses were full of her smell and he wondered if she'd taste as good. Jack didn't think it was possible, but he became more aroused.

Suddenly the one thing he wanted was being offered to him on a silver platter. Heaven alone knew how often he'd fantasised about it. Even during the years he had been married to Anna the fantasy had continued. He could control it during his waking hours but in his sleep…that was another matter. Many times poor Anna had had to put up with him crying out Laura's name. It was another reason their marriage hadn't survived.

He looked into Laura's entrancing blue eyes. Even slightly red and puffy, they called to him. Could he do it? Absolutely! But the real question was—should he?

It was obvious that today had been an emotional milestone. Whatever had taken place between her and Gwen had also taken an emotional toll. She had sought him out as a reaction to the day's events. It was history repeating itself.

Was it right to take what she was offering and to hang with the consequences? Forget that in the cold light of tomorrow morning she might just hate herself. Be appalled at her actions, as she had been a decade ago? Hate him even?

She wasn't thinking straight, Jack knew that with certainty. Why else would she forget her fidelity to Isaac?

Could he live with the hate and loathing in her eyes? Yes, screamed his hormones.

'No,' he said quietly, shaking his head.

She smiled knowingly at him and laughed a deep, throaty laugh.

'Oh, Jack.' She sighed his name. 'It's so easy,' she whispered, tracing his dry lips with the tip of her finger. Then she closed the distance between their lips and he was lost. She was sucking the breath from his body and he didn't care. Her kiss was searing his lips, her tongue licked flames into his mouth. She was setting him alight as easily as a spark to tinder-dry grassland.

Her fingers caressed his scalp. It was a wonderfully erotic sensation.

'Hmm,' Laura sighed against his mouth. 'You taste fabulous, Jack,' she said, snuggling into his chest. 'Have you been drinking?'

Drinking? Had he? His brain was still fogged by raging sexual desire. He struggled to grasp the question. Oh, yes, he'd had a couple of drinks earlier in the bar.

'Beer,' he croaked.

'Oh, dear.' She laughed. 'A lot?'

'No.' Not nearly enough!

But if Laura heard his strangled reply she showed no signs. She'd found his nipple and was twirling a finger round and round, and before he could think straight again she had lowered her mouth to it. His body practically convulsed with desire as her moist mouth closed over the sensitive flesh.

He gripped her hips urgently, forgetting his resolve, and pushed her back onto the bed. This time their passion was equal. Their lips roved and explored together. Faces, necks, ears. Her hands stroked his back and he shuddered as his naked flesh formed goose-bumps beneath her nails.

Jack groaned. He wanted her badly. Years of fantasising and the reality far exceeded his wildest dreams. Somehow her clothes were gone and he was able to caress her bare flesh. His fingers followed the smooth rise of her breasts to their peaks. She moaned and raked her nails down his back as she bit into the hard tanned flesh of his shoulder.

'Oh, Jack, don't stop.'

Stop? Was she insane? He was a slave to the smoothness of her skin. Hypnotised by its silky movement. Drugged by its heady, perfumed aroma.

'You are so beautiful,' he said, kissing her hair, her neck.

'Don't talk, Jack. Touch me,' she begged, guiding his hand to her breasts and kissing his mouth with a runaway passion.

Needing no further encouragement, he rolled her over and over on the soft mattress, kicking at the linen entangling his legs.

The remote for the television fell off the bed, crashing to the floor. The TV blared on.

'A solemn day of remembrance in Newvalley…'

Startled out of their passionate embrace by the roaring commentary, Jack's attention inevitably turned to the coverage of the service.

Laura couldn't believe it was on *again* as she madly groped around the floor in the half-light for the remote control. She didn't want to hear about it another time today. She nearly cheered with relief when she located the offensive little black gadget and flicked the television off. She didn't want to be reminded about today. She needed to obliterate it from her memory, if only for tonight.

'Hey,' Jack said, whisking the remote from her, switching it back on and reducing the volume.

'Jack, please…'

'Shh. Just a moment,' he said distractedly, engrossed in the footage. Laura was left with little choice but to sit there and watch it as well. She didn't want to but there was something compelling about it, her eyes drawn inevitably to the screen.

By the time the piece had finished, Laura could tell the mood had gone. Jack was sitting very erect and staring vacantly at the screen. Their breathing, which had been noisy and fast, had settled completely. She needed to regain some control over the situation. She needed to spend the night in his arms, lose herself in their safety—even more so now after the graphic television images.

She pushed the 'off' button and he turned to look at her. She smiled at him, ignoring the shuttered look, and lightly touched his shoulder.

'Now…where were we?' she whispered in her best seductress voice.

Jack observed her from somewhere outside his body. Sitting naked on his bed—so sexy, so desirable. What had he been thinking? What had happened to his resolve? Those big blue eyes had. She'd looked at him with those eyes full of invitation and he had given in to his base male desires. His highly intelligent brain had bowed to his underdeveloped hormones.

'No,' he said, getting up from the bed, mustering all his willpower to put some space between her and his still raging hormones.

'Jack?' she asked, pulling the sheet over her nakedness.

'I can't, Laura.'

'Can't?'

'Won't.'

'Won't?'

'Laura, I think if we do this tonight you may well end up regretting it tomorrow. Today's been tough for you, I know, but ultimately I don't think you'll thank me for taking advantage of your vulnerability.'

'Sometimes, Jack, I swear you suffer from multiple personality disorder. You switch from Jack the person to Jack the shrink in a bat of an eyelid.'

He smiled at the picture this painted. Some kind of benign Dr Jekyll and Mr Hyde, switching masks constantly. He sighed and rubbed his eyes.

'I think at the moment you're just reverting to type. You're repeating what you did ten years ago to feel safe because this whole Neve thing has thrown you for a loop. You're coming to me because I was there for you before.'

'I don't need any of the psycho bullshit, Jack,' she snapped, stripping back the sheets and pulling her clothes on. 'I suppose you're going to tell me that I'll thank you in the morning.'

'Maybe not in the morning, no. But I hope that one day you'll be able to see that taking advantage of you in an emotionally vulnerable state, to have sex with you, no matter how tempting, just wouldn't be right.'

'Didn't notice you being so reticent ten years ago.'

If she'd slapped his face it couldn't have been more startling. He sighed. Just because her acid comment had come out of left field, it didn't make it any less right.

'No, you're right, I wasn't. But I should have been.'

'Oh, for goodness' sake, Jack.' She shut her eyes and took a deep breath. 'It's not like we planned it.'

'No, but if I'd known then what I know now…'

'I don't think it would have mattered, Jack. I think our night together was as inevitable as the earth turning.'

'It was just too close, you know?' he asked, almost pleading with her to understand. 'The horror was still too fresh…but I should have been stronger.'

'Oh, Jack,' she sighed, her anger over his rejection dissipating. He seemed so vulnerable right now. 'It's not like I was your patient. Don't be so hard on yourself. Are you telling me you regret it?'

'No.' He shook his head slowly. 'I know I should but I don't—I can't. What happened between us was one of the most moving experiences of my life. It was like our souls connected.'

'Yes,' Laura whispered. He had summed it up perfectly.

'Do you?'

'Do I what?'

'Do you regret it?'

'No, never. I think you're right, it was a meeting of souls. I think it was our destiny to be together that night.'

How could she regret it? Their time together had produced Isaac and she would be eternally grateful to whatever cosmic force that had been working that day for sending Jack to her rescue.

'I think I should leave now,' she said quietly.

'It might be for the best,' Jack agreed, feeling his resolve weakening already.

Laura closed the door quietly behind her. Jack took a few deep breaths. He clenched his fists hard, suppressing the overwhelming desire to call her back. His conscience was clear. He had done the right thing. So how come he didn't feel any better?

CHAPTER SEVEN

THE next morning they said their goodbyes after breakfast and checked out. Laura breathed a sigh of relief, knowing they were heading home. It had been cathartic but exhausting.

As they drove in companionable silence through the streets of Newvalley, Laura couldn't help but reflect on her time there. It had been an experience. Confronting her past. Rediscovering Neve. Meeting the regulars. Facing the press again and all the implications their renewed interest encompassed.

It had felt strange, coming back here after ten years of deliberately staying away. And now, as Newvalley became a tiny dot in the distance, it felt strange to be leaving.

'How are you feeling?' Jack's voice broke into her reverie.

'I don't know. Relieved. Bereft. A little torn. Guilty that I'm leaving them behind again. Guilty that I can leave at all. But bloody glad to be going home. Doesn't make much sense, does it?'

'No, that's fine. You articulate your feelings well.'

The kilometres flew by. They chatted about the service and Jack filled Laura in on who was who in greater detail. She asked him about the rescue people she had met at the service and he filled her in on them as well.

'What was it like, Jack? On the outside? What do you remember?'

Jack's face took on a distant look. 'I remember the dust. The air was thick with it. It was stifling and made the air stale.'

Laura nodded. She remembered the dust, too. Choking her. It had been like trying to breathe styrofoam beads.

'I remember that it was hot. Very hot. I remember the bodies.'

Jack's mind took him back to that day. Visions of the carnage that was once a building crowded his mind. The devastation had been overwhelming. A six-storey building reduced to a pile of rubble, all twisted metal and crumbled concrete. The scale of the destruction had been awesome. The building had borne the brunt of Mother Nature's tantrum.

The rescue teams had been so sure that they would haul victim after victim out alive. Even now he remembered the eagerness, their positivity. They had attacked the mountain of debris with vigour and determination, always aware that time was of the essence.

Jack had shared their desperation, clawing at the rubble with his bare hands while they waited for specialised equipment to arrive. Calling out, as they all had, hoping to contact those trapped beneath the mountain or at least reassure them that efforts were being made to get them out.

He remembered the first ebbing of their confidence. The instability of the structure forcing them to stop for their own safety and not to worsen it for those who might still have been alive underneath. Aftershocks had been common, causing mad scrambles off the site. The loss of time had increased their frustration tenfold. Nobody had spoken the words but they had all known—if anyone had actually survived the impact, their chances were getting slimmer and slimmer.

And then they started to find the victims. Or parts of them anyway. Traumatically severed limbs were the most common. Jack could remember being called over to assess the first one they found. An arm protruded from the rubble. The workers were excited, hoping they'd made their first save.

Jack felt for a radial pulse and then a brachial as the rescue workers dug gingerly around the arm to expose the rest of the person, frantically calling out to the owner of the arm.

There was no pulse evident so Jack hadn't held out much

hope. But he'd still expected to find a whole person and it was a shock for them all to realise there was no body attached to the arm.

He shuddered, thinking about it now. But that had just been the beginning. Dismembered corpses, their intestines lying in the dirt. Arms, legs, fingers amputated by tons of falling concrete. Heads flattened, leaking brain matter. Bones that had been crushed almost to powder, crumbled as if they were as soft as fresh ricotta cheese. Congealed pools of blood, the metallic odour mixing with the ever-present dust, creating a nauseating mix. It hadn't been for the squeamish.

As the hours passed they kept at it but with silent resilience instead of confident bravado. And then in the late afternoon Jack heard his name being shouted. They'd found one alive. Elation spurred Jack to the spot where several workers were huddled. A woman lay barely breathing, crushed by a slab of concrete from her abdomen down to her ankles. Her right arm up to her shoulder was also pinned by concrete.

Jack felt her carotid pulse, alarmed at its fragile beat. She was barely conscious, just alive.

'Help me,' she whispered to him, a weak squeeze from her free hand imploring him.

'We're here now, we've got you. We're going to get you out,' he assured her.

Jack sprang into action, working with a paramedic and a nurse, even though every medical instinct he possessed knew it was futile. She'd been crushed for about ten hours beneath a massive concrete slab. There was no circulation to her feet and she could neither move nor feel them.

Her blood pressure was unrecordable so Jack knew she was haemorrhaging somewhere. A specialised fibre-optic camera snaked beneath the slab told him her trapped arm was partially severed. She was slowly exsanguinating from the leaking brachial artery.

She was going to die if they didn't free her but, sadly, she was going to die if they did. The build-up of toxins from crushed cells in her lower body would flood her almost collapsed circulation the minute they removed the slab, sending her heart into fibrillation and then cardiac arrest.

But she'd survived thus far, Jack thought, so maybe they would get a miracle here today.

'Can…can I get a drink?' she whispered. 'I'm so thirsty…'

Jack saw the nurse about to deny the girl's request and shook his head at her slightly, his eyes communicating his reasons. She nodded back at him. Jack asked for water and then held her head up and let her slake her thirst.

Normally in a situation like this they wouldn't want a patient so badly injured to drink. The full scale of her injuries were unknown but it didn't take a genius to figure that she would need major surgical intervention, and with probable abdominal trauma anything by mouth would be foolish.

But this was not a normal situation. She wasn't going to live long enough to have an operation. Might as well grant the poor girl her last wish. Make her last few moments as comfortable as possible.

Jack cannulated her free arm with more good luck than medical expertise. Her circulating blood volume was so depleted her peripheral vessels had totally collapsed.

They pushed in a plasma supplement as fast as they could, trying to replace some lost volume. An alkaline solution ran concurrently in the vain hope it would help buffer the toxic cloud that was going to swamp her system when the slabs came off. A defibrillator was charged and ready to go for what Jack feared was an imminent cardiac fibrillation.

'What's that for?' she whispered, seeing the machine out of the corner of her eye.

Jack was stuck between a rock and a hard place. What to tell her? The truth? Or give a half-truth so the last few minutes of her life weren't occupied with the terrifying reality of her imminent demise?

'It's just a precaution,' he assured her. 'When you've been

crushed by something for a long time, some toxins can build up. It's there just in case.'

Tears gathered in her eyes and she sobbed, 'Please, I don't want to die. Don't let me die.'

'Hey,' Jack soothed, squeezing her good hand, 'we've got you now. Just a few minutes and you'll be free.'

Jack had injected into his words a confidence he didn't feel. He didn't want her to die either, and he would fight to keep her alive with everything he had. But they needed a miracle.

He let her hand go to move away at the instruction of the cutting crew, but her hand clutched at his.

'Where are you going?' she asked. 'Don't leave me. I don't want to be alone.'

'I'm moving just two metres away while they remove this slab, and then I'm coming straight back, I promise.'

She cried as he left and Jack couldn't remember a time when he had felt worse. The concrete was dispensed with quickly, and Jack flew back to her side to see a smile of such sweet relief curve her dry, dusty lips and brighten her dimmed eyes.

'Thank you, that feels so good,' she whispered to Jack, who had to put his ear close to her mouth to catch her words. Then her face stilled and her eyes stared and Jack yelled for the defibrillator.

The trace on the screen was as he expected. They worked on her for several minutes before Jack reluctantly called an end to it.

Laura was silent as he recounted the story. She sat very still, not wanting to disturb his recollections. Her heart went out to him. How very, very awful to have seen the things he had. To have made the decisions he'd had to make.

'I'm sorry, Jack.' She covered his hand, resting on the gear lever, with her own. 'I never realised…I didn't know there'd been someone else. What was her name?'

'Jo-anne.'

'How old was she?'

'Same age as you. So young…too young.'

Laura reflected again on how lucky she had been. Luckiest of all had been to be found by Jack and having him to lean on throughout the ordeal.

'Why did you never tell me about her?'

'I never really talk about her. I guess because I've always felt…guilty that I couldn't save her.'

'Oh, Jack, no one could have saved her,' she whispered gently.

'I know that, rationally. And I've come to terms with it over the years, but my guilt is also about how quickly I put her behind me.'

'What do you mean?'

'I heard you not long after the Jo-anne thing. I knew I had to put what happened aside or I'd be no use to you. She was there…fuelling my desperation, but I obliterated all thoughts of her while I was with you. I think maybe she deserved more thought than that.'

'Oh, Jack!' Laura's heart contracted at the husky tone of his voice. 'I feel so selfish. I've often thought about the rescue team and the wonderful job they did and how awful it must have been for them. But I never really thought about how awful it must have been for you. You seemed so strong, like you'd been doing it all your life.'

'On the contrary, I just happened to be the on-duty registrar at the Newvalley General that day. I was automatically deployed as part of the hospital major disaster plan. I'd never really been involved in an incident on such a grand scale. So I just hung around a lot, pitched in where I could.'

'I'm sure it was appreciated,' she murmured.

'It was just so…slow. You know?'

He turned to her, his eyes imploring, apologetic almost. His voice mirrored the frustration from a decade ago as if it were yesterday. Laura could tell his mind was still back at the site, as if talking about it with her for the first time had imprisoned him in a decade-old nightmare. Unable to escape. It seemed strange now, listening to his anguish, that they'd never really talked about it before. Not like this.

'The more we dug, the longer it took. The site was unstable. We had to keep stopping work until they could shore up areas. And we just kept on finding bodies.'

'Oh, Jack.' Her voice trembled, affected by the despair haunting his voice.

'They ordered me home twice after Jo-anne. They were just about to forcibly remove me from the site when I heard your voice.'

'And there was no way I was going to let you leave me.' She smiled ruefully, recalling her constant need for assurance that he wouldn't go away.

'It never entered my mind.' No way would he have left another girl, not for a second, not even if they had demanded it. They would have had to have knocked him unconscious to remove him. Laura had been desperate for him to stay with her, talk to her, and he had been desperate to ensure she would not be another Jo-anne.

Being the first to hear Laura's cries for help had connected them somehow. He'd felt the gravity of that connection weigh heavily against him. Learning that she was unhurt had boosted his spirit. After the tragedy of Jo-anne he had needed this to turn out OK. They all had.

'Oh, Jack, I was too involved in my own situation to give a thought to what you'd been through. Do you wish you hadn't?'

'Hadn't what?' His brows crumpled together.

'Heard me.'

'No. Never. I can't describe to you how much I needed—we all needed—to hear something. Somebody. After Jo-anne… we were all very demoralised. I probably needed you almost as much as you needed me. I think a piece of me would have always been missing if no one had come out. It would have been as if all our efforts were in vain.'

'Well, they weren't.' She squeezed his hand again.

'No.' He smiled solemnly.

Jack turned his eyes back to the road and thanked the fates again that they had been able to rescue Laura. He remembered how he'd felt that day, talking to her, trying to keep her positive and focussed on her rescue.

It had been such a slow process, with rubble being gingerly removed or cut away. Fibre-optic cameras trying to locate her exact position and assess what was needed to get her out. Engineers, city planners, search-and-rescue experts calculating and co-ordinating each stage of the process. Everyone working through the night, aided by special lights.

A part of him felt helpless that all he was doing was lying on his stomach, talking into a crevice in the rubble above where she was located. He wanted to do more. But, as the team assured him, his was the most important job. He was her lifeline and his role was paramount to her rescue.

He was constantly frightened that one of the frequent aftershocks would hit her position and the tons of concrete and rubble entombing and protecting her would become lethal weapons. Every time she fell silent his anxiety increased tenfold. She wanted to sleep but he jollied and pushed and harassed and kept her talking to the very end.

One of the cameras allowed them to see inside her cramped position and have a constant visual of her. It was just as reassuring for Jack as it was for Laura. They were also able to pump some fresh air into the space, which was thick and stale with dust and exhaled carbon dioxide.

And then they got close enough that he was able to hold her hand. He remembered the overwhelming emotion the first time he touched her skin and she grabbed hold and held tight. The relief, the joy, the anticipation that they were getting closer and she would soon be free. Never had touching another human being felt so perfect.

He turned and looked at Laura as she stared out the window. It still felt perfect a decade later. That deeply rooted need to protect her, born from the rubble of Newvalley, still governed his actions, his feelings today. Except she no longer needed his protection. She didn't need rescuing any more. So what was left for him?

They made good time and stopped for lunch about midday with only another four or five hours to get them back to Brisbane. They stopped in a small town that consisted of a petrol station, a bakery, three houses and an ambulance station.

Jack and Laura followed their noses to the bakery, which sold the most mouth-watering, crusty pies they'd ever seen. Laura's stomach growled as the wonderful aroma tempted her tastebuds.

'How about we eat over there?' Jack indicated a shady park across the road. He pulled a picnic rug out of his boot and they found a grassy spot under a big tree.

They munched through their lunch in companionable silence. Jack stretched out on his back.

'Do you mind if I have a quick kip? I didn't sleep well last night. Forty winks should recharge my batteries.'

Laura blushed at his reference to last night. She hadn't slept well either. She'd had a fire in her belly that had kept her feverish all night.

'Sure.' She nodded quickly, not wanting to revisit the subject of last night.

It was pleasant in the park. A blue sky, uncluttered by clouds, hung overhead. The smells of eucalyptus and earth filled her nostrils. She reclined next to Jack, very aware of the slumbering man beside her. He was much too tempting asleep. He looked lonely and vulnerable and Laura wanted to snuggle into him, put her head on his shoulder.

She watched him as he slept, his breathing deep and even, and thought about their conversation in the car. He had really been through an emotional wringer as well. Listening to him describe the carnage of the collapsed building site had given her the shivers.

He'd re-created not just the physical landscape but he'd evoked the emotional landscape also. It was like he'd painted a three-dimensional picture for her where the desperation and heartbreak were as tangible as the twisted debris.

She thought about Jo-anne and the well of emotion that rose in her throat almost prompted her to trail her fingers down his face. She suppressed the urge and sighed. It seemed they both had ghosts from Newvalley living with them.

His remorse, still present a decade later, over Jo-anne obviously nagged at him. And her recent discovery of Neve locked deep in her psyche had been, unbeknownst to her, a stumbling block to her full psychological recovery.

They would both have to live with the consequences of having known these two people. Jack had to live with setting Jo-anne aside to concentrate on *her*, and she had to cope with burying Neve in order to survive her ordeal. At least they had confronted the things that had festered deep in their subconscious. The trip to Newvalley had given them both some closure on that front, even if their relationship was still fettered by the chains of the past.

Laura's attention drifted to a group of children playing on the adventure playground not far away. They ranged in age from about two to ten, she judged. They scampered energetically over the equipment, obviously pleased to be outside and stretching their legs.

The heat of the sun and the laughter of the children, combined with the hum of insects, lulled Laura to sleep. She lay on her side, using her outstretched arm as a pillow. It really was a beautiful day.

Laura was unsure how long she'd been sleeping when the screams of a child woke her. Jack woke, too, sitting bolt upright and looking temporarily disorientated before springing into action. Laura followed closely behind.

The ruckus was coming from the climbing frame. A group

of people surrounded a little boy who lay crying on the ground, clutching his leg.

'Excuse me.' Jack pushed his way through the onlookers. 'I'm a doctor, can I help?' He addressed a woman who was comforting the child and appeared to be his mother.

'Oh, yes.' She instantly looked relieved. 'He fell off the frame. He's hurt his leg.'

Jack knelt down beside the injured boy and fished around in his pocket. 'Laura, take my keys, grab my medical bag out of the boot, please.'

Laura hurried to the car and back again with the requested bag, the child's crying spurring her along. She knelt beside Jack and opened it quickly, assessing its contents for usefulness. It took only one look at the leg to see that at least one bone, maybe both, were broken in his lower leg. The middle of his shin was misshapen and obviously causing the little boy a great deal of pain and distress.

'My name's Jack. What's your name?' Jack asked the boy as he gently assessed the fractured limb. The little boy sobbed anew.

'Tell the doctor your name,' his stressed mother prompted.

'I bet it's Jim. Jungle Jim,' he teased the boy. 'How old are you, then, Jungle Jim?'

The boy continued to cry. Jack made an elaborate gesture, scratching his head and musing deep in thought.

'Two? You two?' he joked with the obviously older boy. Laura thought he might be eight.

'No,' said the boy, sniffing indignantly. 'I'll be nine tomorrow.'

Laura never ceased to be amazed at how easily distracted from pain children were. She had seen it often enough in her work. A broken bone was exceptionally painful.

'Wow. Nine.' Jack whistled. 'Boy, you are old.'

Nine. The same age as Isaac. Laura watched in admiration as Jack slowly drew the boy out of his shell. The boy's cries subsided and he let Jack look at his leg. In a short time he had developed a rapport with the child and had managed to not only secure his co-operation but take his mind off the pain.

'Well, now, Jim. I'm afraid you've broken your leg. See this bit here?' He pointed to the fractured segment. 'That's the broken bit.'

The boy's bottom lip started to wobble and he was seconds away from crying again.

'Hey, it's OK. You know why?' The boy shook his head. 'Because we can fix it. I'm going to splint your leg and then Mummy and Daddy are going to drive you to the ambulance station down the road and they'll take care of you. OK? Ever been in an ambulance before?'

The boy's eyes widened at the prospect of the adventure ahead. 'Will they put the siren on?' he sniffed.

'I reckon they might.' Jack nodded.

'Cool!'

Laura passed Jack a thick crêpe bandage and helped as he splinted the broken leg to his other leg. They were as gentle as possible but the child was obviously in pain. When they were satisfied it was secure, they lifted him up and carried him to the car. They laid him down in the back seat and his grateful mother climbed in beside him.

'Drive him up the road to the ambulance station. They'll take it from here.'

'Say thank you to the doctor,' the harried mother prompted her son.

'That's OK, Jim. Any time,' said Jack, and offered his hand to the boy.

'My name's Henry,' he said in a small voice as he shook Jack's hand.

'Pleased to meet you, Henry.' Jack smiled.

Laura smiled, too, noticing the pleasure on Jack's face. Jack's rapport with children was amazing. It was a pity he couldn't see how great he was with kids! The fact that Henry had finally surrendered his name spoke volumes about the boy's trust in Jack. He obviously thought Jack was pretty neat.

'Will it need a cast?' Henry's mother asked.

'Depends on how badly broken it is,' Jack explained. 'If it's a clean break, a cast will be fine, but if it's not he may need an operation and some pins to hold the bone in place. They won't know that until they've taken an X-ray.'

'An operation?' she asked, her voice quavering.

'Maybe. Let's not get ahead of ourselves. Just get him to the ambulance first, right?'

'Yes, of course,' she said, thanking him again.

Jack pressed his card into her hand. 'Call me when you know what's happening.'

She looked at it. 'Says here you're a psychiatrist.'

'That's right.'

'You seem to know some about bones as well.'

'Oh, I still remember a bit about orthopaedics.' He laughed, ruffling his young patient's hair and waving as the car headed for the ambulance station.

They watched the car until it disappeared from sight. Laura turned to Jack, studying his strong profile.

'What?' he asked, noticing her interest.

'Nothing.' She shrugged and headed back for their blanket.

'Hey, no fair,' he joked, catching her up. 'What were you thinking?'

'Just that you were very good with Henry.'

She didn't want to say what she'd been really thinking. That he'd make a terrific father.

'Why are you so surprised?'

'Oh, you know,' she floundered. 'You don't seem to…like kids very much.'

'What gives you that impression?'

'Past conversations.'

'What past conversation?'

'When I was trapped you told me that children and marriage and the whole family thing were low on your list of priorities and that you wouldn't have time for children with your busy, brilliant career.'

'True. But that doesn't mean that I don't like them. In fact, I have ten nieces and nephews and I like them very much.'

So he liked them but he just didn't want them cluttering up his life. Oh, Isaac. She wouldn't have him treated as an unfortunate inconvenience by his father. The more she got to know Jack the more convinced she was that she'd made the right decision years ago. As hard as it had been to decide to keep his child a secret, his words kept on justifying it.

'Do you never want to be a father?' The question formed in her mind out of despair and slipped out before she could stop it.

He stared at her for a few seconds and she saw something flicker deep in his eyes. He busied himself with packing their belongings.

'Just because someone likes children, it doesn't mean they want to have their own, Laura.'

'It's a good start,' she said quietly, arms folded, watching with dismay his withdrawal from her.

'Come on, we'd better hit the road.'

Laura watched his back as she lagged behind. What was it with him? He'd been so good with Henry. A boy the same age as his own son. He'd been gentle and kind and had managed to get down to the boy's level. And with Andrew at the hospital. He'd been especially good with Andrew.

Laura suddenly felt misty-eyed. How Isaac would love Jack. She pictured them walking side by side, holding hands. Isaac looking up into his father's face with love and pride, the way he always did with her. Asking his endless questions and listening intently to the answers.

She allowed her mind to drift into fantasyland. What a relief it would be to have someone to share the parenting with. To not have to feel so totally responsible for Isaac every single second. To give the decision-making to someone else for a change. To share all those things that parents the world over did every day.

It was all so foreign to Laura and suddenly something she wanted dearly.

CHAPTER EIGHT

JACK'S expression was closed as he opened the door for Laura and she put on her seat belt. She watched in the rear-view mirror as Jack stowed the blanket and medical bag away and slammed the boot down hard. The tyres spun on the loose gravel as he accelerated away from the kerb.

The silence in the car was awkward now. Laura felt uncomfortable. She stole glances at Jack's forbidding profile, increasing her anxiety. She cast around for something to say to end the charged silence.

'I can't.' There. He had said it.

'Can't what?' she asked, her relief that he was still talking to her taking precedence over his cryptic comment.

'I'm infertile.'

What? No you're not, she almost blurted out. What on earth was he talking about? She lived with the proof of his fertility. A nine-year-old called Isaac.

Her silence was killing him. He had obviously shocked her. But he couldn't let her carry on thinking he didn't like children. He couldn't believe she had ever thought that in the first place. OK, he'd told her that he had other priorities that didn't involve family life, but it was quite a leap to assume that he disliked children.

He'd been stewing on her comments since she'd uttered them. He had to set the record straight, correct her wild assumptions. Even if it meant talking about stuff that very few people knew about.

'Cat got your tongue?' he jibed, none too gently. Why didn't she say something? Anything?

'But how…? I mean, I don't understand.'

'I got mumps shortly after I married Anna.'

'Oh.'

Realisation dawned. The mumps had made him infertile. A not uncommon side-effect of the infection in adult men.

'Yes. Oh.'

Laura started to become aware of the wider implications of his startling admission. He was infertile. He'd conceived Isaac before his bout of the mumps. So Isaac was the only child he would ever have. Ever.

Poor Jack. What a dreadful blow it must have been. Newly married and faced suddenly with most couples' worst nightmare. Not being able to have children.

'How was Anna about that?'

He laughed harshly. 'It broke our marriage up… eventually.'

'I'm so sorry, Jack.' She wanted to touch him. Give him some comfort.

'Don't be. It was a long time ago.' He turned and smiled a sad smile.

'Want to talk about it?'

'Going to play amateur psychiatrist?' He laughed.

'No, just good friend. Someone who knows a little about how life can hurt you.'

His laughter quietened and his mood became sombre again. He searched for the right place to begin.

'Funnily enough,' he said, his voice slightly husky, 'we had a ten-year plan when we first got married, and it didn't involve children. We both had our careers to concentrate on, you know?'

Laura nodded. 'Then, after we'd been married for six months, I got mumps. The minute my infertility was confirmed, having a baby was all we could focus on. Suddenly it was *the* most important thing in our lives.'

'Well, that's only natural,' Laura said, encouraging him to continue.

'We tried everything. Nothing worked. We were basically on the IVF treadmill our entire married life. Seems we were both duds. Anna turned out to be not particularly fertile either. Put together, we stood no chance. Anna was a hormonal wreck most of the time from the injections, and I grew more and more disillusioned.'

'It must have been awful.'

'We had to use donor sperm, which really hurt. I know it shouldn't have mattered but I really wanted *my* child, you know? With my genes. But Anna wanted a baby so badly I gave in and consoled myself with the fact that at least the baby would have one set of our genes.'

'Of course you wanted your own biological child, Jack. That's normal,' Laura soothed. Oh, boy, she thought. What is he going to say when he finds out he's had his own biological son for nine years?

'After three years, the fertility experts recommended we try for adoption. By this stage our marriage was stretched to breaking point. We were arguing all the time and somehow Anna always got round to blaming me.'

'Oh, dear.'

'Which, of course, was right. Unintentionally maybe, but it was my fault.'

'Catching mumps wasn't your fault.'

'I felt angry and inadequate enough, without Anna throwing it in my face every time we argued. And we argued plenty.'

'Did you try to adopt?'

'Well, Anna jumped at the idea but it was like adding insult to injury for me. I was stubborn and pig-headed and refused to contemplate having a child that wasn't one of ours at least, biologically. She said that was stupid. She said just because we wouldn't be the birth parents, it didn't mean we couldn't love someone else's child. But I wanted my own child, right or wrong, and things got steadily worse until we didn't have a marriage any more. We had a minefield.'

'Oh, Jack,' Laura whispered, guilt at her own deceit intensifying her feelings of sorrow for Jack.

'So we split. Anna remarried a few months after the divorce was final. She's since had a baby.'

'Did she fall pregnant naturally?'

'Yes. Seems I was the real fly in the ointment.'

'That must be hard for you.'

'No, not really. We didn't part on the best terms but I'm happy for her. I'm sure she's a great mother.'

'How does that make you feel?'

'Wow.' He laughed and turned to face her. 'You are good at this.'

She laughed back.

'It makes me feel determined. Determined not to go through all that again. Stuff up another relationship through my inability to conceive a child.'

'What?' she asked incredulously. 'You're going to shut yourself off from the possibility of loving again? Being in a long-term relationship?'

'I'm not going to lie to you, Laura. Not being able to father a child hurts like hell. It's a wound that never heals. Apart from Newvalley, nothing this devastating has ever happened to me. I always took my fertility for granted. I guess somewhere deep down I always thought I'd make a pretty good dad. My nieces and nephews adore me.'

'I'm sure they do.' She smiled.

'If I was to take that step, any future partner will know the truth up front and have to accept that children aren't on the agenda.'

'But what about adoption?'

'No,' he said quietly. 'I know I could love someone else's baby, but I want my own child. I don't care how selfish that sounds. I want a child with my superior intellect and my good looks.' He laughed but it lacked warmth. 'A child who comes from me. If I can't have that, I'd rather go without.'

Laura digested this information as Jack turned his attention back to driving. The subject seemed to be closed. She studied him as he drove. Under all his matter-of-factness she could feel his hurt.

She felt a surge of emotion ripple through her body, squeezing her heart and bringing a lump to her throat. She loved him. She supposed she always had, but sitting here next to him as he bled from the wounds inflicted by his infertility, she was certain of it.

He'd been her magnetic north since he'd heard her cries from beneath the rubble. She'd lived a long time ignoring it, but now he was back in her life it could be ignored no longer.

He deserved to know about Isaac. His puzzling attitude towards children was now explained. It wasn't that he didn't like them or didn't want them, but the fact that he couldn't have any that was the source of his bitterness.

In fact, he did want them. So he deserved to know about Isaac. Maybe it would make the pain of his infertility a little easier to bear if he knew he'd already created a life.

Laura knew she needed to tell him. But she hesitated. Not right now. She needed a little perspective before rushing headlong into uncharted territory. She needed to think about how and when to tell him.

Out in the open now, her love for Jack was growing stronger by the second. She yearned to be able to reach across, squeeze his thigh and confess her love to him. But now wasn't the right time.

Laura was even starting to hope that he might have feelings for her. But how was he going to react when she finally told him about Isaac? Love could shrivel up and die as quickly as it had bloomed. Jack's marriage had proved that. Would he hate her for denying him his son? And what would he do about it when she told him the truth?

It was nine o'clock when Jack turned the car engine off outside Laura's house. The streets were damp. It seemed the clouds of two days ago had delivered on their promise. Had it only been two days? It felt like a lifetime to Laura. She'd discovered so much about herself, not least of all her love for him.

'Home again, home again.' Jack's voice broke into Laura's thoughts.

'Yes.' She smiled.

'What are your plans for the next few days?' he asked.

'I'm rostered on a afternoon shift on Thursday.'

'Laura.' his voice was stern. 'You're not going to go straight back to work are you?'

'Of course I am.'

'Don't you think it's a little too soon?'

'I *need* to work, Jack.'

'Seems to me it's become a real crutch.'

'I *like* my work.' Laura could feel herself getting cross. 'Look, we've had a very trying weekend but we've made it through on friendly terms. Don't spoil it.'

He shrugged, raising his hands in surrender. He couldn't help it—he worried about her. Yes, their trip to Newvalley had been cathartic but it didn't mean that Laura should rush headlong back into her life. She would probably experience a period of readjustment. 'You shouldn't rush back.'

'I can't afford to take too much time off. I've got Isaac to support.' Oh, dear. Was it too late to bite her tongue off?

'*You* support him?'

She was silent.

'He doesn't work?'

'It's complicated, Jack,' she sighed.

'I bet!' He fumed. 'Doesn't he know what you've been through? Doesn't he understand what stress being the breadwinner can place you under?'

'Oh, Jack,' she said. 'It's all right, really.'

'Where is he anyway? You said he was away?'

'On holiday.' She closed her eyes in the darkened car interior. Laura realised that the more she said, the worse Isaac sounded.

Jack was angry. His fists bunched at his sides. A feeling

of helplessness compounded his frustration. Laura was mixed up with some lazy, bludging swine and there was nothing he could do because her love for him blazed in her eyes like a beacon. It threw a light into the gloom of the car so bright it was practically blinding.

'When will he be back?'

'Friday.'

Jack heard the anticipation in her voice and jealousy stabbed at his heart like a knife. His mobile rang and he answered it impatiently.

Laura watched as he conducted a brief conversation, relieved at the cessation of his cross-examination. It gave her time to gather her thoughts.

'That was Arlene Summerton.'

'Who?'

'Henry's mother.'

'Oh, right. How is he?'

'Fine. The ambulance transported him to the nearest hospital. It was a clean break of the tibia. He's got a cast on and is tucked up in bed.'

'Great.' She beamed.

'Want to know the best bit?' She nodded. 'The ambos even put the siren on for him.'

She laughed and he joined her. For a moment they both forgot their earlier antagonism and basked in the glow of a happy ending for a little boy.

'Well, anyway,' Laura said, opening the door, 'it's been a long day. I'm beat. Goodnight, Jack.' She smiled and got out of the car.

'I'd like to meet Isaac one day,' he said as he got out of the car and retrieved her bag from the boot. Yeah. Meet the lazy toad!

She regarded him seriously, disguising her inner turmoil. Her heart palpitated wildly. Sure he would. For reasons even he wasn't aware of yet. At least this was an opportunity to finally be honest concerning Isaac in some regard.

'I'd really like that. Soon. I promise.'

Jack was taken aback by her sincerity. He could tell she really meant it. She wanted them to meet but in her own time. He should be happy but that emotion seemed unattainable in this situation. She'd had an effect on him years ago which had been hard to shake. He didn't want to think about how he felt now about a woman who was very obviously in love with another man. He just didn't want to go there. But he needed to meet Isaac, if only to satisfy his own curiosity.

'Thanks for coming to Newvalley, Laura. It meant a lot to everybody, you being there. It meant a lot to me.'

'Thanks for insisting.'

'Glad you went?'

'I don't know yet,' she said, her voice husky with memories. 'Goodnight, Jack,' she called over her shoulder.

''Night,' he replied, watching her open her gate and then the front door. It was a matter of seconds but he missed her already.

The next day, Laura picked up the phone and dialled America. Isaac and her parents were coming home in a couple of days but Laura needed to talk to someone now. She couldn't wait. Her mum had always been her sounding-board. There was so much to tell her.

Memories of Neve were with her all the time now, like a silent partner. Laura could feel her presence almost as a tangible force. It was wonderful to share Neve with her mother, the one person who knew more about her and what she'd been through, since the earthquake, than anyone else. Her mother was delighted to hear about the memorial service and relieved to know Laura had finally attended.

Laura's news about Jack and his infertility and her love for him didn't elicit the same positive response.

'You don't seem pleased,' she had prompted.

'A lot's happened in your life over the last couple of weeks.'

'You can say that again!'

'Perhaps a little too much, too quickly.'

'Oh, Mum. I didn't realise I'd been carrying this weight around until the other day. I haven't felt this light since before Newvalley. I guess I'm impatient now. I want to tell Jack about Isaac. What do you think?'

'I don't know, Laura. What do *you* think?'

'He deserves to know, Mum. Isaac is his son.'

'He's always deserved to know, Laura.'

'Yes, I know, but that was before. Before I knew about his infertility and how much he loves children and how desperately he wants one of his own. I did what I thought was right at the time. I really thought Isaac was a complication he wouldn't want.'

'And if he's angry with you? What if he hates you for keeping his son a secret from him?'

'He won't. I just know he's going to be thrilled when I tell him.'

'We'll be home soon, darling. Don't do anything hasty. Wait until we've had a chance to have a proper talk. OK?'

'OK, OK.' They chatted for a few more minutes before ringing off.

Laura spent the day in rose-coloured glasses, fantasising about their happy family unit. She pictured them together, all laughing and joking and holding hands. Father and son kicking a ball, chasing each other around the park.

She was a little too wrapped up in her rekindled love to pay heed to the misgivings in her mother's voice. She was too busy with her fantasies to think about how she was going to tell Isaac about his father. Or if Jack would hate her for her deceit, as her mother had implied. She just had to pick the right time to tell him. It would all be in the telling.

CHAPTER NINE

LAURA arrived bright and early for her afternoon shift the next day. She found Marie catching up on some paperwork in her office. The unit had quietened down during Laura's absence and Marie was taking full advantage.

It was always difficult, juggling clinical duties with the other demands of the position. Laura knew that only too well. She had relieved Marie a couple of times and disliked how all the responsibilities that came with being the boss took her away from the bedside. How Marie did it full time she couldn't fathom. But someone had to be in charge and Marie was the best.

'Hi.' She poked her head into Marie's office.

'Laura! How are you?' Marie gave Laura a hug.

'Great. I feel really good.' She beamed.

'Well, I was going to order you to have more time off but, well…you're glowing, girl.'

'Thanks. I'm very grateful to you and Jack for forcing my hand. Attending the service was cathartic, to say the least. I should have gone years ago.'

Laura left Marie to her pen-pushing and got on with her duties. She found the allocation book at the nurses' station and looked at the list of afternoon staff, assessing the skill mix and assigning nurses to patients accordingly.

It was good to see that they had three beds spare. This significantly eased the workload on everyone. Still, it wouldn't be the first time that three beds were filled over the course of a shift.

She gowned up and entered Mr Reid's room, taking in the array of equipment that seemed to multiply every time she saw him. A dialysis machine took up one corner of the room to try and correct his kidney failure. Blood was pumped out of his body through the filter, acting as an artificial kidney, and back again.

Laura had allocated two nurses for Mr Reid. The workload in his room was incredible and it looked like the filter on the dialysis machine would need changing some time this shift also. This was a job that took two experienced people a good hour. Add to that his multiple intravenous drugs, requiring a full sterile scrub each time his lines were accessed, and Mr Reid's care was a full-time job for two nurses.

Laura grabbed a penlight and inspected the filter. She noticed the dark clots forming at either end of the filter and elsewhere in the circuit. A quick look at Mr Reid's numbers revealed that the filter was becoming less efficient, dragging smaller and smaller amounts of fluid off each cycle. It would definitely need a new one before they went home for the night.

She moved on. It was a relief to see Jason Smith doing better. His CAT scan the other day had revealed further bleeding in his brain and he had been rushed to the operating theatre. Since the collection had been drained there had been a steady improvement in his neurological symptoms.

It was too hard to tell at the moment what the long-term effects would be and Jason would require months of rehabilitation but they were hopeful that, in time, he would make a full recovery.

Laura was in the middle of writing out a red additive label to go on an infusion she was helping Steve, Jason's bedside nurse, draw up when Jenny interrupted.

'Laura. Is Marie still here? We have an emergency situation.'

'What's happened?' asked Marie, who had just arrived at the nurses' station and had heard Jenny.

'There's been an accident. Something's happened causing part of the building to collapse at the construction site for the new public car park.'

'The one here at the hospital?' Marie asked.

'That's right. Preliminary reports say there are five men that are unaccounted for. The medical superintendent wants us to send a team to the site.'

Laura's heart thudded loudly. It was beating so hard she was sure it was going to fracture a rib.

'Right,' said Marie, already preparing for action, going first to the storeroom and retrieving the packs they used for such situations. 'You're going, I assume.' She spoke to Jenny.

'Yes, we'll leave the registrar here to cover.'

'Lucky we're not busy. We can spare two nurses from the late shift and I'd say when the early shift knocks off there'll be quite a few more volunteers.'

Laura busied herself, checking the packs and gathering extra drugs and equipment that might be needed. Anything to stop her hands from shaking.

'Cas is preparing its resus area for multiple casualties.' Jenny confirmed. 'They'll send staff when they're set up. But with Laura and you, we'll have a damn fine team.'

'No,' said Marie. 'Laura can stay and run things here.'

Jenny stopped in mid-stride. 'I want the best staff available to be at that site, Marie,' she said, looking from one to the other.

'Yes, but we still need a senior person here and—'

'It's OK, Marie,' Laura interrupted quietly. 'I'll be fine, really. Actually, I'd like to go,' she added, suddenly feeling stronger and more positive about the impending experience. 'I could be a real asset out there, particularly if anyone's trapped.'

Years of annual external disaster practice and her own hands-on experience had honed Laura for such a moment. Perhaps this had been her life purpose all along. Why the events of ten years ago had happened. Had it been preparing her for this?

Only the other day in Newvalley she had questioned the

reasons for being the sole survivor. Felt that there had to be some grander plan for her. That she had been spared because she had a destiny to fulfil. Was this it? This could be her chance to justify her living when everyone else had died. For Jo-anne. For all of them. She felt the ghosts of Newvalley rally round her. She wouldn't let them down.

Laura was becoming more convinced that facing something like this would be the ultimate test. If she could handle this, she could prove to herself and Jack that she could make it in her chosen specialty. She could also prove that she was truly beyond the psychological scars inflicted at Newvalley.

'Whatever,' Jenny said, impatience in her voice. 'Sort it out fast, huh? We need to get there stat.'

'I'm going,' said Laura, zipping the last pack decisively and thrusting it towards Marie. 'Let's do it.'

Laura grabbed the other pack and gave the bag of extras to Jenny as she strode for the doors. The team travelled at a near jog, lugging the cumbersome packs down stairs, along corridors and out through St Jude's main entrance. It was only a short walk through the lush grounds to the site.

No one on the team was prepared for the sight that greeted them. Except Laura. The group was silenced as they surveyed the massive structural damage. Luckily, work had not long begun on the car park, so the damage wasn't as bad as it could have been if the structure had been near completion.

'Right,' said Jenny, putting on her hard hat. 'Let's get to it, then.'

Everyone busied themselves, preparing for casualties, setting up the basics, waiting for a call from the rescue workers. It could be a while as they'd only just started to penetrate the mess of concrete and steel.

Laura was on autopilot, her brain full of preparations for every contingency. She busied herself organising some wardsmen to set up a canvas shelter to provide some shade, and left them to it as the first casualty arrived at their makeshift emergency room.

Laura, Jenny and Marie sprang into action, working on the dust-encrusted survivor quickly and efficiently. He had already been collared and was conscious but distressed and in severe pain. Laura tried to soothe him as they administered oxygen and gained intravenous access.

'It's OK, mate. What's your name?' Laura asked, holding his hand.

'Dave,' he said, looking at her with wild eyes.

'Dave, I'm Laura. We're going to look after you. You're out now. We've got you.'

'My mates,' he said, trying to sit up, 'my mates.'

'Dave, it's OK. They're helping them now.' Laura remembered how important it had been for her to have her fears allayed. If she had known while she'd still been trapped that everyone else had perished, about Jo-anne and Neve, she would have really cracked up.

He groaned again. 'My legs, my legs.'

'We're checking your leg now, Dave. Does it hurt anywhere else?'

Marie cut up both legs of his protective work trousers with a pair of sturdy shears. She hacked through his boots also until both limbs were fully exposed. The distal end of his legs and the ankles on both sides had obviously borne the brunt of something extremely heavy. The bones in his legs were smashed, pulverised.

'Right,' said Jenny as Laura threw her an alarmed look. 'We'd better splint these. Let me do a quick check of his neurological function and for other injuries, then we can give him some morphine to help with the pain.'

Laura prepared the specialised trauma splints that inflated to mould to and cushion the broken limb. The regular beeping of the portable monitor in the background reassured them that his vital signs were at least stable.

Jenny was satisfied that there was no altered level of consciousness that would indicate a head injury and make the administering of a narcotic agent inadvisable. She gave Laura a verbal order for morphine and Laura pushed it quickly into Dave's drip so it could enter his system immediately. Dave's thrashing quietened as the drug took effect.

Jenny was examining his chest and abdomen when they heard the high-pitched blipping on the monitor, which indicated their patient's oxygen saturations, change tone.

'Dave?' Laura shook him. 'You OK?'

'My ribs hurt,' he murmured as the tone continued to change, getting lower and lower, chronicling the continued fall of his saturations.

Laura noticed the blue tinge around his mouth. 'Becoming cyanotic,' she noted.

Jenny nodded as she listened to his chest. 'Huge bruised area right lower chest, decreased breath sounds. He's got a pneumothorax. Marie, I need a chest tube. Laura! Gloves.'

With no time for a scrub procedure, Jenny snapped on the gloves, taking care to keep them sterile. Marie opened a prepackaged kit containing all that was needed. Jenny quickly swabbed the area, pierced the skin and pushed the tube into place in one smooth practised movement in the mid-axilla line. A special valve set-up was attached to the end of the tube, allowing air to escape but not be sucked back in.

'Saturations rising,' said Laura, her heart pounding. The lung, which had deflated due to a build-up of air in the thoracic cavity, was obviously starting to reinflate. 'Lips pinking up.'

Jenny smiled. They all did. When he got down to Casualty they would connect his chest tube to a special underwater seal drain, which would remain *in situ* until the lung had fully inflated again. His saturations climbed back to normal.

'Right, let's get these splints on and get him down to Casualty.'

Laura grimaced as she helped Marie and Jenny slide the splints into place. The grating sound of broken bone fragments grinding against each other, or crepitus as it was known medically, set her teeth on edge. It was like fingernails being drawn down a blackboard.

Jenny was finally satisfied that they had done all they could to stabilise Dave for transport. Laura volunteered to accompany the stretcher as Dave seemed reluctant to let her go. She handed over to the Casualty staff and returned to the site just in time for their next customer.

The beefy young man was rolling from side to side on the narrow stretcher clutching his head, which was bleeding profusely. Laura wasn't too concerned about all the blood. She knew that head lacerations could bleed a lot, making even a minor cut appear more serious.

On closer examination, however, Laura realised that the large fleshy clot oozing freely and hanging on tenuously to the back of his head was, in fact, his scalp. The entire skin covering the top of his head had been degloved, sheared off his skull, like he'd been scalped. It looked horrific but, Laura acknowledged, if this was his only injury, he was a relatively lucky man.

Laura felt the hair on the back of her neck prickle and her skin break out in goose-bumps as the young man, who looked barely out of his teens, suddenly cried out for his mother.

'Help me. Mum, help me, help me!'

It seemed a strange thing to say for a man who, despite his young years, looked like he could be a bouncer instead of a builder. Big men did cry.

Ten years vanished in an instant. Neve had called out to her mother. Laura remembered the panic and anguish in her voice and heard it reflected in their patients'. She took a steadying breath and pushed the unsettling flashback aside to reassure and calm the frightened young man. Just as she had done with Neve.

It didn't really work and he continued to be combative.

'Let's get him some pain relief to stop him thrashing around so I can examine better. He seems intact neurologically despite his gruesome appearance.'

Laura and Marie checked the ampoule of morphine.

'Rabbit.' Marie raised her voice to be heard over the young man's din.

Laura raised an eyebrow. Obviously his mates had a sense of humour. They couldn't have chosen a less apt nickname.

Marie shrugged and gave Laura her don't ask look. 'Hold still, Rabbit, I'm going to give you a needle to help with the pain.'

That got his attention. 'A needle? Jeez, aren't I hurting enough?'

Marie winked at Laura and they both stifled their laughter. It was good to find a little comic relief in such a serious situation. Rabbit had just been pulled out from a collapsed structure, he looked like he'd landed head first on a land mine and he was worried about a needle hurting him?

Once the injection was administered he became much more agreeable and Jenny was able to cannulate him as a precaution and assess him further. Laura tended to his head wound, irrigating the area with sterile saline to better visualise the skull and appraise the damage. His bone looked intact, with no obvious fracturing or depressed areas of skull. She flapped the skin back in place, applying a temporary non-adhesive dressing, and roughly bandaged it in place, using Rabbit's chin as an anchor.

Apart from a marathon stitching job, which would probably take the better part of an hour, their patient was relatively unscathed. They would want to X-ray his skull when he got to Casualty to be certain that the force, which had scalped him, hadn't caused further damage to Rabbit's brain.

Again Laura accompanied the stretcher to the casualty department, handing over her patient and turning around again to go back for more.

At the same time Jack was heading towards the site, having just been informed of the collapse. He'd rung the unit, knowing that Laura was rostered on and knowing that Intensive Care would have sent a team to help.

He cursed her stupidity as he steamed up a grassy incline, taking a short-cut. He heard a jackhammer start up and saw and smelt the dust long before he arrived at the site. The dust took him right back to Newvalley.

He felt his chest tighten as images from a decade ago flashed into his mind. The distant sound of sirens added to the effect. Gory images of mangled bodies, crumbled bones, death and destruction flashed on his inward eye.

He had to get to Laura. His desperation to get to her now almost equalled that of ten years ago. OK, maybe she'd be fine. But what if she wasn't?

Laura felt good as she headed back to their temporary medical area. Really good. Positive. Like she was helping and making a difference. A spring in her step powered her up the incline that lead to the site.

And then a jackhammer thudded to life and it stopped her in her tracks. It pierced her contentment like a bullet, shattering it as easily as a bullet shattering bone. Her reaction was unexpected but she couldn't stop it. The noise was inside her head, shaking her grey matter, the incredibly loud sound tearing at her eardrums. Driving her to her knees.

Suddenly the world seemed upside down. She could feel her heart thudding faster and faster and her breaths becoming shorter and shallower. The surrounding hospital buildings seemed to loom menacingly, and she felt as tiny and fragile as an ant. Had her earlier flashback with Rabbit been a warning of worse to come?

Realising she was losing her grip, she tried to employ the breathing techniques she had learned long ago. But the first deep breath filled her lungs with dust and she was back under layers of concrete again, breathing the stale air, thick with dust. Coughing and coughing, her lungs bursting for a fresh supply.

Every noise around her seemed magnified. Her reactions intensified tenfold. A dropped tool caused her to jump more violently than a newborn. An expletive uttered by a workman became amplified to a screeching insult.

The total carnage of the area seemed to be closing in on her. Getting nearer and nearer until she was sure she could hear the cries of the trapped men beneath. They had to get them out.

Get them out. *Get them out*, she screamed silently. Her body was slick with sweat. She started to tremble. The tremors worsened until she was shaking. You have to get them out. Her heartbeat roared in her ears, louder than the jackhammers. Her vision blurred from tears coursing down her face.

'Laura!'

She could hear someone calling her name but that wasn't important. They had to be saved.

'Save them,' she yelled at the person shaking her.

'Laura. It's Jack.'

'Save them, Jack. Save them. Save me.' She pounded on his chest.

Jack was angry. Whose damn-fool idea had it been it to let Laura get into this situation? He hugged her close, her body quivering against his. He pulled her down by the makeshift triage area and sat her on the ground, searching around for something useful amongst the numerous medical items.

He spied an oxygen mask and put it against her face, ordering her to breathe in and out. He didn't attach it to a flow, knowing that the close confines of the plastic would force her to re-breathe her carbon dioxide and stop her hyperventilating.

He had to get her far away from here. There wasn't much he could do professionally at the site today, and the rescue teams were already shifting debris. He would be needed more tomorrow and in the following days to help with staff debriefing. For the moment it was more appropriate and important to stay with Laura.

'Jack, what happened?' Marie came running, spying them sitting nearby.

'I think she must have had a flashback, Marie. What the hell is she doing here anyway?' he demanded in an angry whisper, gently stroking Laura's hair.

'She insisted, Jack. I tried to tell her I didn't think it was a good idea but she wanted to come. She can be very stubborn.'

'Yes, I'm sorry,' he sighed. 'I know that better than anyone.'

'Will she be all right?'

'Should be, if I can get her breathing slower. And get her the hell away from here.'

'Sure. Whatever you think. We'll have more staff joining us soon. I really must get back,' she said as another stretcher was brought down to them.

Jack rocked Laura gently and talked softly in his soothing voice. He removed the mask as her breathing settled into a more normal pattern.

'Better now?'

She nodded, unable to speak. She felt calmer now. In control. That was the worst part about flashbacks. The loss of control. It didn't take much—a voice, a smell, a sound—and, wham, you were right back there, living it all again.

'Where are we going?' she asked as Jack helped her up.

'As far away from here as possible,' he said, his mouth a grim line.

The further Laura's feet took her from the site, the lighter her step became. She followed his lead. Wherever he wanted to take her at the moment was fine. She was beyond objecting.

They ended up in his car. Laura stared out of the window at nothing in particular. She had failed. If she had survived Newvalley in order to help at today's disaster site, then she had failed. She had been an unworthy choice of survivor. She had let them all down.

The journey passed in a blur and before she knew it they'd pulled up outside a lovely renovated cottage in the trendy suburb of Paddington.

'Yours?' she asked.

'Yes.'

'It's beautiful.'

'Thank you.'

He showed her in and gave her a tour. Polished floors, ornate ceilings, a huge rear deck with sweeping city views. It had everything. He'd obviously done very well for himself. Posh car. Gorgeous house. Enough room for kids and a dog, too, judging by the large, fenced back yard. Laura was too shattered to dwell on that irony.

She stifled a yawn, along with the fantasy of her and Isaac living here with Jack as a family.

'You look done in,' he observed quietly.

'I guess a nervous breakdown will do that to you.'

'You didn't have a nervous breakdown, Laura.'

'Didn't I? So I'm not going mad, then?'

'It was a flashback. That's all.'

'I don't have one for years and suddenly I have three in a week? What's happening to me?'

'Laura, you put yourself in a situation fraught with potential triggers. I would have been amazed if you hadn't had one. In fact, I don't know how you haven't had one at work before, given the stresses of your job.'

'I love my work, Jack. I don't know what I'll do if I can't do that.'

'Don't jump the gun, Laura.' He sighed at the stricken look on her face.

'What if you were right all along? Maybe I shouldn't be working in a critical care area. I'm a failure…'

'No, you're not.'

'No? I just failed my first real challenge. How could I have been so blind? I've let my own selfish interests override the basic principle of patient care. Do no harm. What if I'd been with a patient and…' Her voice broke.

'You weren't.'

'I could never forgive myself if I went to pieces at work like that. I've been in plenty of situations before that have been hairy to say the least. I've always been in control.'

'This situation was just a little too close to home. You had a perfectly normal, human reaction to it.'

'My work means everything to me. What am I going to do?'

Her voice wobbled as she felt the tears threaten to break free. Oh, God! She was going to cry! What was happening to her?

He held out his arms and she fell into them, grateful for a place to hide while she unloaded her feelings. He carried her through to his bedroom and lay down with her on his bed. He held her as she cried and stayed with her until she slept, still in her uniform.

Jack eased away and rolled off the bed. He watched the even rise and fall of her chest. A rush of pure tenderness welled inside him. He loved her. All these years and he'd never known it. Or maybe he always had and had been in denial for a decade. She'd certainly been under his skin all this time.

Anna had seen it. Towards the end, when their marriage had lurched from bad to worse, she had accused him of being in love with Laura. She had thrown it in his face often. You don't want to have babies with me because you've never stopped loving her—he remembered her bitter words. He had dismissed it at the time but maybe she'd had more insight than he had given her credit for.

Laura turned in her sleep, rolling on her side. Her uniform rode up her stockinged leg. His eyes slowly took in the Lycra-clad flesh. The shapeliness of her calf and thigh. Further up he admired the curve of her hip and the dip of her waist. The white fabric of her uniform, twisted slightly, pulled tautly across the swell of her breasts. Its zipper ran from her cleavage to her belly. His fingers itched to slide the zip down.

Her face, relaxed in sleep, was truly beautiful. It was tranquil and serene, two qualities not there when she was awake. All her defences were down and she looked carefree and untroubled. Just as she must have always looked before the events of Newvalley.

Her lips, slackened by her slumber, called to him. Full and luscious and kissable. Even as he watched them, transfixed by their perfection, they uttered something he couldn't quite catch. Her tongue darted out to moisten them before she shifted again, rolling onto her stomach, her head turned away from him.

Now he was greeted by the sight of her bottom. Rising gradually from the hollow of her back, it was slight, petite. Just like the rest of her. A totally delectable package. His heart swelled with love. Other parts of him suffered from a major swelling problem, too.

He wanted to gather her in his arms and wake her up with his kisses. Run his hands over every inch of her skin. Make love to her as they had done before. Tell her that he loved her. He took two paces towards her, his legs meeting the side of the bed. He hesitated. All he had to do was reach out and his hands would be on her, rejoicing in the feel of her. But despite his spiralling need, he knew he couldn't do it.

He turned and strode from the room, not stopping until he reached the back deck. He gripped the balustrade, oblivious to the sun casting its shadows on the sandstone retaining wall and the breathtaking sweep of the city as it wound down for the day.

Isaac. Damn him! He'd never met the man but already his antagonism towards him weighed heavier than the huge quarry boulders of the retaining wall. His hands bunched into fists and he swore out loud in frustration. He was in love with someone else's woman. It was a no-win situation.

If only she hadn't walked out on him ten years ago. If only she'd stayed and given their relationship a chance beyond a one-night stand. His love for her warred with his anger.

His stomach growled and, thankful for something to divert his attention from a problem that was already causing an ulcer, he rummaged through the kitchen cupboards. It was hardly a gourmet effort but a sandwich and a mug of freshly percolated coffee hit the spot.

Jack had no idea how long he sat on the back deck, sprawled in his squatter's chair. The sun set and dusk fell softly over the city. The first stars winked and shimmered as the sky darkened and then lightened to a silvery glow as a full moon dangled high above the lights of Brisbane's skyscrapers.

The view from his deck always gave him pleasure but tonight Jack wondered if he'd ever feel pleasure again. His mind was like a revolving door, circling endlessly, trying to sort things out. Thoughts would enter and then stay on board, never reaching their destination but unable to get off. He literally felt dizzy.

He shook his head, deciding another cup of coffee and some ice cream might further distract him from the ever-turning cogs in his brain. He set the percolator to make a fresh pot and decided to turn the television on to catch any news about the building collapse. He kept the volume low, just loud enough so he could hear it in the kitchen.

Finally a news update imparted the information he wanted. All five men had been pulled from the rubble within two hours. Two were critically injured and the others had minor injuries. Laura would be glad to hear that, he thought as he switched the television off and returned to his chair on the deck. He placed his coffee on a nearby table and started on the ice cream.

Laura woke to the earthy smell of coffee. Her stomach growled. It took a few moments to orientate herself.

Realisation of where she was and how she'd come to be here filtered slowly through her sleep-fogged brain. She remembered her earlier sense of failure and was relieved that it didn't seem as acute now. She must have needed the sleep to gain some perspective. How long had she been slumbering?

Her stomach rumbled again and she followed her nose through the gloom to the hot pot of coffee. The exhaust-fan light above the stove was the only light on in the entire house, it seemed.

She heard some noises coming from the deck area and carried her mug out with her.

'Hi,' she said.

Her quiet greeting disturbed not only the night air but Jack's equilibrium. He'd heard her shuffling in the kitchen, so he'd had time to prepare himself. He looked at her and decided he needed more time.

'Feeling better?'

'Much. How long was I asleep?'

'Four hours.'

'Wow. Guess I needed it, huh?'

'Guess you did.' He smiled.

'Ooh. Ice cream. What flavour?' she asked.

'Butterscotch.' He smiled again, the spoon halfway between the bowl and his mouth.

'My favourite.'

'Want a taste?' he invited huskily, offering her his laden spoon. Beads of melted ice cream ran down the portion on the spoon. Laura's mouth watered instantly. He shifted his outstretched legs, clearing room for her to sit on the extended leg of the squatter's chair. He spooned it into her mouth.

Laura's lips closed around the cold metal and she sighed as the spoon slowly slipped from her mouth and her tastebuds savoured the sweet, cold flavour.

Jack would have liked nothing more than to feed her the entire bowl, especially if she continued to show her appreciation in ways that were tantalising his own tastebuds. He thrust the bowl towards her instead.

'I can get my own,' she protested.

'It's OK. I couldn't eat any more.' It was true. He'd much rather watch her eat it.

'Well, we wouldn't want to waste it, would we?' she joked, taking the bowl and shifting to her own chair.

They didn't talk. Laura was busy satisfying her hunger and Jack was busy stoking his up to fever pitch. The moonlight was bright enough for him to see a smudge of ice cream at the corner of her mouth that she had missed. He didn't seem to be able to drag his eyes away from the temptation it presented. He wanted to lick it off so badly he could almost taste her soft lips coated in butterscotch.

'You're staring.' Her voice intruded on his fantasy.

'You have…' He pointed. 'You've left some ice cream…behind.'

Laura became aware of an undercurrent ebbing from him. He seemed tense and intense at the same time. The way he was staring at her face—no, her lips—made her hands tremble. She suddenly seemed incapable of movement. Her tongue felt swollen and useless. She willed it to remove the ice cream from the corner of her mouth. She sucked in a breath as their eyes communicated what their bodies longed to do.

A car braking and skidding out on the street shattered their trance-like connection. Laura's tongue finally received the signal from her brain and it darted out, wiping the remains of butterscotch away. She rose hastily, grabbing the railing and leaning against it heavily.

The moonlight coated her skin in silver, accentuating her paleness. She looked like she was made of alabaster. With her eyes shut and her face basking in the moon's glow, she looked like a statue. A beautiful, priceless piece of art. Jack could resist her no longer. He moved until his shirt grazed her back. He could hear her breath stuttering into the night air. His joined hers, their combined huskiness speaking volumes into the silence.

'Laura, I can't…' He wanted to tell her that no matter how unwise it was, he couldn't deny his need any longer.

He didn't need to explain it to her. She knew how he felt and reciprocated. She wanted him to make love to her so intensely her whole body ached.

When he kissed her, it was like coming home. So utterly right. So deeply perfect. His love for her became infinite. He tried to convey the depth of his emotions in the kiss. He knew he couldn't tell her but that didn't mean he couldn't show her.

Laura moaned and clung to him. She loved him so deeply she thought she would burst. The desire to tell him was overwhelming. But it wasn't the right time. She wanted there to be honesty about everything between them before she confessed her love. He needed to know about Isaac first. She'd have to settle for telling him with her actions.

Jack picked her up for the second time that day, carrying her through to his room and easing her to her feet at the foot of his bed.

'I know I should be stronger than this, Laura, but I…' I love you. 'I just can't stop it any longer.'

'I don't want you to stop,' she whispered.

Their clothes disappeared with their inhibitions, the desire to be naked together all-consuming.

'You are even more beautiful than I remember,' he whispered when her body was fully revealed to him.

'You make me feel beautiful,' she whispered back, and kissed him again. She could still taste butterscotch. It was the sweetest kiss she'd ever known.

Their kisses became deeper, longer, more urgent. Mouths tasted, hands caressed. They hurtled headlong towards nirvana. Each kiss was like their last, each touch increasing the ecstasy until they could bear the unfulfilled pleasure no longer.

Laura shut her eyes in anticipation of the fulfilment of a ten-year-old fantasy. How often had she dreamt of this moment?

'Open your eyes,' he commanded softly. She opened them. 'I want to look into your eyes.'

They rose together. They peaked together. They fell together. If the world ended tonight, she would die a happy woman. It had been worth the wait.

CHAPTER TEN

SOME time later they eased apart, sweat beading on their naked bodies. Laura snuggled into Jack's side, her head on his shoulder. For the first time in years she didn't feel empty. She was in love and for tonight she was going to enjoy how that felt.

She'd spent a decade trying not to articulate her feelings for Jack. Trying not to think about him, period. No easy task when she lived with someone who walked like him, talked like him and looked exactly like him. A miniature Jack.

She sighed contentedly as Jack's fingers stroked lightly up and down her arm. Gooseflesh puckered the skin.

'I saw the news earlier,' said Jack.

'What did it say? Is it bad? Do I want to know?'

'Everyone was out in two hours. Two critical, the others hardly a scratch.'

'Oh, Jack.' She raised herself up on her elbow, her eyes shining. 'That's fantastic! I thought… Well, I tried not to think, but I know exactly how they must have felt. Trapped. Waiting for someone to dig them out.'

'There was a happy ending to this one, Laura.'

She smiled at him and kissed him lightly on the mouth. She lay on her stomach, her chin on his chest.

'I suppose the two criticals will be on the unit,' she mused.

'I guess.' He watched her face as she grappled with the implications.

'I don't know if I can nurse them, Jack. A few hours ago I'd have relished the idea but what if hearing them talk about their experiences triggers something in me again?'

He remained silent, stroking her back, letting her work it through for herself.

'Pretty selfish, huh?'

'Why so?'

'They've been through hell and I'm thinking of myself. I could be a real help to those men. No one else on the unit but me will know what they've been through emotionally and mentally. I mean *really* know, first hand. I could be such an asset to their recovery.'

'That's why they pay people like me.'

'So who debriefs the debriefers?'

He laughed and traced the outline of her mouth with his finger. She bit down gently and growled low in her throat. He laughed some more, an edge of sexual excitement brightening his dark eyes. 'This is how I like to debrief.'

'Seriously, Jack. My work is important to me. What if I can't cut it any more?'

'Laura, I think you're getting ahead of yourself.'

'No, Jack. I don't think I am. I so wanted to succeed out there today. I can't help but think I survived Newvalley for a reason and today was it. I wanted to prove myself a worthy choice.'

'You have nothing to prove, Laura.'

'Just as well. I didn't prove anything, did I?'

'All it proves is what I've been saying all along. You need to reduce your exposure to stressful situations. It doesn't mean you have to give it up altogether. Maybe you just need to cut your hours back. Stresses build up and have a cumulative effect. If you're not working as often, you'll have less stressful situations to deal with.

'Think of it as a crossroads in your life. You can keep going, maybe alter the path a little, or you can change direction completely. Nursing offers many specialty areas. Maybe you just need to revise your options.'

He was right. She'd given a lot of years to intensive care nursing but that didn't mean she couldn't do something different. Most of all she didn't have to make up her mind right here and now. His words were liberating.

'I think I might just heed your advice and take some time off work. I've got plenty owing.'

'Good girl.' He grinned at her and she hit him over the head with her pillow for his patronising comment. She knew he didn't mean it but he looked so smug at the moment he deserved to have the smile wiped off his face.

'Where are you going?' he asked as she slipped out of the bed. He missed her nearness.

'I'm starving. I need more ice cream.'

'Good choice.' He grinned again.

The kitchen was darker now, the moon higher in the sky. She turned on the light, squinting at the wall clock. Nearly midnight. She opened the freezer and located the tub of butterscotch ice cream. She hummed a happy tune, determined not to think about tomorrow. For the moment she was just going to rejoice in tonight.

Laura grabbed two spoons out of a drawer, deciding against bowls. It would be far more decadent to eat straight out of the container. Her gaze fell on some snapshots pinned to a corkboard. It was Jack with a variety of children from toddlers to teens. They were great pictures, full of happiness and love. Obviously family.

It seemed the Rileys shared a strong family resemblance. These were probably Isaac's cousins. The similarities were staggering.

She felt wistful tears gather in her eyes. She looked at the man she loved, goofing around with the kids in the photos, and it confirmed what she'd always known—Jack would make a great father.

It wasn't fair that so many people in the world today were terrible parents and yet others who would have excelled at it weren't able to. Jack would have been the best. Could still be the best?

She carried the ice cream in to Jack and they sat naked on the bed, feeding each other.

'Jack,' she said, wiping up the remnants in the container

with her finger, 'are those kids in the kitchen your nieces and nephews?'

'Sure are. They're great kids, too.'

'Ah. A proud uncle,' she teased. 'You like it?'

'I love it. And they adore me, too, of course.'

She laughed. Of course they would. He was easy to adore. Maybe she should tell him right now about Isaac. They were on the right subject and, given what just happened between them, she hoped he'd give her a fair hearing. Laura so wanted to tell him about his son. If he became angry then so be it. She was sure he would come around.

After all, she hadn't kept Isaac from him out of any malicious intent. In fact, quite the opposite. She'd done it to help him, so he could have a career and make a name for himself. She'd done it so he could realise his dreams.

She felt sure that if he knew how she'd agonised about it, how difficult her decision had been, he would understand.

'Hey. Why so serious?'

'I've been meaning to talk to you about something.' Her heart pounded. It was now or never. Would he forgive her? Be able to see it for the selfless act it had been?

'Then talk.' He smiled and she felt encouraged to continue.

The phone rang. 'Sorry,' he said. 'I'm on call. I'd better take this.'

'Sure.' She nodded.

Giving Jack some privacy, Laura gathered their spoons and the empty ice-cream container and took them into the kitchen. She rinsed the spoons under the hot tap and left them to drain.

She didn't hear Jack and she started when he hugged her from behind.

'You seem a million miles away.'

'Who was that?'

'The hospital. I'm really sorry but I'm going to have to leave. Simon Adams is having a bit of a meltdown. He's somehow managed to barricade himself into a toilet and he's threatening to commit suicide.'

'Oh, no! Poor Simon. Poor Andrew! It's OK, Jack—go. You must go.'

'I don't want to leave,' he groaned into her hair, and she turned in his arms, receiving a deep lingering kiss. 'You wanted to tell me something,' he prompted, hugging her close. Any more kisses of that ilk and they'd be back in bed.

'It doesn't matter. I'll tell you another time.'

'Are you sure?' Jack felt torn between his concern for his patient and his desire to stay with Laura.

'Go,' she commanded.

'Will you be here when I get back?' He tried not to think of how she had disappeared on him once before. He didn't want to face that kind of devastation again.

'Actually, I think I might go home.' Isaac was coming home later. There were so many things she had to organise and she should try and get some sleep. If she stayed, sleep wouldn't be high on their list of priorities.

'Do you have to?' Disappointment shrouded his words.

'There's no telling how long you'll be. Besides, you need to concentrate when you get to the hospital.' She stood on tiptoe and kissed him. 'It'll be too distracting for you if I'm here, keeping the bed warm.'

'Damn right about that,' he said, claiming her mouth for some more of her sweet lips.

'Go.' She shoved him gently from her, licking her moist lips, savouring his taste.

Jack whistled a happy tune as he sped towards the hospital. He'd dallied too long at home and needed to make up some time. Making love to Laura again had been perfect. He loved her with every fibre of his being. He loved everything about her. But what about Isaac?

He quashed the thought as soon as it reared its ugly head. He was in love and nothing was going to spoil how he felt tonight. Besides, Isaac wasn't here, was he? Maybe she was having second thoughts about Isaac. Maybe she'd call it all off and begin anew with him?

Laura hugged herself as the taxi driver covered the distance between Jack's place and hers. Thankfully she'd scored about the only silent taxi driver in Brisbane. She didn't want to make small talk with a stranger, she wanted to be alone with her thoughts. Rerun the events of the night. Each moment, each kiss.

Letting herself in, her eyes fell on a framed photo of Isaac. Not long from now she'd be at the airport, scanning the arrival crowds for his face. Not long from now she hoped to be introducing Jack to his son.

She went to bed, her mind grappling with the words she would use to tell Jack he was a father. She didn't have to worry about Isaac. She knew he'd take it with his usual boyish aplomb. She'd told him he would meet his father one day when he was a little older and, although they never talked about it much, Laura knew he looked forward to that time very much.

She gave up trying to find the right words. She might just have to wing it. But however she told Jack, she needed to do it soon. The next time she was talking to him. Definitely.

The next morning Laura was enjoying a relaxing soak in the bath, reliving their love-making again, when the cordless phone chirruped near her ear.

'Hello,' she answered, holding the phone with the help of a shoulder as she dried off her hands.

'Hi. It's me.'

'Yes.' She'd known it would be.

'Sorry I had to leave last night.'

'Couldn't be helped,' she dismissed. 'Everything turn out all right?'

'Eventually. It was a bit hairy for a while but once he'd surrendered the knife—'

'Knife!' she said, alarmed. Was Jack's job dangerous?

'Only a butter knife. Anyway, we had a long talk and he agreed that he needed to stay with us for a while longer.'

'Sounds like a good idea.'

'You were going to tell me something last night before we were interrupted.'

'Oh, yes… Doesn't matter. I'll tell you later,' she stalled.

OK. She had vowed to tell him the very next time she talked to him, but not like this. She couldn't tell him over the phone she'd been keeping his nine-year-old son a secret from him. She needed to impart how she'd grappled with the problem for ages. This was something she had to tell him face to face. Next time she *saw* him, she'd tell all.

'Now you have me really intrigued.' He laughed. It sounded so sexy her toes curled. 'About last night…' he said.

'Yes.'

'It was…'

She squirmed at the suggestion implied by his lack of words, causing the water to ripple.

'Are you in the bath?'

'Yes.'

'Ah…so you're naked.'

'As a jaybird.' She laughed.

He felt his body react as images of her wet, slippery body cavorted through his mind.

'I wish I was there with you.'

'Really?' A smile curved her lips.

'Really. The things I could do.'

'Really?' she blushed, suddenly feeling very hot in the deep warm bath. The husky undercurrent in his voice was unmistakable.

'Hmm.'

'So.' She licked her lips. 'What are *you* wearing?'

'I'm in bed. I didn't get a whole lot of sleep last night, what with work and a gorgeous blonde.'

His innuendo brought even more colour to her cheeks. 'And what do you wear to bed?'

'Nothing.'

'So you're naked, too?'

'As a jaybird.'

'So…we're both…naked.'

Images of his naked reclining body joined the tantalising memories of last night. She had to physically squeeze her thighs together to suppress the urgent need to feel him inside her. The water temperature seemed to increase to boiling point.

'Stay there. I'm coming over,' he said.

'No,' she said, sitting up, trying to keep her alarm from her voice.

Isaac was due home soon. Jack couldn't see him before she had a chance to tell him about his son. He'd have to be blind not to guess from looking at Isaac that he was his own flesh and blood. She wanted to prepare him before he actually saw Isaac.

Besides, she had to leave in a few hours and if Jack came over now… The next time they made love she wanted there to be total honesty between them. She wanted this secret to be gone for ever.

'I have to go to the airport shortly.'

'OK. What are you doing after that?'

'Jack.' She laughed softly.

'What's at the airport?'

Laura hesitated. What could she say? She was tired of the lies and half-truths she'd been telling.

'Oh, that's right. I remember you said Isaac was coming home today.' His voice lost its flirty tone. It was flat and expressionless now. 'What time's his flight?'

'Two o'clock.'

Jack felt his happiness evaporate. What a reality check. He could no longer avoid thinking about the subject he'd deliberately not thought about last night. What had he been thinking? He'd fallen in love with another man's woman. It wasn't going to be happily ever after. Just because she'd slept with him, it hadn't erased her love for Isaac. But just how committed was she to him? She claimed she loved Isaac and yet she'd spent last night with him. How could she do that?

'What was last night about, Laura? Was I one last fling before your lover returned?' Jack could feel the anger burning his stomach lining. His abdominal muscles were bunched so tight he doubted a scalpel could penetrate them.

'It wasn't like that, Jack. I didn't plan it.' The pain in his voice was unbearable, she didn't want to hurt him.

'I thought last night meant something.'

'Of course it did. It was beautiful. But…you've always known about him, Jack.'

'And how will he feel about you and me? About what we did?'

She was silent. Where had their light-hearted banter gone?

'You're not going to tell him, are you?'

'It's complicated,' she said, clutching the phone, her eyes closed.

'Yes. So you've said.'

'Look, last night was great. It was more than that. It was inevitable. Just like in the beginning.'

'Oh, I get it,' he said bitterly. 'I was unfinished business. Something you had to get out of your system?'

'No! Oh, Jack, it's—'

'Complicated,' he supplied harshly.

'It is,' she insisted. 'Once you've met Isaac, you'll understand. Please, trust me.'

'I don't want to meet him,' he said sullenly.

'I really think you should.'

'No, Laura. I don't want to see you together. Watch him touch you, kiss you. You do love him, don't you, Laura?'

'Yes, but…'

Jack felt his muscles tense even further. They contracted as if they'd been struck. 'But what? You want both of us?'

'Yes. In different ways, yes.'

'Too bad, Laura. I don't share and he's a fool if he does.' He banged the phone down.

Good job, Jack, he cursed silently. It had started out with such promise and then the subject of Isaac had reared its ugly head and jealousy had taken over. He picked up the phone and started to dial her number and beg her forgiveness. He hadn't meant to get angry but the thought of her heart belonging to someone else was sending him a little crazy.

But he was going to have to deal with it. Like it or not, Isaac was in her life. He put the phone down. He'd go over tomorrow, he should be more in control by then. He owed her an apology. And maybe she was right. Maybe if he met Isaac and saw how happy they were together he could be more at peace with the situation.

He wanted her to be happy, didn't he?

CHAPTER ELEVEN

LAURA winced as the loud click of disconnection ricocheted around her ear canal. Jack was angry. She couldn't blame him. If she put herself in his shoes momentarily, her behaviour did seem appalling. Sleeping with him while supposedly being in a committed relationship. What was he supposed to think?

Tomorrow she would go and see him, tell him everything. But today she wanted to focus on Isaac. Devote her time to him. She couldn't wait to feel his little body hugging her again.

The phone call had put a dampener on Laura's mood. She still felt deflated two hours later, waiting at the arrival gate for Isaac and her parents. Not even the anticipation of seeing her little man again after so long lifted the gloom.

'Mum, Mum, Mum.' Isaac's excited yelling broke into her thoughts.

'Isaac.' She waved, watching her lanky nine-year-old dodge and weave through the crowd coming out of the arrival doors. He ducked under the roped area and reached her in a couple of strides.

Laura felt absurdly tearful. He seemed to have grown even more in the fortnight he'd been away. She hugged him fiercely, relieved to have him home with her again. She didn't realise how much she had missed him until this moment. Her heart swelled with love and she kissed his short spiky hair.

'I missed you Zac-Zac,' she whispered, using the nickname he'd been given as a baby. She squeezed his body closer.

'I missed you, too, Mum.'

'What? Even at Disneyland?'

'At night-time. I missed your goodnight kiss.'

'Oh, Isaac,' she whispered, hugging him again. 'Doesn't Granny give good kisses?'

'Yeah. She's second best.'

'Isaac Henry Scott, you take that back,' his grandmother said with mock severity.

'Hi, Mum.' Laura hugged her. 'Where's Dad?'

'He's bringing up the rear. How are you?' Her worried eyes searched Laura's.

'I'm fine, Mum,' she reassured softly, giving her mother's hand a squeeze. She would be soon anyway.

There was much excitement for the rest of the afternoon, with Isaac taking centre stage. Eager to show and tell her everything, his joy was palpable. Laura had cooked his favourite meal and her parents joined them. By seven o'clock Isaac was fast asleep in front of the television.

'I'm not surprised,' his grandfather said, scooping him up. 'He didn't sleep a wink on the plane. I'll put him to bed.'

'Thanks, Dad.'

The women watched affectionately as the two males in their lives left the room.

'So, come on. Tell me.'

Laura filled her in on everything that had happened while they'd been in America. About going to Newvalley and Neve and about Jack, his infertility, how he thought Isaac was her partner, and what had happened after her episode at the building collapse at work.

'You're in love with him,' said Barbara Scott.

'Yes.'

'What are you going to do?'

'I have to tell him about Isaac.'

'I agree.'

'Want to do it for me?' she joked.

'There's just some things you have to do yourself, darling.'

'I know.'

'How do you think he'll take it?'

'Well, he's angry with me at the moment so I don't know how pleased he'll be. It'll be a shock. But I really think that once the initial surprise has worn off he'll be ecstatic. He's going to make such a great father.'

'Do you think he'll resent you for the missing years?'

'I don't know, Mum. I don't think he could resent me any more than he does at the moment. At least he'll know that Isaac isn't a lover.'

Her parents left soon after that. They were exhausted and Laura was again reminded of their advancing years.

She wandered into Isaac's room and sat on the edge of his bed. She watched the rise and fall of his chest and was struck anew by his resemblance to Jack. She'd always thought he looked like his father but it hadn't been until she'd seen Jack again that she'd realised they were exactly alike. Isaac was a carbon copy of his father.

He mumbled in his sleep and Laura lay down next to him, hugging his body to hers. She had missed this so much. With all the things distracting her recently, she hadn't realised how much she had truly missed her dear little boy. Night-time cuddles had always been a ritual for them and she had missed that the most.

Laura fell asleep on Isaac's bed, waking a few hours later. She stumbled through the house, switching off the television and lights as she went. She undressed and crawled into her bed, giving little thought to what the new day would bring. No way would she be able to sleep if she started to think about tomorrow and Jack and Isaac and the rest of her life.

Isaac slept late the next morning. Jet-lag had finally caught up with him. Laura checked on him before she had breakfast and he was still sleeping soundly half an hour later.

She felt unsettled after her argument with Jack the previous day. Marie had left several messages on her answering-machine, so Laura decided to ring her at home to explain what had happened at the site. Marie was very understanding and relieved that her friend was feeling better. Laura rang off but not before Marie had promised to arrange an immediate leave of absence.

She took her coffee out to the deck with the morning paper, spreading it out on the red cedar table, and settled into the comfortable canvas chair. At least it was a distraction from her thoughts.

Ten minutes later the doorbell rang. Laura, still in her sleepwear, pulled the gown closer. Who could that be at nine o'clock Saturday morning? It was probably her parents.

She was floored to find a repentant Jack standing there, a bouquet in his hand.

'Jack!'

'Can I come in? I'm sorry for yesterday.' He pushed the flowers into her arms.

Jack was aware that turning up unannounced would surprise her. But she looked nervous and jittery as well. She didn't invite him in and stood there staring, apparently dumbstruck.

She may have been unable to speak but her mind was racing. This couldn't be happening. She knew he expected to be invited in and she could hardly refuse when he'd come bearing an apology and gifts.

It was OK for now as long as Isaac continued to sleep. And Jack's arrival had presented her with the perfect opportunity. But she had to tell him immediately in case Isaac decided to put in an appearance.

Next problem. How to get him through the house to the deck without him noticing an array of children's toys and photos of Isaac dotted throughout the house. She noticed the way his gaze was concentrating on her cleavage and knew she could use feminine wiles as well as the next girl for a good cause.

'Come through,' she invited, letting the robe slip off her shoulder to reveal a fair portion of shoulder and neck and breast. He smiled at her and she felt the intensity of his gaze burning through the back of her gown.

'Go out and sit down. I was just reading the paper,' she said nervously, hastily arranging the flowers in a vase. 'Coffee?'

'Yes, please,' he called from the deck.

He started to thumb through the paper. Was she nervous about him meeting Isaac? Was she worried that the flowers might upset him? Maybe he shouldn't have brought them. His coffee being plonked in front of him interrupted his thoughts and he noticed her hand trembling.

She sat opposite him. They sipped at their drinks for a short while.

'I'm sorry for just turning up. I'm going away for a few days to a seminar in Sydney tomorrow, and I wanted to see you to apologise for the things I said.' He noticed her gaze preoccupied with the area behind his head.

'Apology accepted,' she said, distracted by her busy thoughts. If he was going away she had to tell him now. Where did she start?

'I thought it was time I met Isaac. Has he left already?'

'He's sleeping. Jet-lag.'

'Did he go overseas?'

'America,' she said. Well, like it or not, they were on the right subject. It was just the opening she'd been hoping for. 'Actually, I wanted to talk to you about Isaac.'

'Laura,' he interrupted. 'I need to say something first. I'm sorry about what I said yesterday. I shouldn't have doubted your commitment to Isaac. I think you were right when you said that what happened between us was inevitable. I think we were just fulfilling a destiny that had been written in the stars ten years ago. But I realise that it doesn't negate your feelings for Isaac. Nine years is a long time to be with somebody. I behaved like a real jerk.'

Laura listened to his words. He was unburdening himself and she was grateful for his apology. She sensed it was something he needed to do. But no need was greater at the moment than hers to tell him Isaac was his son, not her lover.

'Finished?' She smiled.

'Sorry, speech over. Friends?' He'd take that if it was all that was available to him. He extended his hand.

'Sure.' She shot him a nervous smile and shook his hand.

Laura opened her mouth to launch into a speech of her own. Jack stood before the first word had a chance to leave her mouth.

'Where are you going?' she asked anxiously.

'To get some more coffee. You?'

'Oh, yes. Yes, please,' she said, grateful for the artificial boost the caffeine would give her. She was going to go mad if she didn't get this off her chest soon. Laura was just beginning to realise how exhausting it was to keep a secret. She felt weighed down by its magnitude. The relief to have everything out in the open would be immense.

Jack went to open the fridge for some milk when a snapshot on the freezer door caught his eye. What was Laura doing with a picture of him as a kid? The one where he'd caught his first fish and the pride was written all over his face?

No. It couldn't be the same picture. He started to notice the differences. This one was in colour and the clothes worn by the boy were a little different. But at a glance it could have been him. He reached for the milk, still staring at the photo.

'Who are you?'

Jack turned and saw the boy from the photo standing in the kitchen doorway. The resemblance had him reeling.

Laura heard Isaac's voice and leapt from her chair, but it was too late. In the few seconds it took for her to get from the deck to the kitchen, father and son were face to face. She searched Jack's face. He looked pale and his expression was stunned, to say the least. She met his gaze and in that instant she saw the penny drop. He had guessed.

'Who are you?' Jack asked.

'I'm Isaac. Are you visiting my mum?' he asked, oblivious to the importance of the occasion.

So *this* was Isaac. This boy who looked exactly as he had looked when he'd been a boy. *This* was Isaac. Looking at him was like peering into a mirror. Snatches of memories flashed through his mind. Running and laughing and playing as a child. Isaac could have been that child.

'Isaac, this is J-John Riley. He's a doctor. We work together.'

'Hi,' said Isaac, offering his outstretched hand. Jack shook it automatically. It was a good, firm grip for a nine-year-old. 'I'm going to watch the cartoons, Mum,' he said, pouring some milk onto his cereal and taking it with him to the lounge room.

They watched him go in silence. Jack continued to stare after him long after he was out of sight.

'He's mine, isn't he?'

'Yes,' she said, sagging against the kitchen bench opposite. It wasn't the way she'd envisaged it would happen, but at least he knew now.

'But...but how?'

'We didn't use any protection, Jack, remember? Six weeks later I had a positive pregnancy test.'

'My father's name is Isaac,' he said, still staring after his son.

'Really? I didn't know that.' But she was happy now that she knew. It was fitting that she had named their son after his paternal grandfather, no matter how unwittingly.

He looked at her. Now the initial shock had worn off, the questions were beginning. His emotions seesawed. Happy, bewildered, excited, angry. He'd had a child all this time and she'd never told him. Why?

'Would you mind telling me why it is that you never told me about my son? Because for the life of me I don't understand it.' His voice was low, a bewildered growl.

'Jack, I can explain.'

'I don't think it's going to matter, Laura. Whatever you say can't justify this. Why didn't you say something? Why have you let me think Isaac, my son, was your lover?' His voice had an unmistakable edge to it.

'Lots of reasons. None of them seem very compelling right now.'

'Indulge me.' His voice was abrupt.

'I never said that he was my partner. You jumped to that conclusion and I decided not to correct your assumption. I thought it would be a good cover for me until I worked out whether I should tell you about Isaac or not. I needed to know before I told you if your attitude towards children had changed.'

'My attitude towards children?'

'I knew you weren't keen on children—'

'Laura, we've been through this. You know that I want children.'

'I know it now, Jack, but I didn't know it ten years ago.'

'I never said I didn't want children.'

'Maybe not in so many words but you implied it. ''A family life is not in my foreseeable future,'' quote, unquote.'

'That didn't mean that I wouldn't want to know if I had fathered a child.' His voice was getting louder now.

'Shh. I don't want Isaac to hear us fighting.'

'We're not fighting.'

'You're practically yelling at me,' she pointed out, trying to remain calm. She had to put herself in his shoes.

'You kept my son from me for nine years.' He slammed his fist down on the kitchen bench. 'I think I have a right to be angry.'

'I didn't do it to hurt you. You said you wanted a career. I decided to go it alone so you could have your career.'

'I could have had a career *and* been a father to Isaac.'

'Jack, I owed you my life. I did this for you. A child would have been too distracting.'

Too distracting? He felt his anger surge like a bomb exploding inside him. 'Who gave you the right to decide what would be distracting for me?' he whispered loudly.

Laura didn't have an answer. His raw anger silenced her arguments.

Jack was breathing hard now. The thought of all of those years. Gone. Wasted. He couldn't get them back. Watching Isaac grow inside her. Being at the birth. Helping to feed and change and bath him. Teaching him how to ride a bike and reading to him. Kissing him goodnight.

He'd missed out on all the firsts because of Laura's mistaken need to protect his career. She'd appointed herself his advocate. Jack noticed a pain in his chest. The pain of regret.

'Were you ever going to tell me?' he demanded.

'I was trying to tell you just now and the other night when you had to go in to the hospital.'

'What does he know about me?'

'That we knew each other briefly. That it didn't work out. And that your name is Jack.'

'That's all?' he asked incredulously.

'He hasn't been too curious yet.' She shrugged.

Jack felt her comment hit him square in the solar plexus. His own child didn't have enough interest in him to want to know more about him. The pain in his chest was a raw ache now. It hurt so much that he had to physically rub his chest to get some relief.

'Jack, I'm sorry. I know I should have told you but I did it with the best intentions.'

'I don't think you were ever going to tell me.'

'I was, Jack…one day. I thought when Isaac was older he'd want to meet you, know more about you.'

'Do you know how much having a child means to me, Laura? Do you have any idea?' he snarled.

She nodded.

'Finding out I was infertile was devastating. I've been

grappling with it ever since. And now I find out that I've had a child all along.'

'Be fair, Jack. How was I to know you'd contracted mumps and become infertile?'

'Would it have mattered?'

'Of course,' she said, hurt by his question. 'Please, I understand this has been a shock but don't be angry with me. What can I do to make it up to you?'

'Can you give me back his first smile? His first step? His first word?'

'No,' she whispered.

'Can you give me nine years' worth of memories that I don't have because *you* decided to play God?'

'No, not the way you want them, but I can in a way. I have this box…it's full of lots of different stuff from Isaac's life—'

'Photos,' he interrupted incredulously. 'You think a few old baby photos are going to make up for years of deceit?'

'It's more than that.' Her voice broke. It was so much more. But looking at Jack now she doubted anything would reach him. His anger was too fresh, his hurt too new. Maybe after he'd calmed down a little he'd be more receptive to the contents of the box. Now obviously wasn't the right time.

He picked up his keys and strode away. 'Where are you going?'

'I can't talk to you at the moment. I have to get out of here.' The disgust in his voice made her flinch.

'Please, don't leave. We need to talk some more.' She placed a restraining hand on his arm.

'Laura, if you had any idea how close I am to wringing your beautiful neck, you'd let me go right now.'

She did so reluctantly and he slammed out of the house. Isaac remained engrossed in the television, oblivious to the confrontation between his parents.

Laura placed her head against the closed door. What a mess! A chill slid down her spine at the emotion she had seen in Jack's eyes. She hadn't seen it before. Was it hate? Did he hate her? And what about Isaac? Would Jack want to be a father to a child that he didn't know?

Her relief that her ten-year secret was out had been short-lived, tempered now with worry and doubt. With Jack refusing to talk to her, there wasn't much she could do at the moment. The ball was in Jack's court now. What would he do with it?

Three thousand, two hundred and ninety-five. Jack had worked it out. He was sitting in his darkened study with only the desk lamp for light. He underlined the figure in bold angry strokes. That's how many goodnight kisses she'd deprived him of, and that was a minimum. He wrote 'Minimum' beside the numbers and traced savagely over the letters until they were thick.

Did Laura's box hold those kisses? When he opened the lid, would they fly out and press themselves against his cheeks? Could a box full of photos give him the feel of baby kisses against his neck? How could she think that could ever be enough?

He returned to his doodling. One kiss a night, three hundred and sixty-five nights a year for nine years. He double-checked his calculations. His jaw clenched as the now familiar ache started in his chest again. His knuckles were white from his strong grip on the pencil. It snapped and Jack looked at it, surprised.

He'd been tense since finding out about Laura's deception. It had only been that morning and yet he'd have sworn that he'd been carrying this anger around for years. Maybe he had. Learning about Isaac seemed to compound his unresolved feelings about his infertility. It seemed to add insult to injury. He rubbed his chest.

The phone rang again. He didn't pick it up, he knew it would be Laura. She'd rung every hour all day. His answering-machine blinked in testimony to this. Her messages had got longer as the day had worn on. He could hear the worry in her voice. She seemed more anxious with each call.

'Jack, please. I know you're home. Please, pick up and talk to me. Don't go away to your seminar with all of this still unresolved between us. Don't go away angry.'

Her voice broke and he laid another brick on the wall he was building around his heart. The beeps went as she hung up. She was hurting. Well, good. If she took her hurt and multiplied it tenfold then she might be in his ballpark.

The rational side of him knew that sooner or later he would have to talk to her about this, but not right now. He was feeling too raw at the moment. Two days away in Sydney was just what the doctor ordered. He needed to have some time and space and distance to think about everything. Get past the anger he felt towards Laura. They would need to be on friendlier terms if he was going to have a relationship with his son.

What a difference a day could make, he thought bitterly. He'd started the day loving her but prepared to sacrifice his feelings and give her to Isaac to…what? His anger was the only thing he could feel. It seemed to have frozen out every other emotion.

All his medical training and rational thought processes had deserted him. Tonight he was just a man. One who had fallen in love with a woman who had deceived him in the worst way for the longest time!

CHAPTER TWELVE

LAURA and her mother sat on the deck, chatting. Isaac was due home in a couple of hours. He'd spent the day with a friend from school whose parents owned a beach house at Noosa. Isaac often accompanied them and always came home sun-kissed and exuberant.

'I'm sure Jack will come round, dear.' Her mother's positivity brought Laura back to the conversation.

'I hope so.'

'He may be angry now but he won't let it get in the way of building a relationship with Isaac.'

'How can you be so sure?'

'Motherly instincts.' She shrugged.

'I'm a mother. How come I don't feel so optimistic?'

'Because you're too involved. This whole thing is about *you*. It's hard to see the forest for the trees when you're standing in the middle of it.'

'I don't know, Mum. I think I've blown it. I'm sure sooner or later he'll want to be involved with Isaac, but will he ever be able to forgive me enough to want to be involved with me? I love him, Mum. I couldn't bear to have him hate me.'

'He just needs some time, darling.' She squeezed her daughter's hand.

'Looks like you and Dad were right all those years ago,' said Laura, staring up at the emptiness of the blue sky, a perfect reflection for the emptiness in her soul. 'I should have told him straight away.'

'Hindsight is always twenty-twenty. What's done is done. Whether it was wiser to tell him then or not is irrelevant now. You can't turn back the clock.'

'You don't know how I wish I could.' Laura's quiet voice was wistful.

'Get in line, darling.' Barbara chuckled. 'I doubt there'd be a single person on the planet who hasn't wished for the same thing.'

'If only I'd listened to you,' Laura groaned.

'Do children ever really listen?' Barbara smiled. 'You weren't exactly thinking straight back then. You had the whole Newvalley thing to deal with and then found out you were pregnant. I don't really think you had the ability to think beyond a day. If you'd been able to project long term you would have realised that Jack had a right to know. But you couldn't. You were dealing with too much as it was. Asking you to think beyond the next day wasn't an option.'

Laura knew what her mother was saying was true. Ten years ago the only way she'd felt she could get through the day had been by taking one thing at a time. Her mother had got to the crux of it as usual.

'If only he hadn't contracted mumps. His infertility and the whole mess with his ex-wife makes my decision not to tell him seem cruel. He's been so consumed by not being able to father a child that finding out he's had one for nine years is like rubbing salt into his wounds.'

'You couldn't have known that he'd become infertile, darling.'

'I know. It's just…oh, it's such a mess. He's so caught up in what he's lost out on, he doesn't realise what he can gain,' said Laura.

'He's hurt and angry right now, but he won't be for ever. He's grieving. Being a father is something he thought he'd never have a shot at and now he knows about Isaac, he's grieving the loss of being the perfect dad.'

'I don't know how to reach him. How do I convince him that what I did was for the best possible reasons? How do I make him realise that we need him?'

'Wait for him to come to you.'

'I can't, Mum. I've done so much wrong. I need to put it right.'

'Everything isn't always a quick fix, darling. It's early days, Laura. When's he due back?'

'He should be back by now.'

'Well, he's had a couple of days to think about it and calm down. Give him some space. You can't push him on this. He'll call you when he's ready.'

'I need to make this better, Mum.'

Barbara's heart broke at the desperation in her daughter's voice. 'Can you do that, darling?'

'No,' Laura said sadly. 'He wants what I can't give him.'

'Oh? What's that?'

'Memories.'

'You can share yours. And there's the box.'

'I tried to tell him about the box the other day but he rejected the idea out of hand. I think he was insulted that I tried to placate him with memorabilia.'

'It's so much more than that, Laura.'

'I know that, but he wasn't in the mood to listen.'

'Maybe now he's had some time to calm down he'll be more receptive to the idea.'

'Maybe. I think I need to really choose my moment to present him with it. I need to know his mood, maybe even have him ask first. There are such personal things inside. I want him to be in awe of his son's life as he looks at everything, not blinded to it by his anger at me.'

Laura waved her mother goodbye half an hour later and reflected on their conversation. Could she wait as long as Jack needed? Maybe his time away had helped him resolve some of his anger. The waiting was driving her mad.

Now she was alone again, without the sensible, calming influence of her mother, she was overcome by the urge to do something. She didn't want to sit by and leave it to chance.

She looked at her watch. Isaac wouldn't be home for at

least another hour. She grabbed her keys and headed out. It might be unwise but she just had to see Jack.

Jack looked like hell as he answered the door. He had a five o'clock shadow and looked like he hadn't slept a wink since the last time she'd seen him. He was in denim cut-offs and a white short-sleeved shirt left unbuttoned. It flapped open, revealing his tanned, smooth chest.

'Laura.' He closed his eyes, emphasising his tiredness. 'I'm really not in the mood.'

'Please, Jack. Hear me out.'

He sighed and opened his eyes, regarding her sceptically. He remained still, not inviting her in. He obviously wasn't going to make it easy. But if she had to do this on his door-step, then so be it.

'You asked me once if I could give you back Isaac's first smile, his first steps. Well I can…in a way. I can't give you the feel of his baby body snuggled against yours or the smell of his baby skin. But I can give you lots of two-dimensional memories.'

'What? Photos?' he mocked, angered by her seemingly simplistic view of it all. It belittled the depth of his hurt.

'Among other things,' she said quietly, swallowing the wave of emotion his harshness had evoked. Tears shone brightly in her eyes. Laura was glad she hadn't brought the box with her, as she had been tempted to do. He wasn't in the most receptive mood.

'Look, whatever my reasons were back then, Jack, it's done now. I can't change it. I wish that I could. I'd give anything to be able to turn back the clock. But I can't. I can only be sorry for it and go on from here. We can go on together if you just try and meet me halfway.'

He remained impassive. A tear trickled down her cheek and she dashed it away. 'If you remember, I wasn't exactly thinking very rationally ten years ago.' Her husky voice was rich with the passion of her thoughts. 'I was so grateful for what you'd done for me in Newvalley, I wanted to repay that. You became my entire focus. I wanted the best for you and that was to be one hundred per cent free to concentrate on your career. A child would have been a major distraction.'

He tried to interrupt but Laura held up her hand. 'Right or wrong, Jack, that's how I felt. That's how my thought processes worked. I wish I could take it back but I can't. But you know what? Nine years is nothing compared to the next twenty or thirty or forty. You've still got a lot of fathering left.'

'Don't lecture me on being a father. I'll take the next forty years but I want the last nine also.'

Laura's dismay was evident. She just couldn't seem to get through to him. She bowed her head and wiped the tears away. Her mobile phone rang and she was grateful for its interruption. His harshness was upsetting.

'Hello,' she answered, emotion choking her voice. She watched Jack at the periphery of her vision, impatience evident in every line of his body.

'What? Calm down, Sally. What's wrong? What's happened?'

Jack heard the alarm creep into her voice and a dreadful feeling of foreboding washed over him.

'Oh, my God! Is he all right?'

Laura looked at him frantically and Jack knew something serious had happened. Please, don't let it be Isaac.

'I'm coming right now. I'll be there in five minutes.'

'Laura?' Jack tried to keep the edge out of his voice as she hit the 'end' button on her mobile. 'What's happened?'

'Isaac…' She sniffed, tears running down her cheeks. 'There's been a car accident. He's being airlifted to St Jude's.'

A thousand questions and emotions crossed his mind but one look at Laura disintegrating in front of him and Jack knew that he needed to take charge. This wasn't the time for explanations or recriminations—this was the time for action.

He strode back inside, collecting his keys and buttoning his shirt as he went. 'Let's go,' he said to an immobile Laura as he brushed past her. 'We'll take my car.'

Laura couldn't speak for the fear that was invading her bones. Please, let Isaac be OK. Please, let him be OK. All the patients she'd ever looked after from motor vehicle accidents marched through her mind. She tried to think of the good ones but the tragedies kept taking over.

In a matter of minutes the car had screeched to a halt outside the children's block at St Jude's. It was a specialised wing of the hospital for paediatric patients. It had its own casualty department, operating theatres and intensive care unit.

'Isaac Scott,' Laura said to the nurse behind the triage desk. 'He was airlifted here from a car accident not long ago.'

'Oh, yes. He's in Theatre at the moment. They've got a bed for him in the PICU. It's on the—'

'I know where it is,' said Laura, already moving towards the lifts.

They travelled in the lift in silence, Jack offering his hand which she took, too numb to be surprised by his supportive gesture. They were slightly out of breath when they reached the waiting room, just outside the swing doors of the unit. Sally Werner was pacing inside.

'Sally!' exclaimed Laura. 'Look at you.' She had a badly bruised cheekbone and her arm in a sling.

'Just a broken collar-bone,' she said dismissively. 'Laura, I'm so sorry. I tried to swerve and avoid it but the car just slammed into us.' She started to cry and Laura rushed to comfort her friend.

'It was an accident, Sally. I don't blame you.'

Bloody dangerous drivers. Jack could feel his anger against the hooligan who had done this to his child build to boiling point. It far surpassed anything he had felt for Laura these last couple of days.

'Who was driving?' he demanded. Probably some teenagers on a joyride.

Laura introduced Jack. Sally seemed too distracted by the day's events to give a second thought to his presence. 'He was a shift worker driving home after a double shift. Fell asleep at the wheel.'

Jack shook his head, the wind taken out of his sails. How many times had he driven home after a marathon shift so tired he could barely think straight? *There, but for the grace of God, go I.* It was his mother's favourite saying. Jack's anger dissipated.

'Is he all right?'

'Yes. Miraculously, everyone else is fine. Minor injuries only.'

'Is Isaac out of Theatre yet?' Laura's only concern right now was her son.

'They said they'd come and get me when he was back.'

'Do you know what his injuries are?'

'They did say but I don't know how much I've taken in. Something about chest injuries. They put a tube into his throat before they transported him.'

Oh, God. They'd intubated him. He had chest injuries. His breathing was obviously compromised. She felt dizzy and swayed slightly. Her back came up against the solid wall of Jack's body as he put a steadying arm around her shoulders. She leaned against him gratefully.

'What else?' Her brain had switched to clinical mode.

'He's got a broken leg. I'm not sure which one and something about…about a haemorrhage in his brain. That's why they're operating now.'

A head injury! Laura felt as if she'd been winded. She felt Jack's hand tighten on her upper arm. Oh, God, her baby! Her baby.

The slogan from a poster flashed through her mind. It was for head injury prevention. WHAT WILL I DO IF I BREAK MY

BRAIN? Head injuries were survivable but too often robbed the victims of any normal life.

She put a halt to her galloping thoughts. She mustn't think the worst before she knew the details. Often laypeople, like Sally, were overwhelmed by critical-care settings, making things seem worse than they actually were. Laura clung to that.

Jack could read the play of emotions on Laura's face and he knew that the nurse in her would be thinking of the worst-case scenario. God knew, he was. Medical professionals tended to do that where their loved ones were concerned. Sometimes it was a curse to know too much.

'Come on, Laura,' he gave her arm a squeeze. 'Let's stop imagining the worst and go and find out.'

They pushed open the front swing doors of the PICU. The registrar on duty approached him.

'Do you want to see somebody?'

'Isaac Scott. He's…he's my son.' Jack stumbled over the words. His son. It sounded so alien.

Laura felt a well of emotion rise and threaten to bubble over at hearing those words come from Jack's mouth. She swallowed hard against the lump in her throat. It felt so good to have him by her side. He was being so strong and it was so good to be able to share the burden of this horrible event.

'Yes, he's in room one.' The doctor indicated a room in the nearby hallway.

'What are his injuries?'

'Well, he's not long back from Theatre, where they evacuated a blood clot from his brain.'

Jack heard Laura gasp and he tightened his hold on her hand. Oh, God. Please, let him be OK.

'No. It sounds worse than it is. We think his head will be OK. It was extradural and only just large enough to operate on. Now the pressure's been released… Of course, we won't know until he wakes up and the cerebral oedema settles.'

'Right. Anything else?' asked Jack. Please, don't let there be any more.

'He has a fractured right tibia and fibula, so that leg's in a cast.'

'Is there more?' Jack shut his eyes. No more. Please, no more.

'He has a right lung contusion, which caused his lung to collapse. It was because of this and his decreased level of consciousness at the accident scene that he was ventilated. He has a chest drain in that side.'

'Is that it?' Jack held his breath. Isaac's injuries were extensive enough.

'Yes. Would you like to see him? You and your wife can go right in.'

We're not married, Jack was about to reply, but let it die on his lips. What did that matter? They were his parents and he was critically injured. Nothing mattered but Isaac getting better. Nothing. Surprisingly, not even Laura's deceit.

Laura thought she'd prepared herself for what she was about to see. After all, an intensive-care environment was her second home. But the fist that rammed into her gut at seeing Isaac nearly knocked her flat.

He looked small and fragile among all the medical machinery. Tubes went in and out and wires crisscrossed his pale body. He looked so still.

Isaac's head was wrapped in a bandage, his broken leg elevated on a pillow. A tube hung from between his ribs, draining the collection of blood and air that had caused his lung to collapse. The air bubbled as it escaped into the water at the bottom of the drain bottle.

Laura gasped and sobbed, staring at her child, not recognising him. He looked so lifeless. So pale. Whiter than the sheet. She noticed a bag of blood running into one of his lines and knew his haemoglobin must be very low.

Jack was shocked, too. No way was this the tanned, happy little boy he'd seen a few days ago. He wanted to rush to his son's side, hug his body with a fierceness he'd never known he could feel. But fear immobilised him. Fear of hurting Isaac more. Fear that he might squeeze him too tight, trying to convey the depth of his love.

This couldn't be happening. Jack threw a general prayer upwards to all the deities he could think of. Don't let him die. He'd only just found Isaac. Surely fate wouldn't be cruel enough to take him away now. His fear for his son was so overwhelming he couldn't even articulate it.

'You can come closer, Jack.'

Laura's words penetrated his statue-still stance. She had moved to Isaac's bedside and was sitting on a chair the nurse had organised for her. Her tear-streaked face pulled at his heart and he noticed she was gripping Isaac's hand like she was never going to let him go. The nurse offered her a tissue and she blew her nose.

'How long's he been back from Theatre?' Jack asked the nurse. He felt himself gaining strength as he switched to thinking like a doctor. Thinking like a father was making him crazy and, looking at Laura, he knew he needed to be strong.

'Nearly an hour.'

'Has he woken up yet?' Isaac's chances for a full recovery increased the sooner he gained consciousness.

'No.' She shook her head and smiled gently.

They sat staring at their son surrounded by all the medical paraphernalia. Their gazes fixed on the monitor with its pretty multicoloured squiggles.

Each line was a different colour—one for his heart rate, another for his blood pressure, one more for his respiratory rate and another representing his oxygen saturations. Their ears were tuned to the low-velocity beeping that occurred every time his heart beat.

As Isaac's nurse bustled around his bed, Laura stole a glance at Jack. His expression was grim. She wished she could read his thoughts. What was he thinking? Was he concentrating all his energies on positive thinking, as she was?

His animosity towards her seemed to have disappeared the moment he'd found out about the accident. Was it gone for good or just put on ice while he concentrated on Isaac's condition?

Two hours later, Jack could bear the silence of the room no longer. Sitting and watching his son's chest as it rose and fell with each ventilated breath, listening to the beep, beep, beep of the monitor was torture.

'Lets go for a walk, stretch our legs.' His voice rasped into the silence.

'No, I'm not leaving. You go, Jack. Get a coffee, something to eat. I'll come get you if there's any change.'

He hesitated. Maybe he shouldn't? But he was already wrecked from his sleepless night and out of his mind with worry. A break would give him a chance to recharge his batteries. He could also get a sandwich or something for Laura as she didn't look like she was leaving at all tonight.

Amazing what a difference a couple of hours could make. He'd been so angry with Laura earlier today and now, only a few hours later? His heart ached for her. He could only imagine how horrible it must be for her to go through this. His anger seemed petty and juvenile compared to this. He felt ashamed at how he had treated her. He stirred his cup of tea a few minutes later and realized that if they got through this night he had a lot of making up to do.

Laura watched the nurse as she adjusted the rate on an infusion. 'You're turning his sedation down?' Laura asked.

'Yes. Let's see if we can't get him to wake up a bit quicker.'

Laura understood the dilemma too well. How much sedation was enough? They trod a fine line. Too much bombed the patient and compromised his respiratory function. Too little and many patients became anxious and agitated, jeopardising their care. They wanted Isaac to wake but wanted him to be calm. He would need ventilating until his lung recovered, so they needed to achieve the right level of sedation.

It was a bizarre feeling, sitting next to her seriously ill son in such a familiar setting. She was so used to being the nurse, the one with the power in a hospital situation. In control.

But she wasn't now. She was a parent, on the other side of the fence, and she felt helpless and dependent. Laura recognised that a good nurse could learn from this experience. She'd been given a peek at the other side. From this day forward she would *know*, truly know, what it was like to be on the other side.

Time moved more slowly than a snail with a headache. Laura and Jack didn't talk. They sat on opposite sides of the bed, holding a hand each, miserable in their worry. Laura stroked Isaac's arm and spoke softly to him from time to time.

Laura looked up as the door opened and was surprised to see her mother and father entering, anxiety stamped on their faces. She'd been so involved with the situation she hadn't even thought to ring them. She felt awful. But having Jack by her side had been all she had cared about.

Tears spilled down Laura's face as her mother and then her father gathered her in their arms.

'Jack rang us,' Barbara whispered, bending over and placing a kiss on Isaac's paper-white cheek.

Laura looked at him through blurry eyes and felt her heart burgeon with her love for him. He was taking care of her again, coming to her rescue when all she'd been able to do was flounder around and barely put one foot in front of the other.

'Thank you,' she mouthed, touched by his thoughtfulness, and he gave her a sad smile.

Her parents stayed for a little while and then tried to convince her to leave the room for a short break for a cup of tea and something to eat. Jack's sandwich had been left untouched.

'No.' She was adamant. 'I need to be here in case he wakes up.'

'I'll be here,' Jack interjected. 'He won't be alone, I promise. You need to keep your strength up, Laura. Just take a short break.'

He reached across Isaac's body and covered her hand with his. He smiled reassuringly and Laura gave herself permission to let go, surrender the reins of mothering for a short while and let Isaac's father take some of the load. How had she managed all these years without him?

Alone with Isaac, Jack felt suddenly helpless. What could he do? Weren't fathers supposed to have all the answers? Weren't they supposed to protect their children from this kind of hurt? He despaired. He didn't how to be a father.

But he did know how to be a psychiatrist. The doctor inside told him to talk. Just talk. About anything. It didn't really matter what. Once recovered, coma patients often told of voices, conversations they had heard while unresponsive.

It seemed somehow fitting that he could offer his son the same thing that he had offered his son's mother all those years ago—the sound of his voice. Laura had told him his words had kept her going and made her stronger. Maybe he could give Isaac the strength he needed to get better through the power of his voice?

So he held his son's hand and told Isaac the story of Laura and himself. Told him that he was his father and that he loved him and wanted him to get better so they could meet properly. How he'd been so angry but now he was just grateful to have found him and had been given a chance to know him and love him. That his mother was a wonderful woman and he loved her very much.

Jack felt tears on his cheeks and realised he was crying. He cursed himself for being such a fool. He had pushed the woman he loved away out of anger. Had he damaged his chances with her? Had he pushed her too far away with his bitterness? He promised himself, promised Isaac, that when Isaac pulled through this he would spend the rest of his life making it up to them.

Laura came back in with her parents and Jack was relieved to see she looked a little refreshed. He thanked God the dim lighting hid the tell-tale signs of his tears. He didn't want Laura to think he had lost it. He had to be strong for her.

The night shift came on and still Isaac hadn't regained consciousness. All his vital signs and his neurological observations were normal, but he hadn't opened his eyes.

Laura was really starting to worry. He should be waking up by now. Yes, all the other signs were encouraging but what if things suddenly got worse instead of better? She remembered Jason, the young man on her unit who had extended the bleed in his brain, remembered how he had fitted and was terrified that Isaac would go the same way.

What if they lost Isaac? She didn't want to think about it, but with Jason fresh in her mind the possibility loomed. Jason didn't die, she reminded herself frantically. No, but no one knew whether he would fully recover either.

What if Jack never got to know his son? How would she ever forgive herself? It was important to her that he knew Isaac. Really knew him. There was only one way that she could think of to accomplish that. It was time for the box.

It was, of course, the worst possible time. But sometimes you didn't get a choice, and if they were going to lose Isaac tonight it was only right and fair that Jack knew as much about him as possible. She'd been waiting for the right time but sometimes the worst time was the best time.

She had kept his son from him for nine years. It was now time for Jack to get acquainted with Isaac.

CHAPTER THIRTEEN

WITH her parents' help, half an hour later Laura led Jack into the deserted parents' lounge. An old, large cardboard box sat in the middle of the floor.

'What's this?' he asked, staring at the box.

'It's the box I told you about. I know it doesn't look much but there's a whole lifetime of memories inside. I know they're not the kind you crave but, I promise you, by the time you've been through it you'll know Isaac almost as well as I do. You said to me once you wanted the last nine years. Well, they're in the box.'

The old angry Jack rebelled at the idea that she honestly thought he could be placated by a tatty box of photos. But mostly, with his anger a thing of the past, he was itching to open it, discover the treasures inside.

With Isaac lying so sick and so still, he desperately wanted to learn about the boy he usually was. Not the pale, unresponsive child but the tanned, exuberant boy who was a carbon copy of himself.

Like a starving man wandering the desert craved an oasis, Jack craved the memories. Any memories or mementoes from his son's childhood were more precious than diamonds or gold. The gravity of Isaac's condition made them priceless.

'You'll need this,' she said, pointing to a nearby video machine and television. 'I'm going to leave you alone. Give you some privacy. I'll come and get you if anything changes.'

Jack barely noticed her leaving so intent was he on the contents of the tattered cardboard box. He dragged it over to a lounge chair and opened the cardboard flaps slowly, almost reverently. This box contained precious treasure.

Jack was stunned at its contents. His heart beat rapidly as he quickly pulled out the contents and placed them on the floor. He wanted to look at everything individually but he wanted to empty the box and get a general overview of its contents. Get some idea of what he should look at first.

Laura was right. It wasn't just photos, although it soon became apparent that every waking and even some sleeping moments of Isaac's life had been snapped for posterity.

He opened a small metal box, the inside of which was lined with plush red velvet. It contained the positive home pregnancy test Laura must have done. He held it and could still detect the faint pink cross, indicating a pregnancy. Isaac's very first picture. Also inside was a lock of his baby hair and his hospital ID tags.

He undid a soft bundle, wrapped in tissue paper. An exquisite ivory gown slipped out. Jack knew it was Isaac's christening outfit. He fingered the fabric, touching the lace and satin, stroked the gorgeous embroidery and beading on the yoke. He buried his face in it and inhaled the faint trace of powder and clean baby skin. It was hard to put down so he laid it across his lap as he investigated further, its silkiness comforting.

The first ultrasound picture was amazing. A fuzzy blur sucking its thumb. The ultrasound video was there also. He put it in the machine and watched the different blurry images of Isaac at twenty weeks gestation. His heart swelled. It was almost as good as being there.

There were numerous videos, all numbered and labelled and stored in chronological order. He would watch them all later. He found another, smaller album at the bottom, which had pictures of Laura at various stages of her pregnancy. It was fair to say she glowed. In the earlier photos she looked peaky, she must have suffered from morning sickness, but as her pregnant stomach grew she looked more and more healthy.

Jack spent all night poring over the contents of the box.

Everything from Isaac's first tooth to his first artwork was here. Seeing and feeling these things helped to answer a lot of questions and fill in a lot of gaps. The masses of photos, all put in albums, all conscientiously kept in order from Isaac's birth until present day, were incredible. They all had dates and comments written beside them by Laura.

He was getting a very rounded picture of the type of person his son was. Jack was continually struck by their resemblance. His mother was going to freak when she met Isaac. His mother was going to freak anyway when she found out she had a nine-year-old grandson she hadn't known about, but particularly when she saw their resemblance. It was uncanny. No way could anyone doubt Isaac's paternity.

He'd kept the videos for last. He didn't start playing them until every photo, every drawing, every memento had been looked at and touched.

Jack's hand trembled as he inserted the video numbered one into his machine. His breath drew in sharply when he realised it was a video of Isaac's birth. He was going to see his son being born after all.

He laughed and cried as he watched the action unfold. Barbara had held the video camera but Laura had certainly been the director.

'Mum, you have to be down the other end,' she said to the camera. A contraction gripped her and she moaned as the intensity increased. 'Mum,' she panted as the pain subsided. 'I'm fully dilated. I've been pushing for half an hour. This baby is going to be here soon. You have to film it.''

'Laura, do you really think…? Well, it's a very private thing to video.'

'It's for Jack, Mum. No one else is going to see it. One day he might want to see this, witness his child coming into the world. Now film,' she yelled as another contraction hit and her body bore down.

Her sentiment and determination to record it for him

touched Jack. He watched transfixed as his son, all ten pounds of him, made his smooth, calm entry into the world.

His breath caught in his throat as his wet, bouncing son, not even two minutes old, suckled greedily at Laura's breast. He already knew that she'd breastfed Isaac for eighteen months. Her pictorial evidence chronicled this. It made him immensely proud that she had nurtured their son.

Dawn was breaking as the last of the videos ended. It seemed the video camera had never been far away. There was footage of practically every day of Isaac's life for the first few months and then it went to weekly and then monthly and six-monthly in recent years. He watched his son grow up on the television screen.

His heart swelled with pride at Isaac's first words and steps and ached when he fell over or learnt one of life's many painful lessons. Every birthday. Every Christmas. His first day at school. She'd missed nothing. Even his first visit to the dentist had been videoed.

He fixed himself some toast and coffee and looked out of the windows at the city skyline slowly becoming visible as the sun shone its light across the sky. His head was full of memories of Isaac. Memories Laura had given him. She had filled in as much of those nine years as was physically possible.

He had behaved badly and said some awful things. She was right. What was done was done. Laura had done what she felt had been right at the time. The rawness of the whole Newvalley disaster had obviously skewed her normal thought processes. She'd been in a vulnerable emotional place back then and Jack could only imagine what it must have been like to discover she was pregnant. As if she hadn't had enough on her plate.

His mind wandered back to the box. It was a gift in the truest sense, given out of love. Yes, he still yearned to have experienced all those memories at first hand but he'd done the next best thing. He could spend the rest of his life growing old with his bitterness or he could accept that the past was something he couldn't change and build a future with Laura and Isaac.

He had promised his son only hours before that he would spend the rest of his life making it up to Laura. The gift that she had just given him cemented this determination. He only hoped she would let him.

Jack entered his son's room quietly. Laura had her head on the bed, Isaac's hand pressed to her cheek. Exhaustion had obviously taken its toll and she'd finally succumbed to sleep.

He debated whether or not to wake to her but he couldn't help himself. There was so much to say to her that he didn't want to wait another second.

He placed gentle hands on her shoulders, lightly massaging the muscles that were tense despite her slumber. She stirred and he dropped a light kiss on the top of her head.

She woke and looked around at him through bleary eyes.

'Oh, no, I must have fallen asleep,' she gasped, her eyes flying to Isaac. 'Has there been any change?' She looked at Jack and then beseechingly at the nurse.

'No change,' she murmured gently.

Laura felt the tears threaten again. 'Wake up, darling,' she whispered to her little boy, and kissed his hand. 'Please, wake up.'

Jack could see her frustration and helplessness building. 'Laura, come outside with me. Take a break. We need to talk.'

She started to protest but was stopped by the look in his eyes. He seemed…happy, and something else? He was looking at her as if he…as if he loved her? The box. Of course, he'd seen inside the box. She took his hand and followed him outside.

Laura didn't dare hope but his mood was promising. The parents' lounge was empty and she noticed the box immediately. His brown eyes gleamed and he prowled around the lounge, a bundle of pent-up energy.

'How can I ever thank you enough?' he said, coming closer, standing in front of her. 'I owe you an apology. I've been a total jerk. I've been so caught up in how wronged I felt that I didn't listen to you. Some psychiatrist, huh?' he laughed nervously.

'What are you trying to say, Jack?' Laura's heart banged painfully against her ribs.

'What you did, keeping that box for me, it's helped me realise that you didn't do any of this to intentionally hurt me. You wouldn't have been so diligent with the box if you'd wanted to hurt me.'

'Yes,' she said softly, holding her breath.

'I guess finding out I was a dad put me in a real spin. I've thought for so many years it was impossible…I reacted badly.'

'Oh.'

'And then Isaac had his accident and I realised that my anger was unimportant. I should have been down on my knees, rejoicing that I was a father, not blaming you for it. I was selfish, only thinking about me.'

'It was a difficult situation.' She shrugged.

'I'm sorry, Laura, how can you ever forgive me?'

'Forgive you? There's nothing to forgive. You reacted like any other person would have done. I'm the one who needs to ask for forgiveness. The decision I made ten years ago was wrong. It wasn't fair to you or to Isaac. I have no excuse, only to say that I really thought I was doing the right thing by you. It was a decision that didn't get easier to reverse as the years went by. I'm so sorry.'

He sat down next to her and pulled her into his arms. He held her for a long time and her heart soared. It was time to tell him how she felt. She needed him to know that she loved him. Had always loved him. And what she'd done, she'd done out of love for him.

'I love you, Jack. I've always loved you.'

Jack was stunned. Laura, the one great love of his life, was admitting something he'd never dared hope for—particularly considering his treatment of her in recent days. His love for her surged forth and he couldn't have stopped it if he'd tried.

She reached out to touch him. Hands that had caressed him. Made love to him. Held and nurtured his child.

'I love you, too, Laura.'

'You…you do?'

'Of course I do.' He looked at the insecurity on her face. Oh, no, what had he done? He'd treated her so badly the last few days. 'I've been a bitter, angry fool. But even when I was hurting so much and so mad at you, deep down I knew I still loved you. It finally broke through my anger last night when I realised Isaac could have been killed and then…when I opened the box. It was like I was falling in love with you all over again. All that stuff you kept for me…thank you, my darling. I love you so much.'

'Oh, Jack. I love you, too. I think from the moment I heard your voice in Newvalley I was a goner.'

'Me, too. I've spent ten years in love with you and didn't know it.'

She fell into his arms and they hugged like the world was going to end then and there. They drew apart, allowing their lips to meet, controlled by some invisible force.

Laura clung to him. Her heart rejoiced and filled with love. Jack loved her. After the despair of the last few days it all seemed too good to be true.

They broke apart again and Laura held him to her as if this was the last time they'd ever see each other.

'I'm so happy at the moment and I shouldn't be. Isaac is still so…critical. I don't have the right to be happy when he's in there fighting for his life.'

'No, Laura, you're wrong. You deserve this happiness more than ever. And with both of his parents in there, rooting for him, loving him, I just know he's going to come through this. The power of our love will get him through this.'

She swallowed a sob and sought solace in his arms again. She prayed he was right. If something happened to Isaac she didn't know what she would do. She doubted even their new-found love could get them through that.

And if he didn't make it, how would Jack then feel about her? Would he still love her, knowing that she'd denied him his son? Would a few precious days and a box of memories suffice, should Isaac die? Or would his love be blinded again by his bitterness at her unintentional deceit?

She shook her head, pushing such morbid thoughts away. She needed to think positively and, as Jack said, believe that the power of their love could reach Isaac and bring him back to them. She would not think about the what-ifs.

'I want to tell Isaac.' His quiet voice broke their reverie.

'So do I,' she admitted with a smile.

'When?'

'I don't know, Jack. He's been through a major trauma. Let's wait until he's recovered. He might be quite shocked. I don't want that to have an adverse affect on him.'

Laura was certain Isaac would be thrilled to meet his father but she wanted him to be fully recovered before he had such potentially life-altering news laid in his lap.

'I know it's unfair of me to ask you to wait, but—'

'Laura.' Jack took her face in his hands and pressed a soft kiss on her mouth. 'It's OK. You are his mother. You know him and you know what's best for him. I'll leave it up to you to decide when the time's right.'

'Jack—'

'Shh.' He placed two fingers against her lips. 'I've waited nine years. A little longer won't matter.'

Laura was tempted to open her mouth and suck them inside. She took a deep breath, suppressing the urge, and almost mewed her disappointment when the pressure of his fingers left her lips. She licked them to savour the taste of him. She saw his pupils dilate as his eyes followed the movement of her tongue.

This was crazy. Their son was inside, fighting for his life. She cleared her throat breaking the moment. 'I think we should get back.'

'Definitely,' he agreed quietly, a smouldering smile the only trace left of the heat that had flared between them.

They went back to Isaac's room together, holding hands, buoyed by their love. They sat beside each other this time, close. Laura leaned against Jack and his hand covered hers as she laced her fingers through Isaac's.

A few moments later the alarms triggered on Isaac's monitor as his heart rate accelerated. Laura felt hers rise in response and immediately prepared for the worse. She leant forward and squeezed Jack's hand tight.

The nurse calmly moved to the opposite side from where they were sitting and shone a small light into Isaac's eyes.

'Hello, Isaac,' she said. 'Can you open your eyes? It's OK, you were in an accident. You're in hospital. Your mum's here. She'd love it if you could open your eyes.'

'I'm here, darling.' Laura leapt up, moving into Isaac's line of vision. Tears filled her eyes. To her eternal relief she found Isaac's brown eyes staring back. Jack's eyes.

They looked a little blank at first and she watched as realisation of his surroundings dawned. Panic crept into them and he started to move his head, shaking it from side to side.

'Mum,' he mouthed around the tube down his throat. 'Mum.'

Laura's relief that he knew who she was overwhelmed her. Tears streamed down her face as she tried to calm Isaac. He began to thrash and tried to bring his hand to his face. His movements caused him to cough as the endotrachael tube irritated his airway. The more he moved, the more he coughed, the more panicked he became.

'I'll just give him a little bolus of sedation,' the nurse said above the ringing of monitor alarms, triggered by Isaac's wild movements.

Laura assured him over and over that everything was fine, that she was there, as the bolus relaxed his agitated movements and he drifted back to sleep. Hopefully, when he woke next time, he would be calmer.

Jack felt a weight lift off his shoulders. He gathered Laura close and held her. Finally, some good news. 'I told you,' he whispered. 'I told you our love would pull him through.'

Laura looked at him, the love shining in her eyes. He had been right. 'Thank you, Jack. Thank you for being here. I love you.'

Time seemed to move at its normal pace again. The atmosphere in the room lightened immeasurably. Isaac woke frequently throughout the day and Laura's presence and assurances helped to keep him calm. He appeared to be orientated and obeyed simple commands, all-important tests to gauge his neurological status.

Isaac's grandparents visited, friends visited, Laura's work colleagues visited. Jack was beginning to feel like the proverbial fifth wheel. Everyone who walked through the door seemed to know Isaac better than him. He tried not to be jealous or feel left out, but it was hard.

He wanted to be there but felt like he didn't belong. He was Isaac's father yet he felt he was intruding on private family moments. He couldn't comfort his son or calm him when he became distressed because Isaac didn't know him. If anything, he was afraid he'd make the situation worse.

So for the next couple of days Jack hung around on the fringes, trying not to intrude. Isaac seemed to accept his presence without question, which only seemed to compound Jack's misery. He desperately wanted to be a part of Isaac's recovery, not just a friendly face that popped in now and then.

Isaac recovered quickly. In two days all the invasive medical tubes had been removed. He remained weak but much improved. Laura could sense Jack's frustration but Isaac's needs were taking precedence for the moment. Her love for him warred with her motherly instincts.

On his third day in hospital Laura was feeling confident enough in Isaac's recovery to leave him for short periods. She left him with her mother and took the opportunity to walk across to the adult section of St Jude's and clear out her locker. She wasn't sure how long she would be off work, and lockers were always at a premium.

The walk was therapeutic in a lot of ways. It gave her the opportunity to stretch her legs, which hadn't moved much in the last few days, and it gave her some time to mull over the problem with Jack. She could sense his alienation but wasn't sure how to get around it.

'Hi,' she said, popping her head into Marie's office, carrying a plastic bag full of personal items.

'Laura.' Marie rose and gave her a big hug. 'How's it all going?'

'Great. Really good. He's improving before my eyes.'

'That's fantastic,' Marie enthused. 'He was so lucky, Laura!'

'Tell me about it. Whenever I think about what could have happened…' Laura shuddered. 'Anyway…it didn't, so good news all round.'

'You want some more good news?' Marie smiled and her face took on a mysterious look.

'Sure. I'm always up for good news.'

Laura followed her boss into Mr Reid's room. He was sitting up in bed, looking better than she'd ever seen him. The room was free of all the extra machines and pumps that a week ago he hadn't been able to do without.

'Oh, my God. Mr Reid,' Laura gasped, amazed at how good he looked. 'Look at you!'

'Yeah, gave you all a bit of a scare, didn't I?'

'You nearly gave me a heart attack the day we had to rush you to Theatre!' she joked.

'I'm going back to the oncology unit tomorrow. My bone marrow's kicked in and doing all the right things, and my kidneys are working again, too.'

'Well, that's just fantastic.' She smiled and squeezed his hand.

'A miracle. That's what it is. I wouldn't have made it without you guys. You do such a great job here. I owe you my life.'

'Nonsense! You just keep getting better. That's all we care about.'

Laura walked back to the paediatric wing with a real spring in her step. Mr Reid's recovery *was* miraculous. She'd seen too many similar patients not pull through. It gave her faith in miracles, especially with Isaac's full recovery almost guaranteed. Things were looking up. If only she could help Jack through this uncertain time. Maybe he would be next in line for a miracle?

CHAPTER FOURTEEN

JACK was waiting outside Isaac's room when Laura arrived back. She smiled at him with a touch of sadness as she saw the unhappiness reflected in his sad brown eyes. He pulled her close and gave her a lingering kiss. It was the first time they'd been alone in a couple of days—if you could call being in the middle of PICU being alone.

'I want to hug him, Laura.'

'I know, Jack. I know.'

'Do you? I'm his *father*. I want to be able to go in there and hug and kiss him as a father.'

'Oh, darling, it must be so frustrating,' she whispered, resting her head against his chest.

'You have no idea,' he murmured. 'And I hate it, I hate it so much. It's worse because I find myself jealous of you and your closeness. I know that's crazy but you've had him for nine years… I barely know him but I love him more than I could ever have imagined.'

'I'm sorry, Jack.' His hurt clawed at her conscience.

'I'm infertile, Laura.' He said it slowly, wanting her to understand the depth of his emotions. 'I never thought I'd have children of my own. Now suddenly I have a son, and I don't want to waste any more time.'

'You must hate me,' she whispered again, burying her face in his shirt. All this anguish she had caused.

'No, my darling.' He lifted her chin until she was looking up at him. 'I know you did what you thought was right. You gave me a son. I love you.' He kissed her to emphasise that love.

'And I promise I'm not deliberately keeping you from him now. It's just that…I can't tell you when the time is going to be right, Jack. I think we're just going to have to play it by ear. I have a feeling that an opportunity will just present itself and we'll know.'

'And if it doesn't?'

'When he's fully recovered we'll tell him anyway.'

They held hands as they walked into the room. Isaac was awake, watching television. Jack couldn't believe how much better his son looked. He ached to hold him in his arms and greet him as a father would. He had to stop himself from rushing to do so.

'Hello.' Isaac's direct gaze assessed him. A reflection of his own. He noticed how Isaac was focussed on their joined hands and Jack let go, feeling like he'd been caught smoking behind the bike sheds.

'Hi,' said Jack, suddenly nervous. 'I bought you something to stop you from getting too bored.' His walk was tentative as he approached Isaac and gave him a brightly wrapped package.

'Cool. Thanks, Dr Riley.' Isaac ripped the paper away and gasped. 'Wow! Mum, it's the latest GameBoy. Excellent.'

Laura smiled across the bed at Jack as she watched the two men in her life talk. It all sounded like German to her but she'd never heard such a beautiful sound. Her heart sang to see father and son together.

An hour later, after a conversation that had required little input from Laura, she ordered an end to the electronic game discussion. Isaac was yawning and, despite appearances, only three days ago he'd been dangerously ill. He needed to rest.

Jack and Laura gazed at his face, drinking in the sight of him, linking hands across his body as he drifted off. Jack mouthed 'Thank you' to Laura. The time they had just spent together had been magical. He actually felt like a father for the first time.

'Mummy?' Isaac's sleepy voice interrupted their intense gaze.

'Yes, sweetie?'

'I had the strangest dream while I was in a coma.' He opened his eyes and once again spied them holding hands.

Laura smothered a smile at Isaac's casual mention of his 'coma'. She removed her hand from Jack's, picked up Isaac's and kissed his fingers. 'Do you remember it?'

'Sort of,' he said, yawning. 'My dad came to visit. He was sitting by my bed and talking to me about how you two met and how much he loved me.'

Jack held his breath. Isaac had heard? He had poured his heart out to his son that night, talking about whatever had popped into his head just to try and make a connection with him. Draw him back from the brink with his voice.

'His voice sounded an awful lot like yours, Dr Riley,' said Isaac, turning his head to look directly at Jack. 'I liked it, it was nice. I wasn't scared any more when I heard it.'

Laura looked at Jack. Had he talked to Isaac about such things when she hadn't been in the room? Was it possible that hearing his father's voice had helped bring him back to them?

Isaac had summed up the power of Jack's voice in one short sentence. Ten years ago she'd also stop being scared. He had talked and she had known that everything was going to be OK.

She raised an eyebrow at Jack, momentarily confused. He stared back, looking at her then at Isaac then back at her with a look of utter amazement. Laura knew from Jack's face that Isaac hadn't just dreamt the conversation.

As unexpected as it was, Isaac had given them the perfect opportunity. Had she not long ago told Jack that the right time would present itself? And here it was. Laura had never been surer of anything.

'Zak-Zak,' she started tentatively, and Isaac swivelled his head toward her. 'You didn't dream it, sweetie. It actually happened. Your father's been here all along.'

Jack felt the hairs on his arms stand to attention as Laura

reached across Isaac and linked her fingers through his. He dared a peek at his son. Isaac seemed very awake now.

'Isaac…' Jack cleared the huskiness from his throat. 'I'm your father, Isaac. I've been so very worried about you.'

'*You're*…you're my dad?'

Jack nodded his head too choked up to answer. Everything hinged on this moment. If Isaac rejected him…he didn't know what he would do. He felt Laura's reassuring squeeze and realised she had a lot at stake, too.

'Are you staying? For good?'

'I'm not going anywhere. Ever.'

'My mum's been lonely for a real long time. She doesn't say anything but I can tell.'

Laura gulped back a lump in her throat. Isaac had noticed something that she hadn't even been aware of. With Jack here by her side now, she realised she *had* been lonely over the years.

'She'll never be lonely again.' Jack's voice was full of solemn promise.

'Do you love her?'

'I love her more than life itself. I love you both more than life itself.'

'Are you going to marry her?'

'Isaac!' Laura, who had disintegrated into a sobbing mess, just had to protest at that one. He was being very grown-up, testing Jack's commitment, but she drew the line at that.

'No, Laura. It's OK.' Jack smiled at her and turned back to his son. 'I'd love to marry your mother. Very much. But I need your approval first.'

Laura thought her heart was going to implode at any second. He wanted to marry her? She couldn't believe what she was hearing.

'Mine?' Isaac's eyes grew large at the importance of it all.

'Sure.' Jack smiled. 'For a long time it's just been your mum and you. You've been the man in her life. I want to make sure it's OK by you first.'

Laura sniffled in the background as Isaac considered the proposition. Jack held his breath. His son was an articulate, intelligent, nine-year-old boy, and he desperately wanted Isaac's approval. It was more important to him than any professional or peer acknowledgment.

'Well,' Isaac said consideringly, 'you do know how to play GameBoy. That's important. And you have a nice voice. And when you hold my mum's hand like that I can see it makes her happy. You probably can't tell at the moment because she's crying so much but, being the man in her life, I can tell.'

Laura laughed through her tears. Had the bang on his head turned him into a nine-year-old sage? He was obviously a lot more observant than she'd given him credit for.

'Looks like I'm going to have to rely on you to help me with your mum's body language,' said Jack seriously.

Isaac sucked in a breath and sighed heavily. 'It sure can be difficult sometimes. Girls are tricky.'

'They can be,' Jack agreed, delighting in his son's personality.

'I reckon it'd be great to have you as my dad,' said Isaac.

Jack's face split into a grin as his heart split wide open. He heard Laura laughing and crying and at that moment he felt like he could conquer the world.

Laura was hugging Isaac and crying all over his chest. She lifted her face and arm and invited Jack into their circle. Finally, he got to feel his son's arms around his neck.

'Hey,' Isaac interrupted. 'You two are supposed to kiss now. I've seen it on all those mushy movies.'

Laura's eyes sparkled with mirth and excitement as much as tears. Never in her wildest dreams could she have hoped for this happy ending. Jack and Isaac and her were going to be a family at last. Her life was complete.

She looked at the man she loved, happier than she had ever seen him. The man who had always been there for her in her times of trial. When she'd been trapped and scared.

When she'd felt like she'd been falling apart at the first memorial service. And then ten years later, when she'd thought she'd put it all behind her, only to discover that it would always be a part of her. Part of her identity.

He'd been there, too, when Neve had emerged from a deeply suppressed part of her memory. And at the building site when she'd been crippled by a flashback.

And now, with Isaac's accident. When their son had been injured and lying unconscious in Intensive Care, despite his anger towards her, he had been there as well.

Their mouths touched, inches above Isaac's face, his arms around their necks, linking them all together. They had fulfilled their destiny.

Two years later…

'Hello.'

'Gwen? It's Jack. Jack Riley.'

'Jack?' Her Irish brogue reached across the oceans.

'Has Laura had the baby?'

'She sure did, an hour ago. We have a daughter.'

'Oh, Jack. How wonderful! A little girl. That's the best news! What are you calling her?'

'Well, that's why I'm ringing, actually. Laura and I have been talking about it and we decided that if the baby was a girl we wanted to call her Neve.'

'Oh, Jack…' Gwen's voice wobbled and broke.

'We'll understand if you don't want us to. We don't want to upset you. Laura just thought it would be a lovely tribute to the memory of your Neve…so that you know that she holds a special place in our hearts. She helped bring Laura and I together in a roundabout kind of way. We don't ever want to forget her.'

'Oh, Jack, that would mean more to me than you could possibly know. God bless you. God bless you both, and our darling little Neve.'

Jack was hanging up the phone as Laura, freshly showered,

plonked herself down on the hospital bed. His heart lurched at her beauty. She glowed. You would never have known she'd just been through a marathon labour and given birth only an hour before.

'Who was that?' she asked, kissing her husband and relieving him of their precious bundle.

'Gwen.'

'What did she say? Did you ask her?'

'She blubbered a lot but she was ecstatic. She's booking a flight as soon as possible to come and see her.'

'Oh, that's fantastic, darling. I can't wait to see the two of them together.' Laura felt a tear slide down her face and Jack hugged his wife and baby close.

They were silent as they drank in the sight of their newborn daughter, swaddled tightly and sleeping peacefully.

'Neve is perfect for her, don't you think? Good closure. I'm so happy Gwen is thrilled. And Isaac. He always wanted a baby sister.'

'They're thrilled? They haven't got anything on me!' he said, the wonder of it all still evident in his voice. 'I still can't believe that we got pregnant,' he said, stroking his finger down his daughter's cheek. 'Do you know how devastating it was to be told my shoe size was higher than my sperm count?' He shook his head. 'Well, we showed them. What they lacked in number they made up in determination. My little guys got there in the end.'

Jack turned to her and lifted her chin so Laura was looking into his eyes. 'Thank you, Laura. Thank you so much. For Isaac. For Neve. For you. You've made my life whole.'

Neve stirred and yawned. Her newborn squeaks were of contentment.

'I aim to please.' She smiled and snuggled into the crook of his arm.

Laura was as content as her newborn daughter. *This* had been her reason for surviving Newvalley. It had taken twelve years to become apparent, but she had never been more sure.

To give Jack the gift of a child. This was why she had survived. Just as he had given her the gift of life, she had reciprocated. She had given him a baby daughter.

They stared at Neve for a long time, watching her sleep. They had been truly blessed.